Collection Editor: *Cory Levine*
Assistant Editors: *Alex Starbuck & John Denning*
Editors, Special Projects: *Jennifer Grünwald & Mark D. Beazley*
Senior Editor, Special Projects: *Jeff Youngquist*
Senior Vice President of Sales: *David Gabriel*

Editor in Chief: *Joe Quesada*
Publisher: *Dan Buckley*
Executive Producer: *Alan Fine*

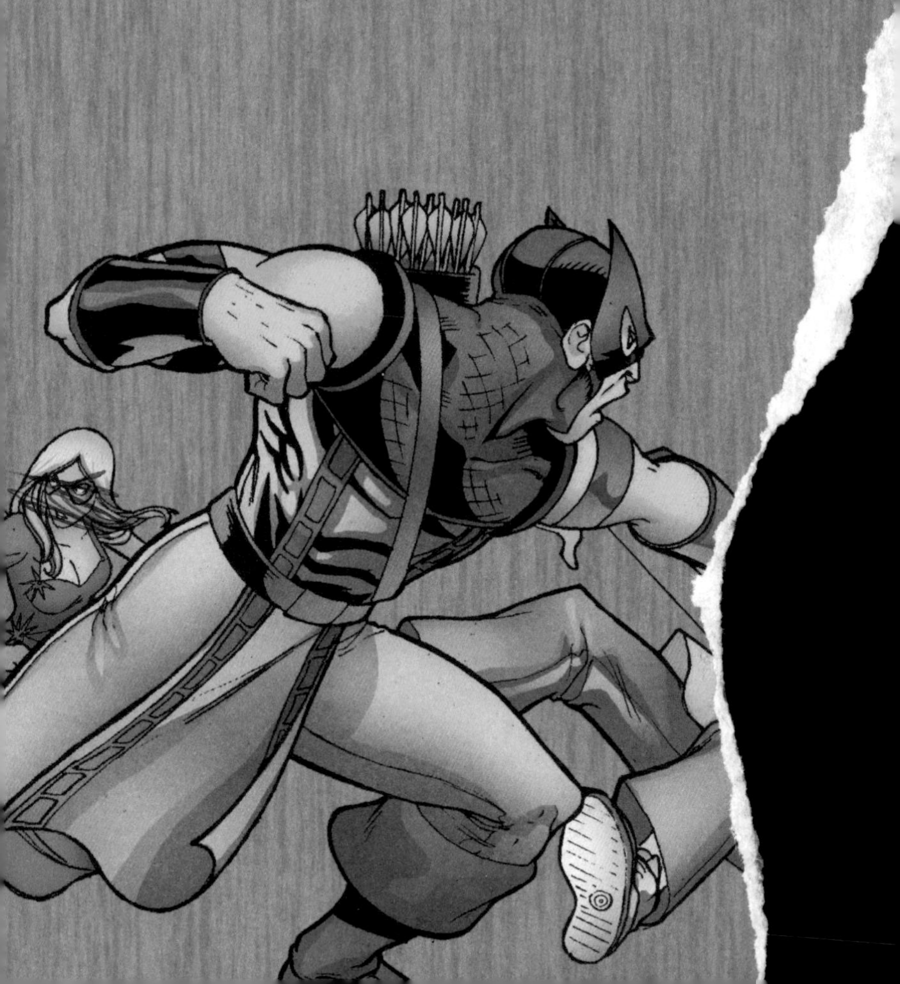

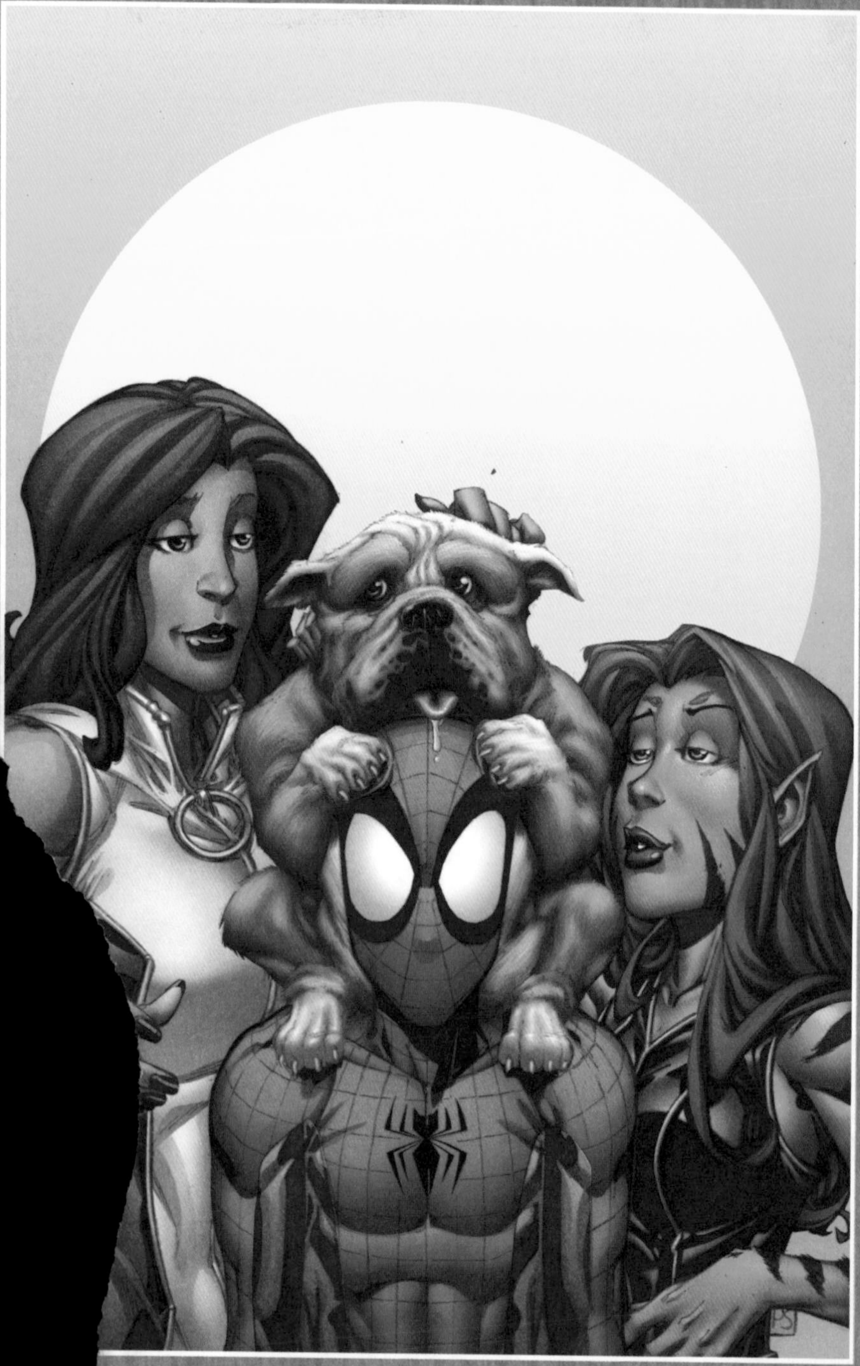

#13

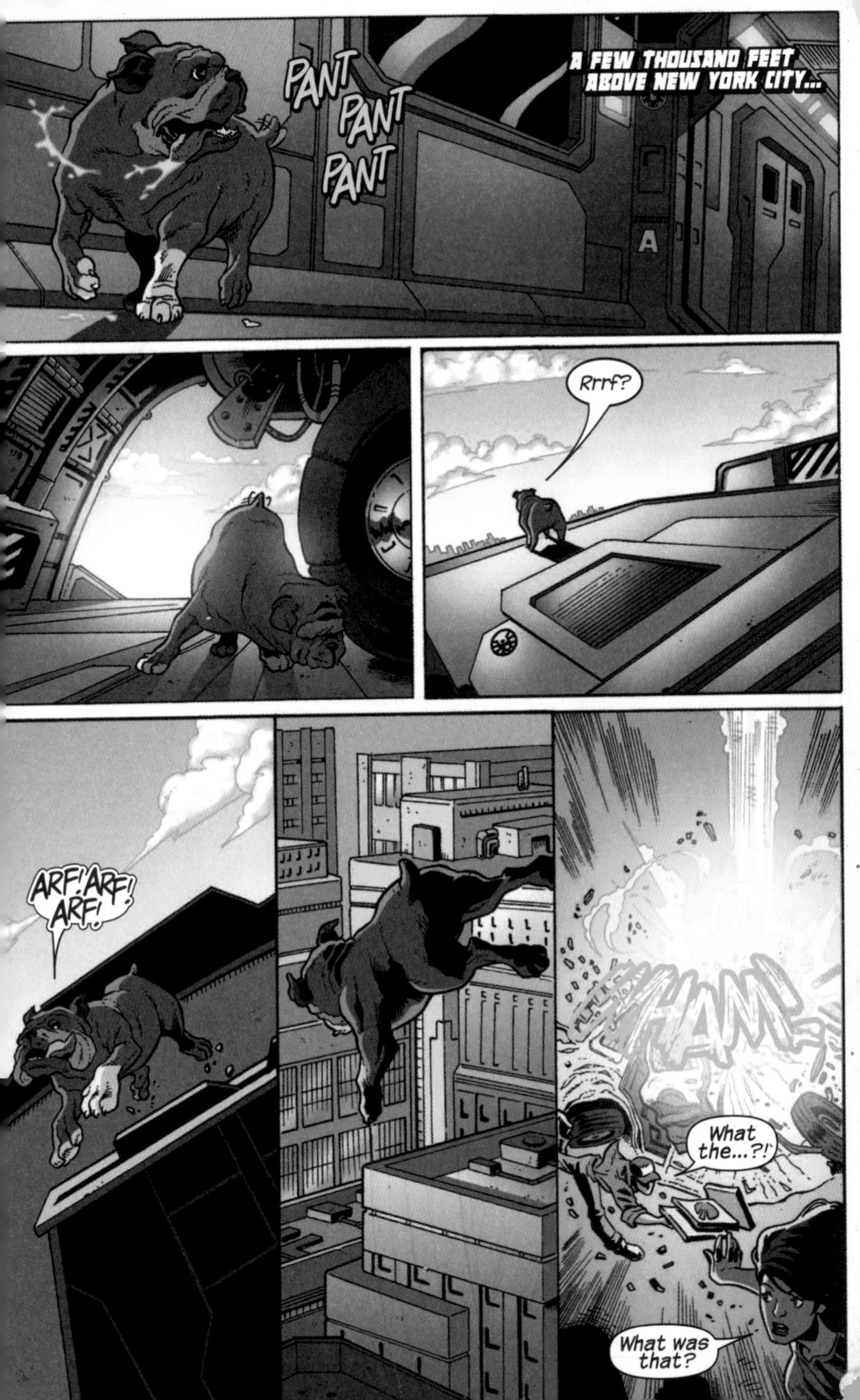
A FEW THOUSAND FEET ABOVE NEW YORK CITY...
PANT PANT PANT
Rrrf?
ARF! ARF! ARF!
WHAM!
What the...?!
What was that?

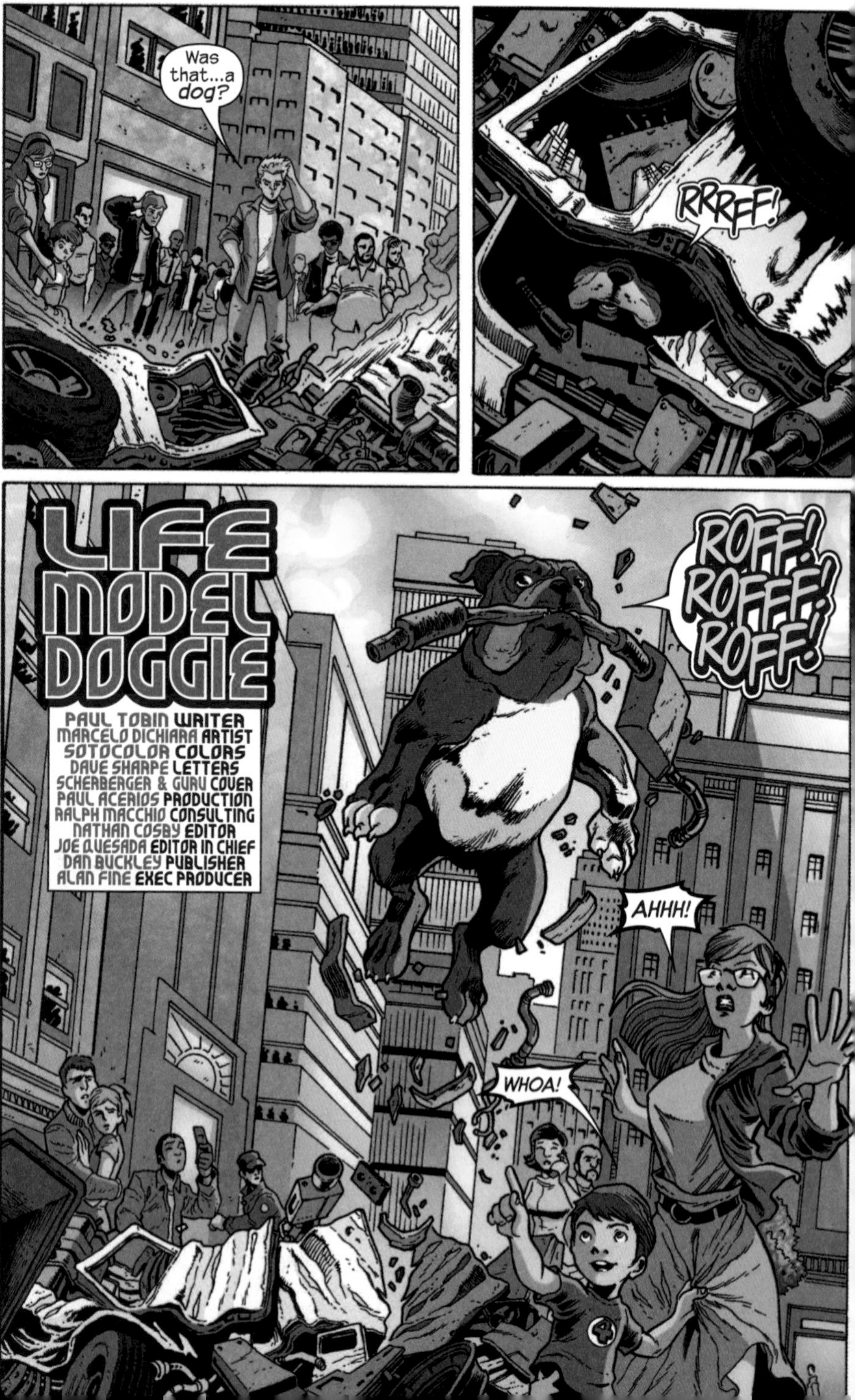
Was that...a dog?
RRRFF!
LIFE MODEL DOGGIE
PAUL TOBIN WRITER
MARCELO DICHIARA ARTIST
SOTOCOLOR COLORS
DAVE SHARPE LETTERS
SCHERBERGER & GURU COVER
PAUL ACERIOS PRODUCTION
RALPH MACCHIO CONSULTING
NATHAN COSBY EDITOR
JOE QUESADA EDITOR IN CHIEF
DAN BUCKLEY PUBLISHER
ALAN FINE EXEC PRODUCER
ROFF! ROFFF! ROFF!
AHHH!
WHOA!

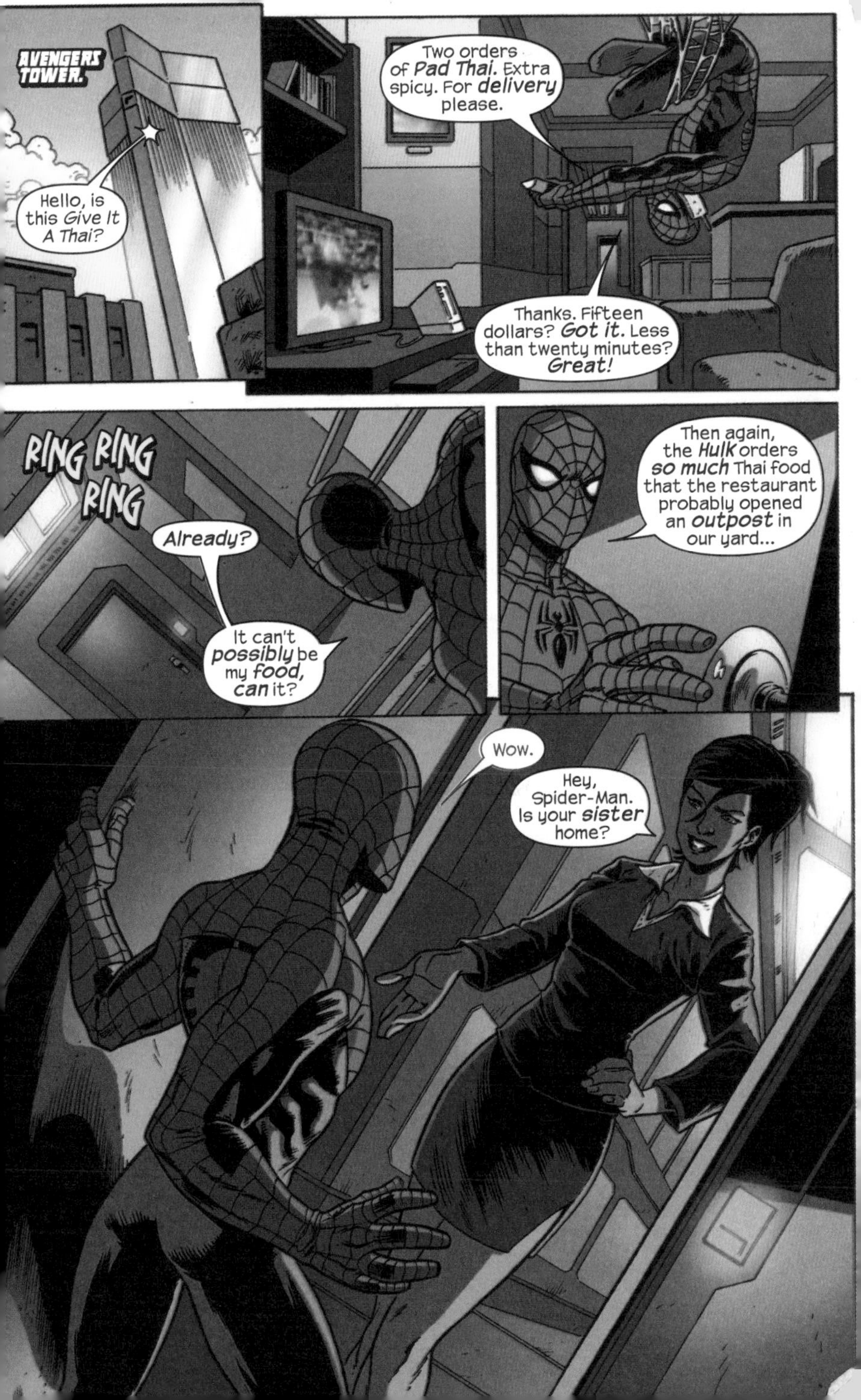
AVENGERS TOWER.
Hello, is this Give It A Thai?
Two orders of Pad Thai. Extra spicy. For delivery please.
Thanks. Fifteen dollars? Got it. Less than twenty minutes? Great!
RING RING RING
Already?
It can't possibly be my food, can it?
Then again, the Hulk orders so much Thai food that the restaurant probably opened an outpost in our yard...
Wow.
Hey, Spider-Man. Is your sister home?

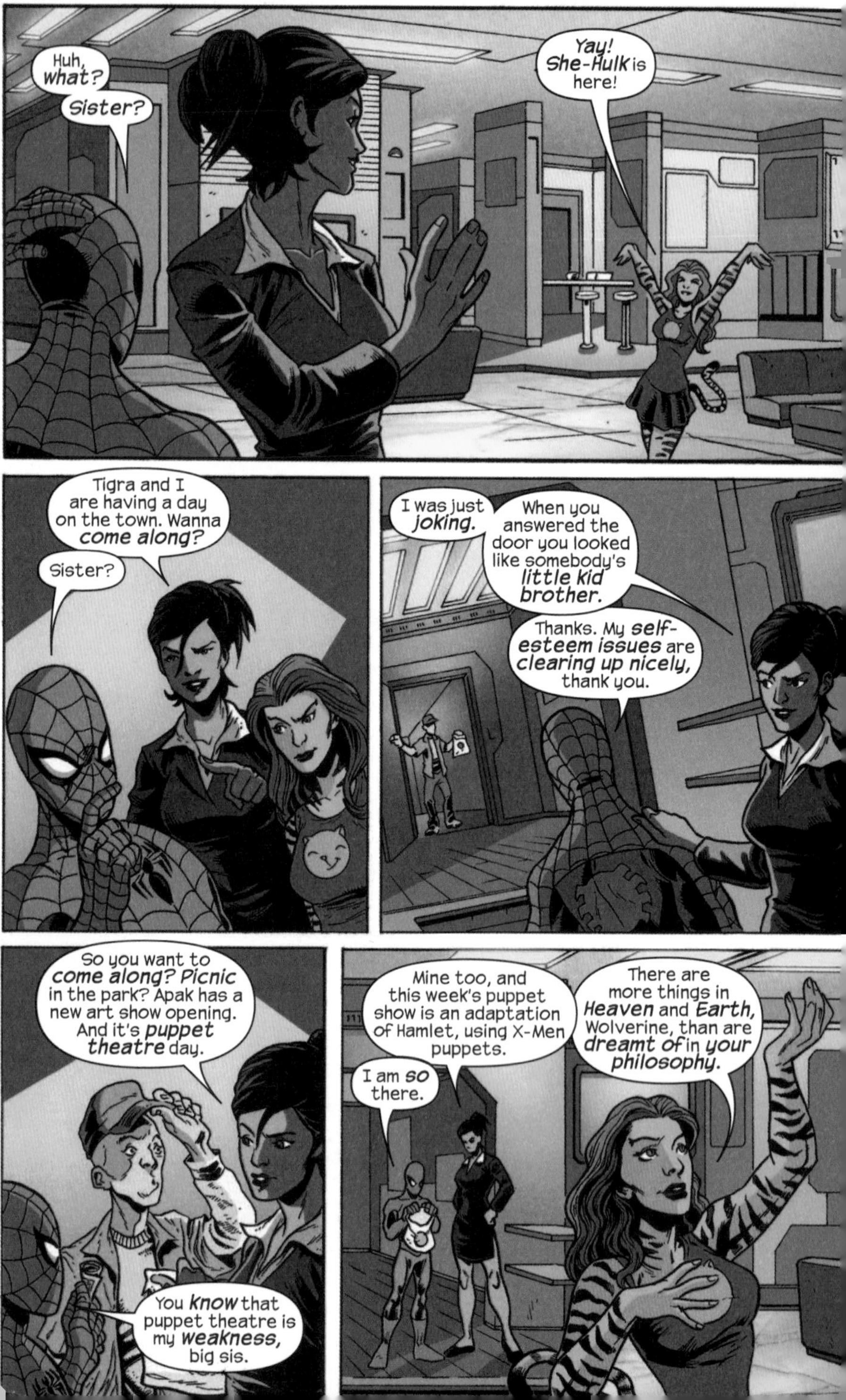
Huh, what?
Sister?
Yay! She-Hulk is here!
Tigra and I are having a day on the town. Wanna come along?
Sister?
I was just joking.
When you answered the door you looked like somebody's little kid brother.
Thanks. My self-esteem issues are clearing up nicely, thank you.
So you want to come along? Picnic in the park? Apak has a new art show opening. And it's puppet theatre day.
You know that puppet theatre is my weakness, big sis.
Mine too, and this week's puppet show is an adaptation of Hamlet, using X-Men puppets.
I am so there.
There are more things in Heaven and Earth, Wolverine, than are dreamt of in your philosophy.

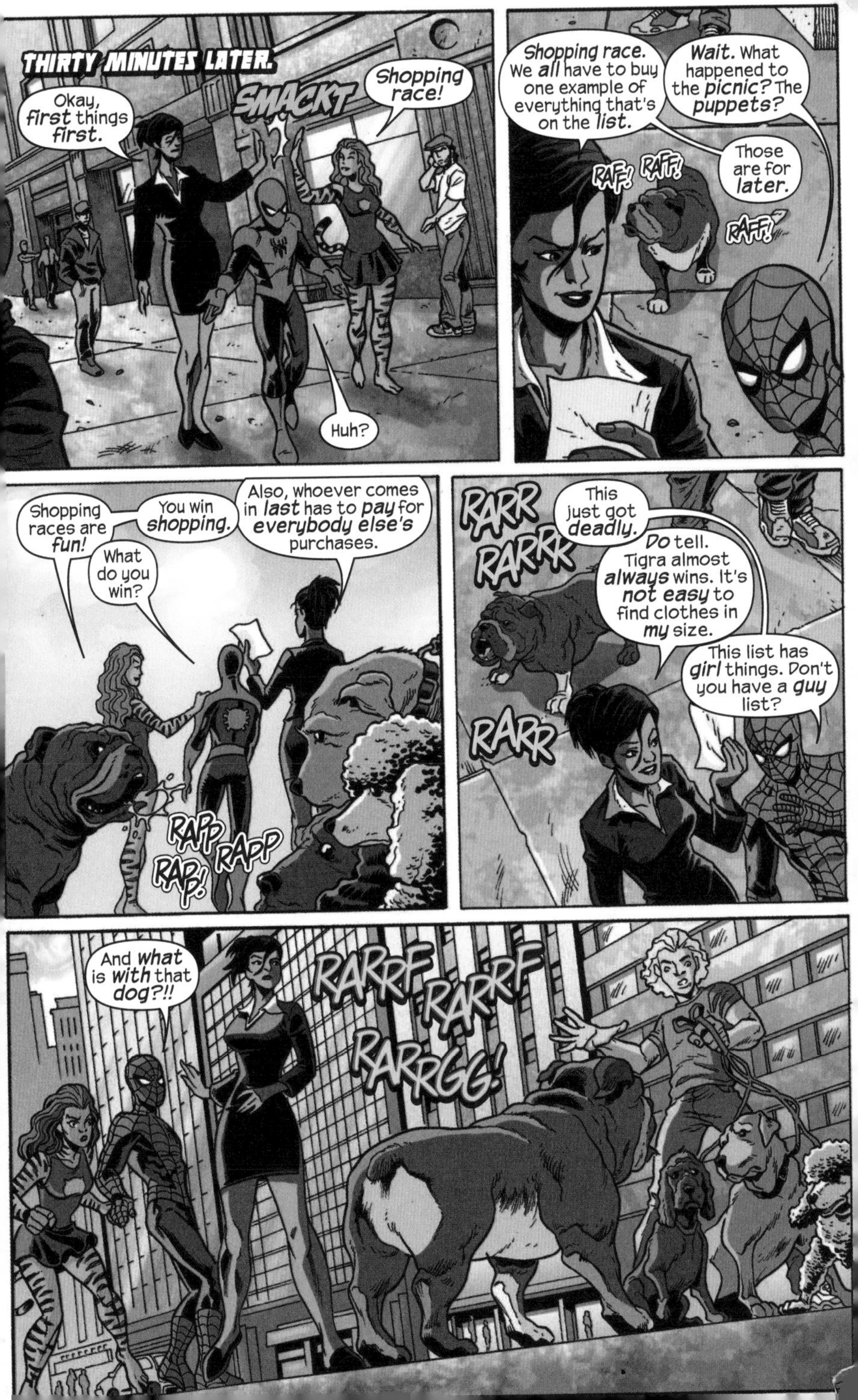
THIRTY MINUTES LATER.
Okay, first things first.
SMACK!
Shopping race!
Huh?
Shopping race. We all have to buy one example of everything that's on the list.
Wait. What happened to the picnic? The puppets?
Those are for later.
RAFF! RAFF!
RAFF!
Shopping races are fun!
You win shopping.
What do you win?
Also, whoever comes in last has to pay for everybody else's purchases.
RAPP RAPP
RAPP!
RARR
RARRR
This just got deadly.
Do tell.
Tigra almost always wins. It's not easy to find clothes in my size.
This list has girl things. Don't you have a guy list?
RARR
And what is with that dog?!!
RARRF RARRF
RARRGG!

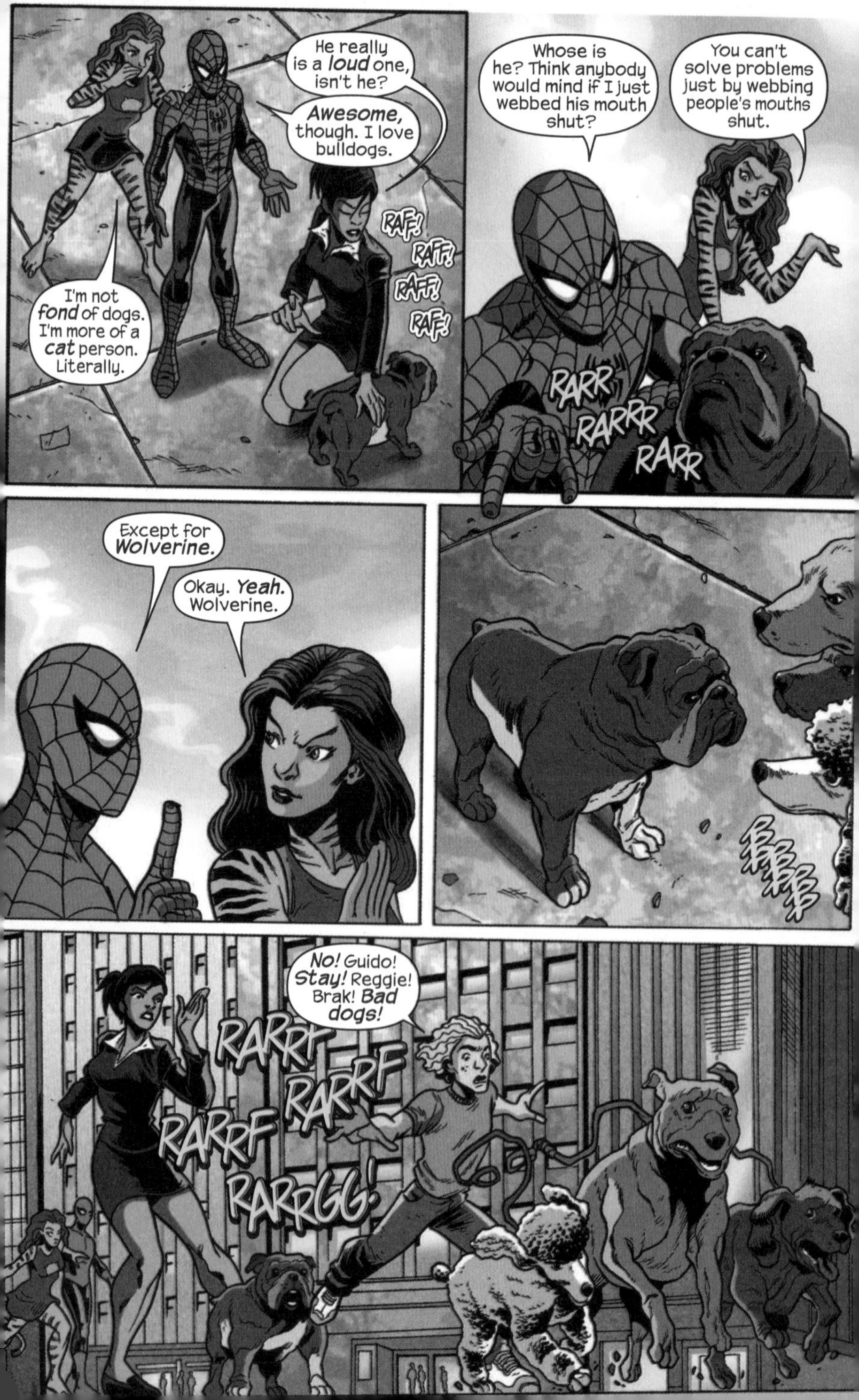
He really is a loud one, isn't he?
Awesome, though. I love bulldogs.
RAFF! RAFF! RAFF! RAFF!
I'm not fond of dogs. I'm more of a cat person. Literally.
Whose is he? Think anybody would mind if I just webbed his mouth shut?
You can't solve problems just by webbing people's mouths shut.
RARR RARRR RARR
Except for Wolverine.
Okay. Yeah. Wolverine.
No! Guido! Stay! Reggie! Brak! Bad dogs!
RARRF RARRF RARRF RARRGG!

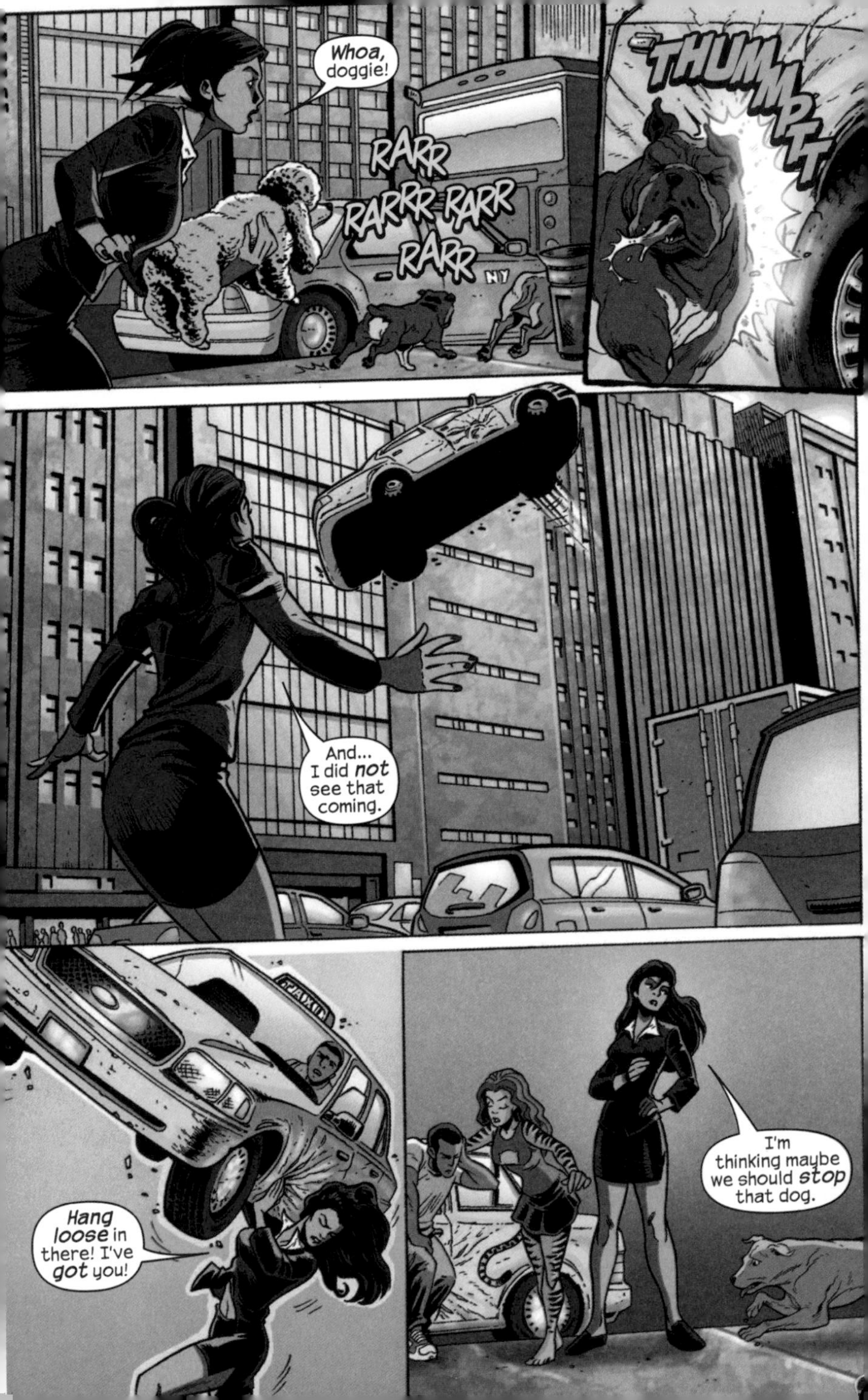
Whoa, doggie!
RARR
RARRR RARR
RARR
THUMMPTT
And... I did *not* see that coming.
Hang loose in there! I've *got* you!
I'm thinking maybe we should *stop* that dog.

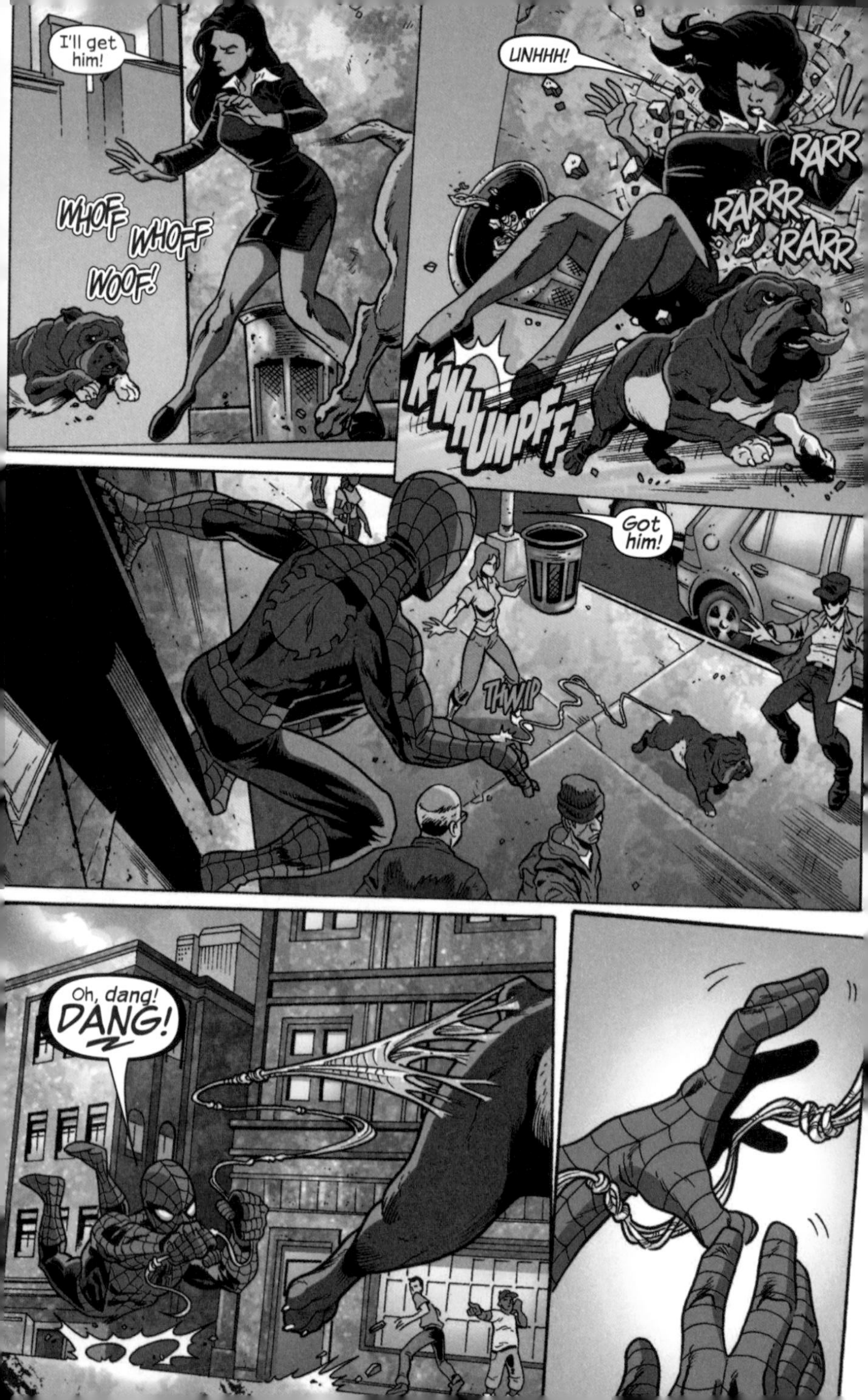
I'll get him!
WHOFF WHOFF WOOF!
UNHHH!
RARR RARRR RARR
K-WHUMPFF
Got him!
THWIP
Oh, dang! DANG!

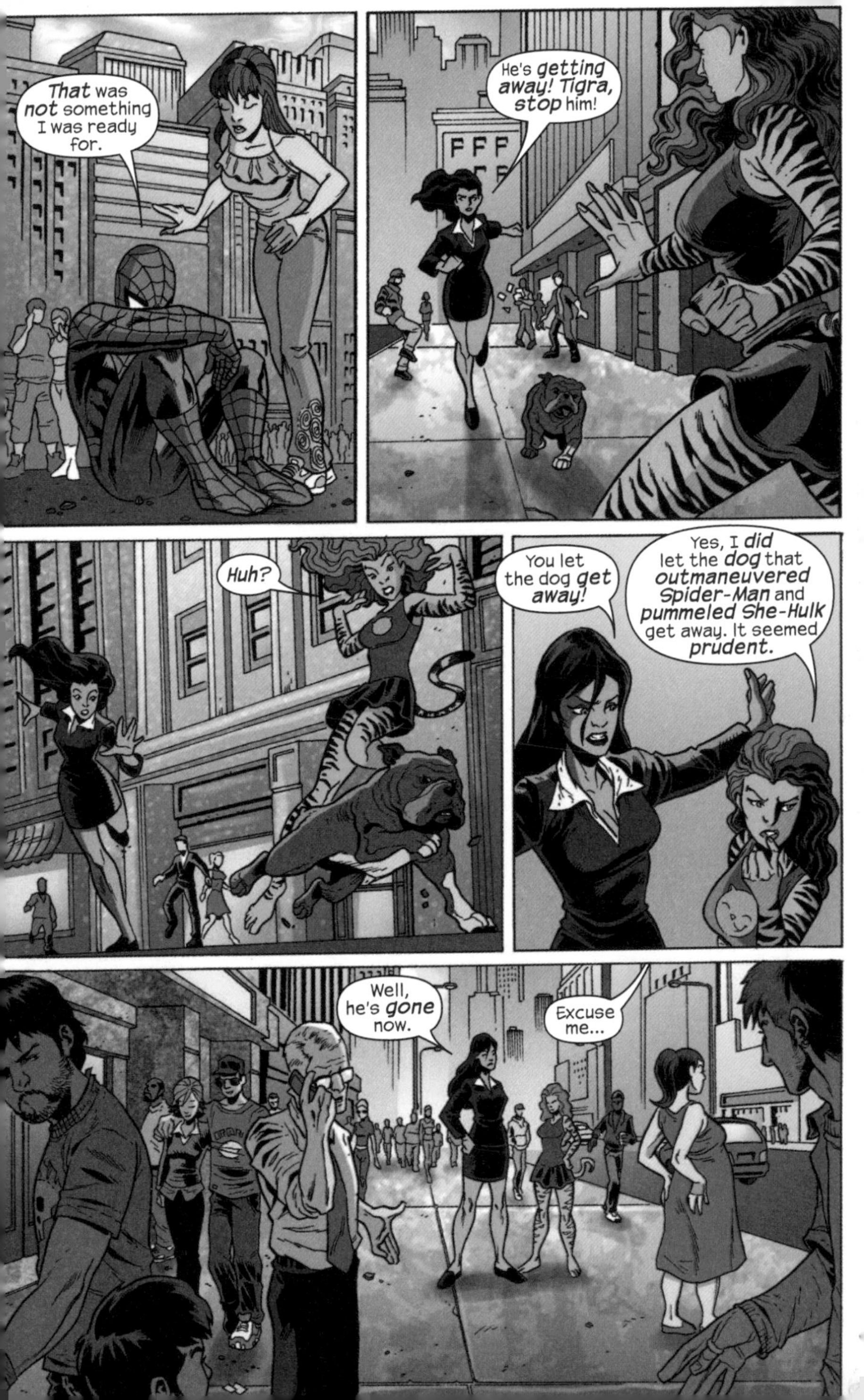
That was not something I was ready for.
He's getting away! Tigra, stop him!
Huh?
You let the dog get away!
Yes, I did let the dog that outmaneuvered Spider-Man and pummeled She-Hulk get away. It seemed prudent.
Well, he's gone now.
Excuse me...

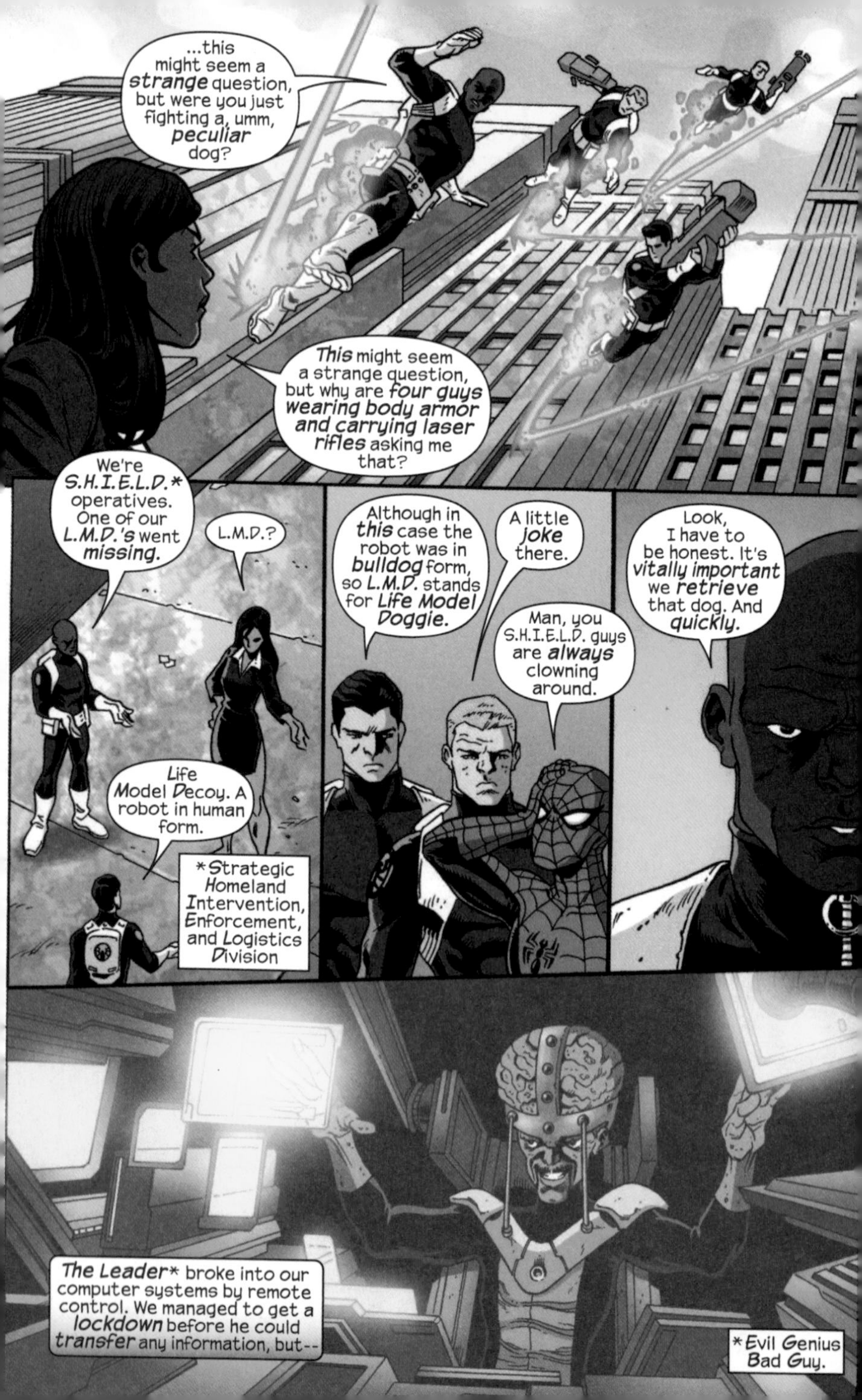
...this might seem a strange question, but were you just fighting a, umm, peculiar dog?
This might seem a strange question, but why are four guys wearing body armor and carrying laser rifles asking me that?
We're S.H.I.E.L.D.* operatives. One of our L.M.D.'s went missing.
L.M.D.?
Life Model Decoy. A robot in human form.
*Strategic Homeland Intervention, Enforcement, and Logistics Division
Although in this case the robot was in bulldog form, so L.M.D. stands for Life Model Doggie.
A little joke there.
Man, you S.H.I.E.L.D. guys are always clowning around.
Look, I have to be honest. It's vitally important we retrieve that dog. And quickly.
The Leader* broke into our computer systems by remote control. We managed to get a lockdown before he could transfer any information, but--
*Evil Genius Bad Guy.

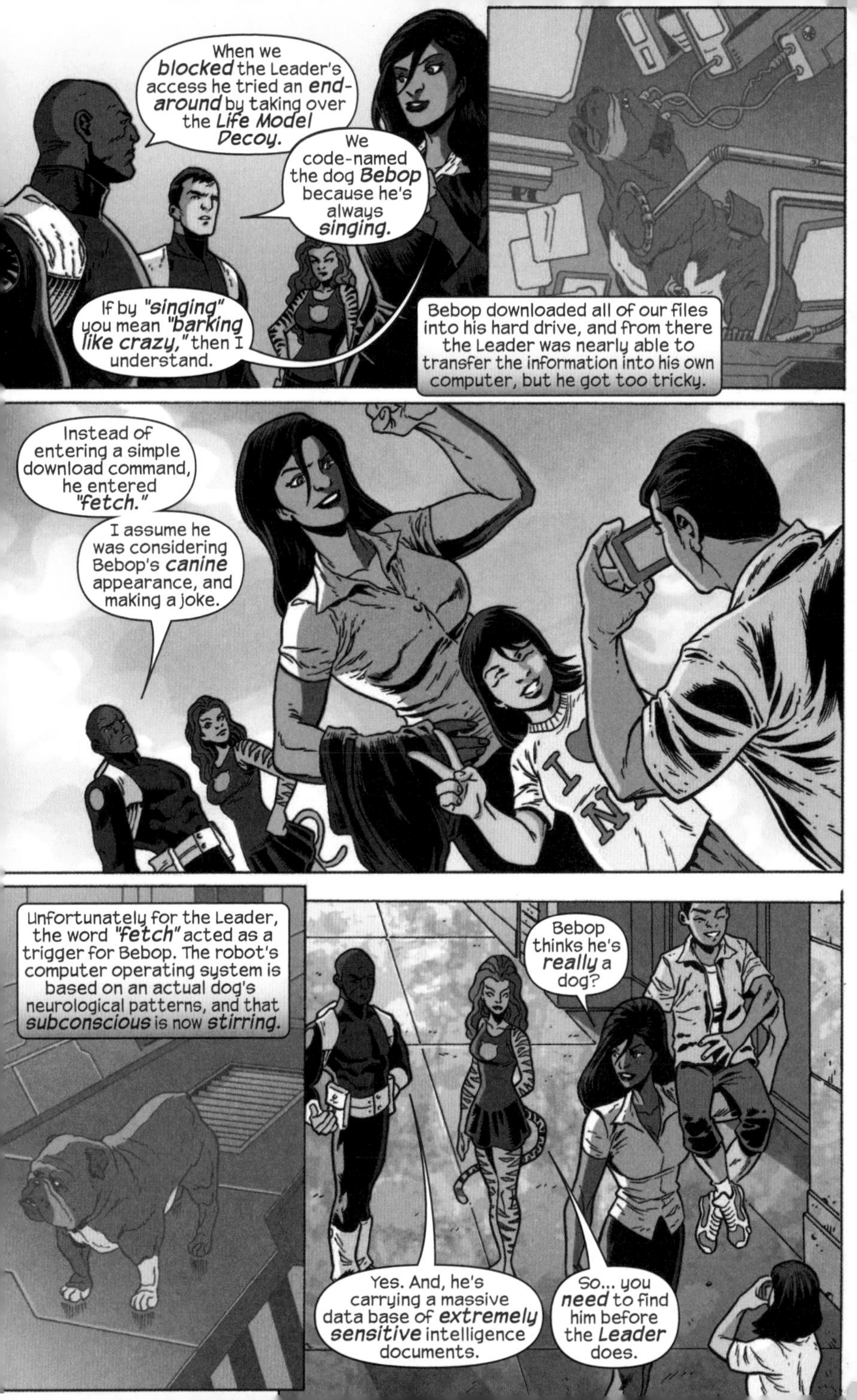
When we blocked the Leader's access he tried an end-around by taking over the Life Model Decoy.
We code-named the dog Bebop because he's always singing.
If by "singing" you mean "barking like crazy," then I understand.
Bebop downloaded all of our files into his hard drive, and from there the Leader was nearly able to transfer the information into his own computer, but he got too tricky.
Instead of entering a simple download command, he entered "fetch."
I assume he was considering Bebop's canine appearance, and making a joke.
Unfortunately for the Leader, the word "fetch" acted as a trigger for Bebop. The robot's computer operating system is based on an actual dog's neurological patterns, and that subconscious is now stirring.
Bebop thinks he's really a dog?
Yes. And, he's carrying a massive data base of extremely sensitive intelligence documents.
So... you need to find him before the Leader does.

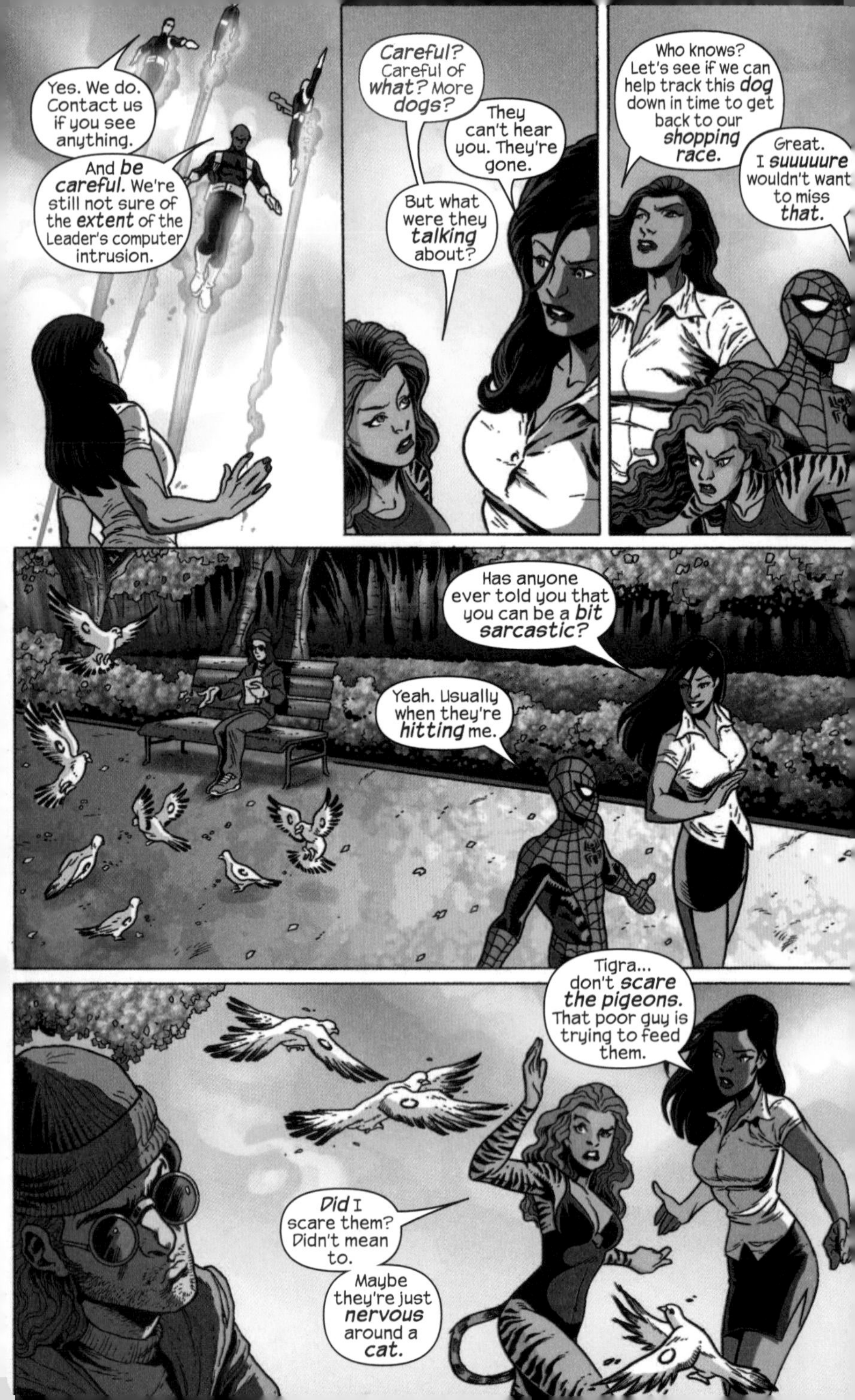
Yes. We do. Contact us if you see anything.
And be careful. We're still not sure of the extent of the Leader's computer intrusion.
Careful? Careful of what? More dogs?
They can't hear you. They're gone.
But what were they talking about?
Who knows? Let's see if we can help track this dog down in time to get back to our shopping race.
Great. I suuuuure wouldn't want to miss that.
Has anyone ever told you that you can be a bit sarcastic?
Yeah. Usually when they're hitting me.
Tigra... don't scare the pigeons. That poor guy is trying to feed them.
Did I scare them? Didn't mean to.
Maybe they're just nervous around a cat.

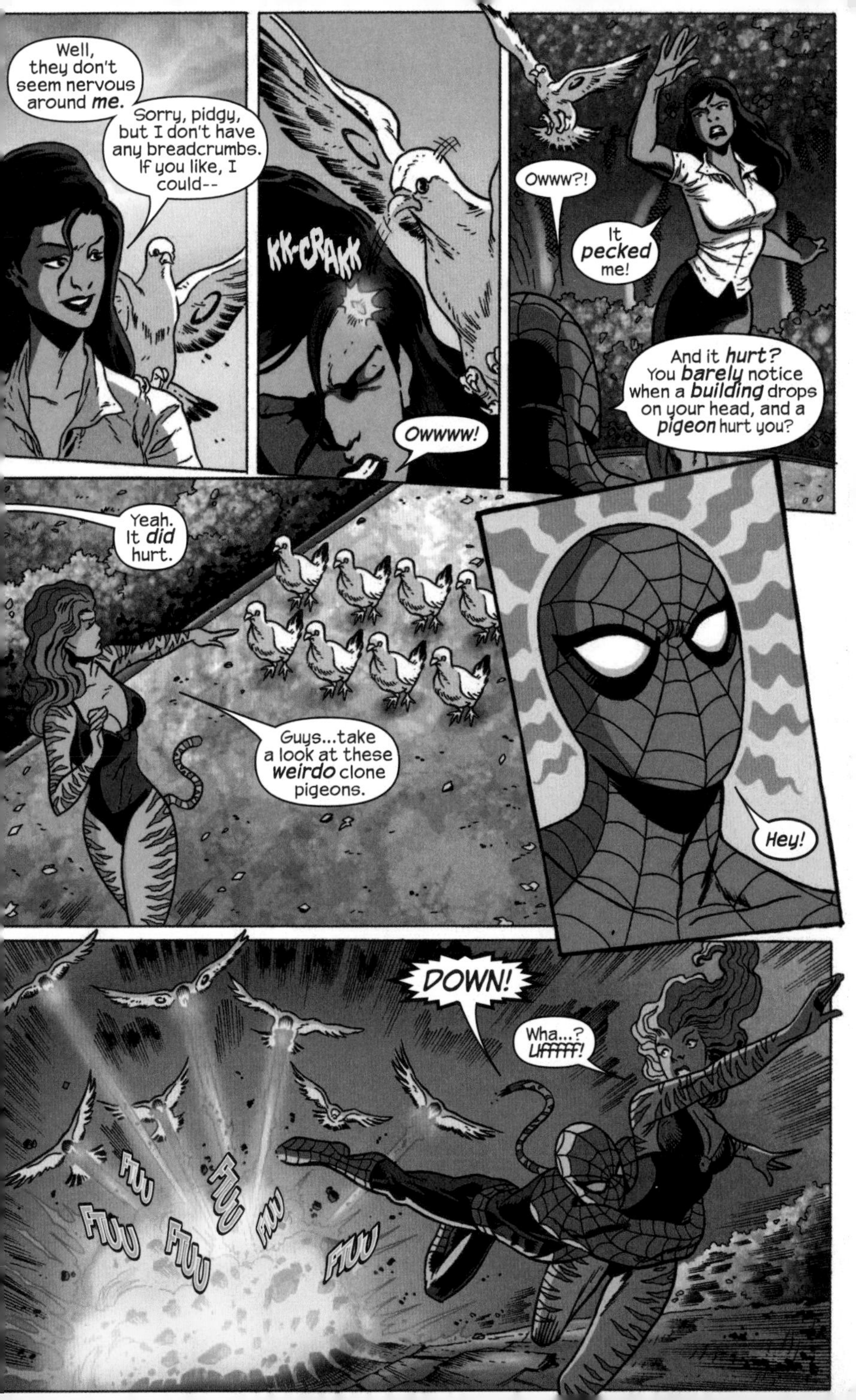
Well, they don't seem nervous around *me*.
Sorry, pidgy, but I don't have any breadcrumbs. If you like, I could--
KK-CRAKK
Owwww!
Owww?!
It *pecked* me!
And it *hurt*? You *barely* notice when a *building* drops on your head, and a *pigeon* hurt you?
Yeah. It *did* hurt.
Guys...take a look at these *weirdo* clone pigeons.
Hey!
DOWN!
Wha...? LIFFFFF!
FTUU
FTUU
FTUU
FTUU
FTUU
FTUU

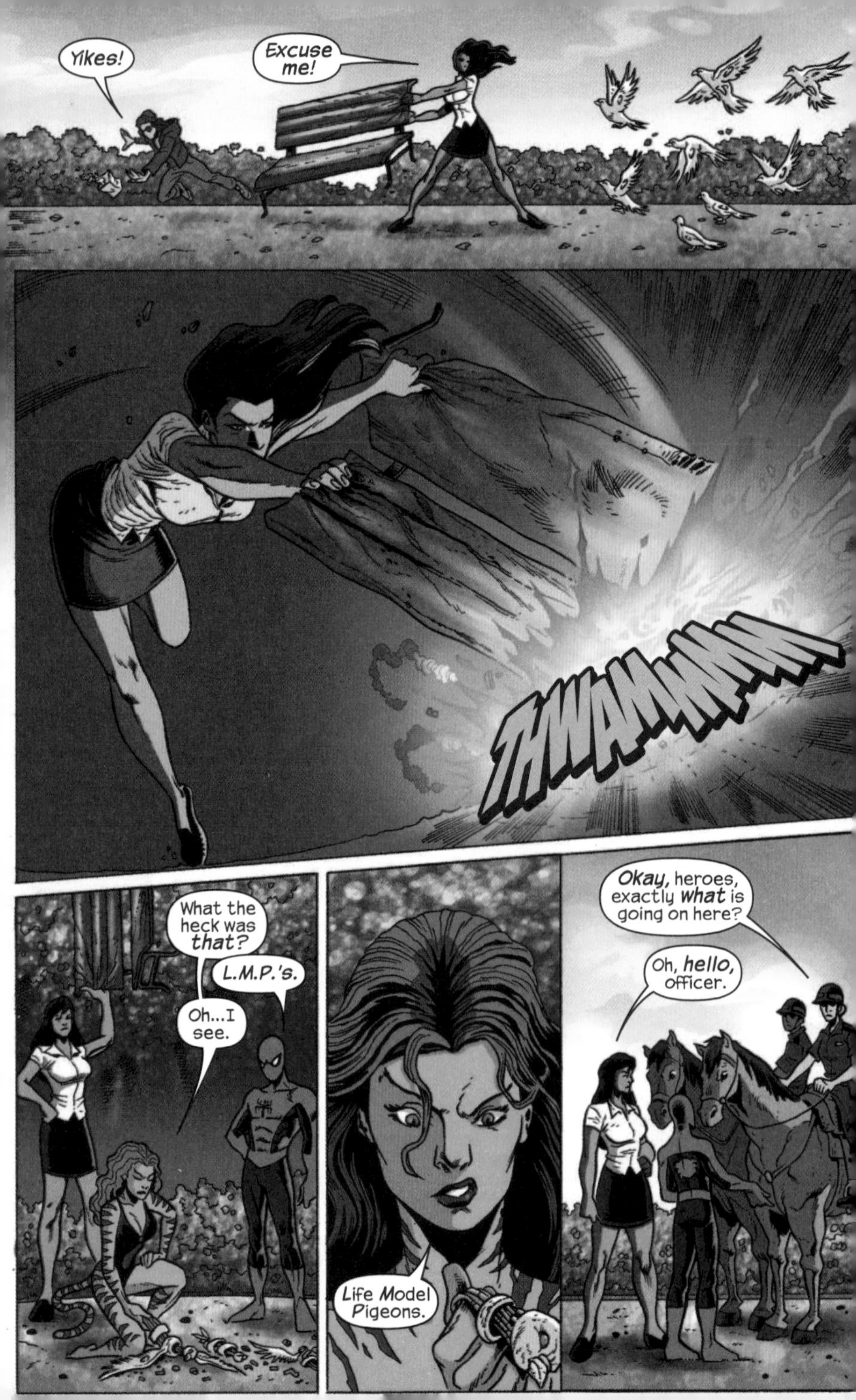

Yikes!
Excuse me!
THWAMMMM
What the heck was that?
L.M.P.'s.
Oh...I see.
Life Model Pigeons.
Okay, heroes, exactly what is going on here?
Oh, hello, officer.

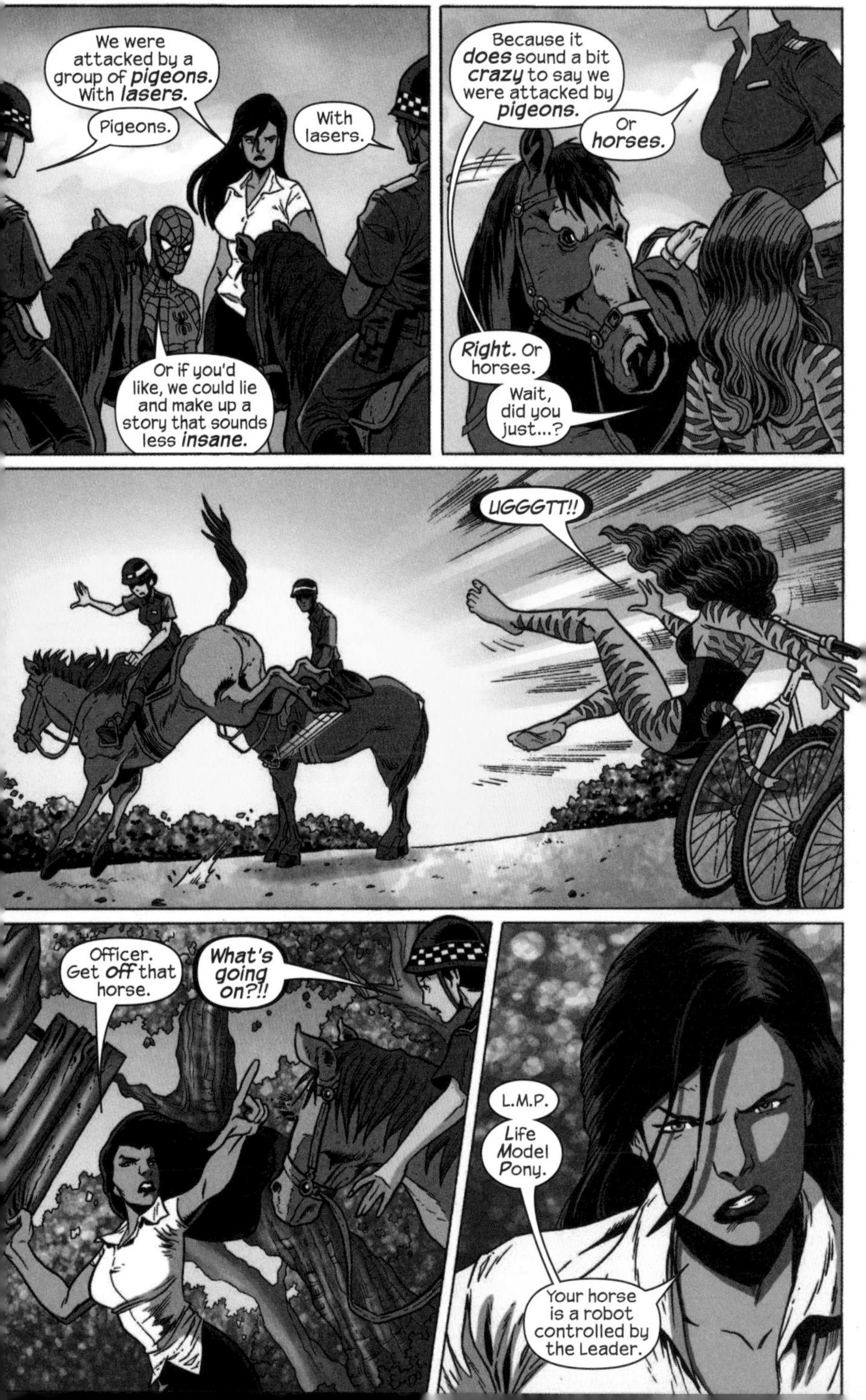
We were attacked by a group of pigeons. With lasers.
Pigeons.
With lasers.
Or if you'd like, we could lie and make up a story that sounds less insane.
Because it does sound a bit crazy to say we were attacked by pigeons.
Or horses.
Right. Or horses.
Wait, did you just...?
UGGGTT!!
Officer. Get off that horse.
What's going on?!!
L.M.P.
Life Model Pony.
Your horse is a robot controlled by the Leader.

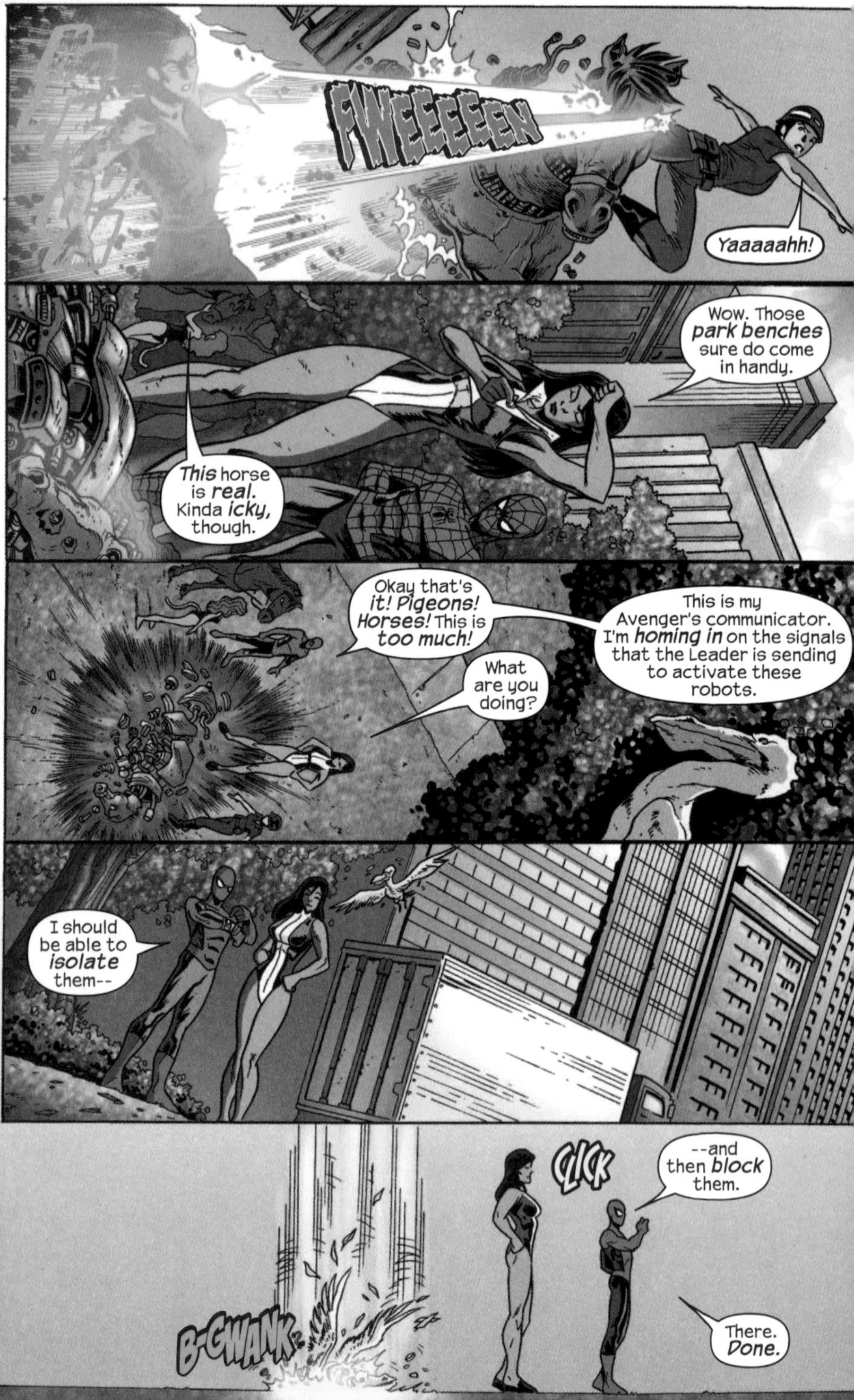
FWEEEEEN
Yaaaaaahh!
Wow. Those park benches sure do come in handy.
This horse is real. Kinda icky, though.
Okay that's it! Pigeons! Horses! This is too much!
This is my Avenger's communicator. I'm homing in on the signals that the Leader is sending to activate these robots.
What are you doing?
I should be able to isolate them--
CLICK
--and then block them.
B-GWANK
There. Done.

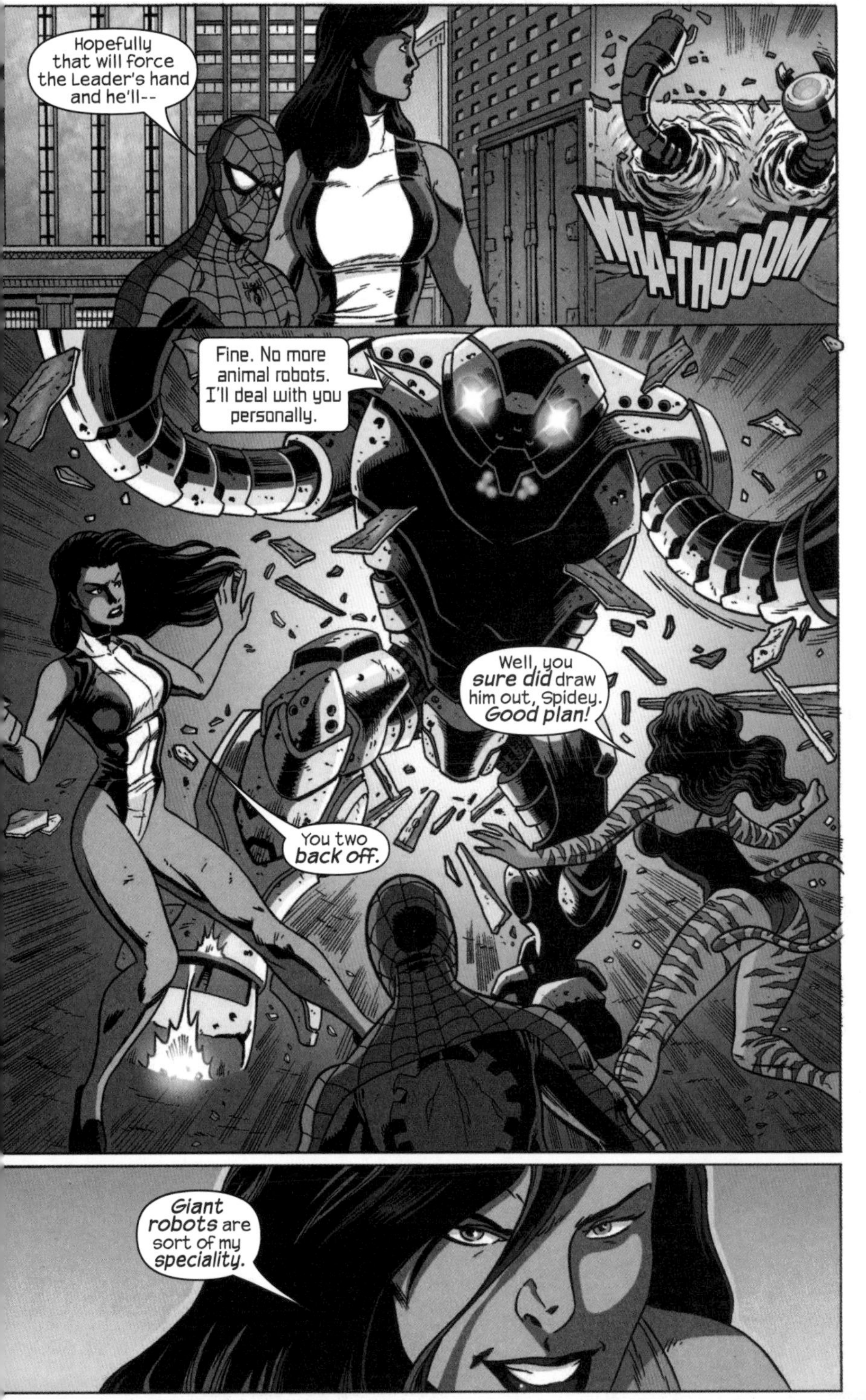
Hopefully that will force the Leader's hand and he'll--
WHA-THOOOM
Fine. No more animal robots. I'll deal with you personally.
Well, you *sure did* draw him out, Spidey. *Good plan!*
You two *back off.*
Giant robots are sort of my *speciality.*

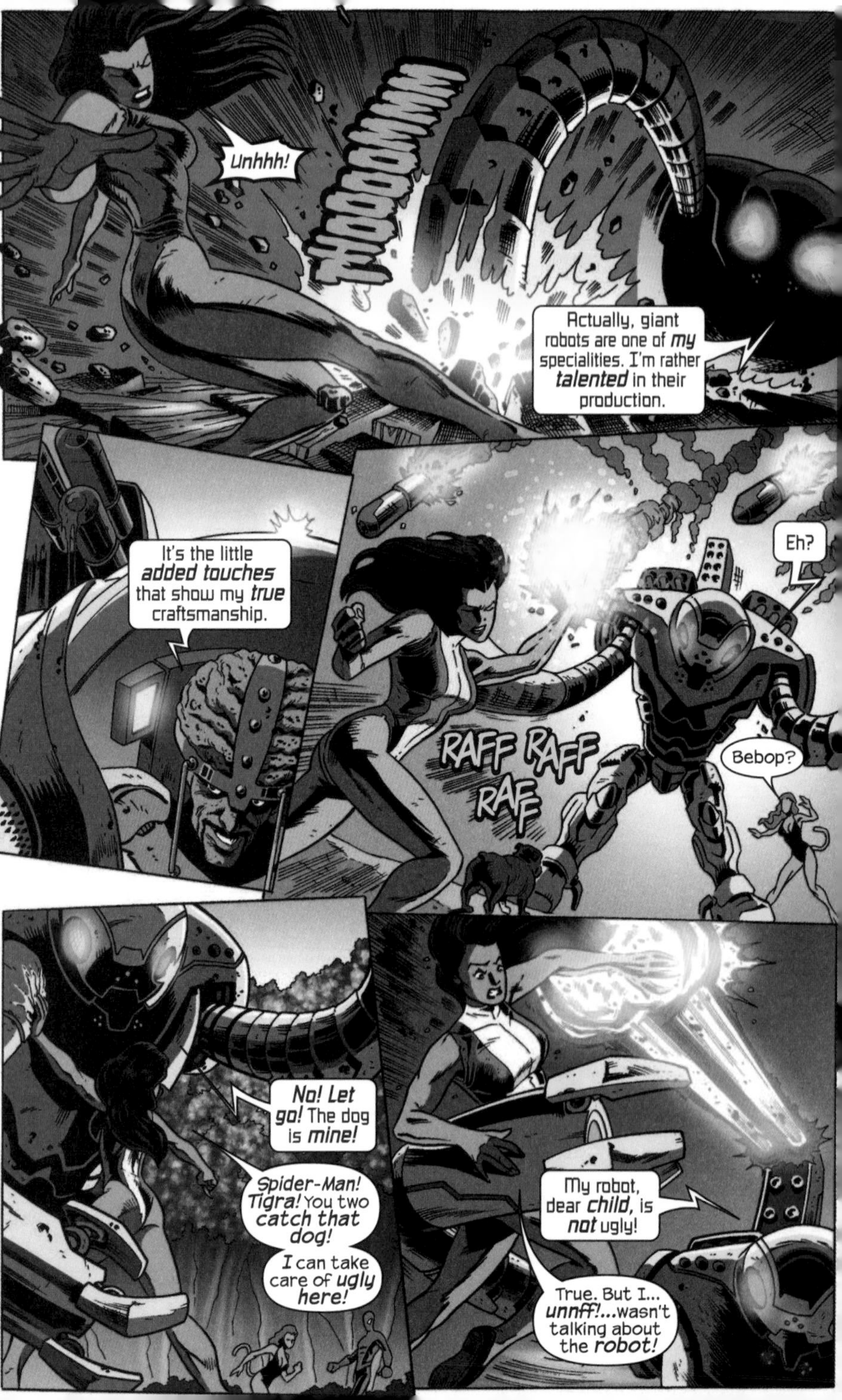

WHOOOOOOOM
Unhhh!
Actually, giant robots are one of my specialities. I'm rather talented in their production.
It's the little added touches that show my true craftsmanship.
Eh?
RAFF RAFF RAFF
Bebop?
No! Let go! The dog is mine!
Spider-Man! Tigra! You two catch that dog!
I can take care of ugly here!
My robot, dear child, is not ugly!
True. But I... unnff!...wasn't talking about the robot!

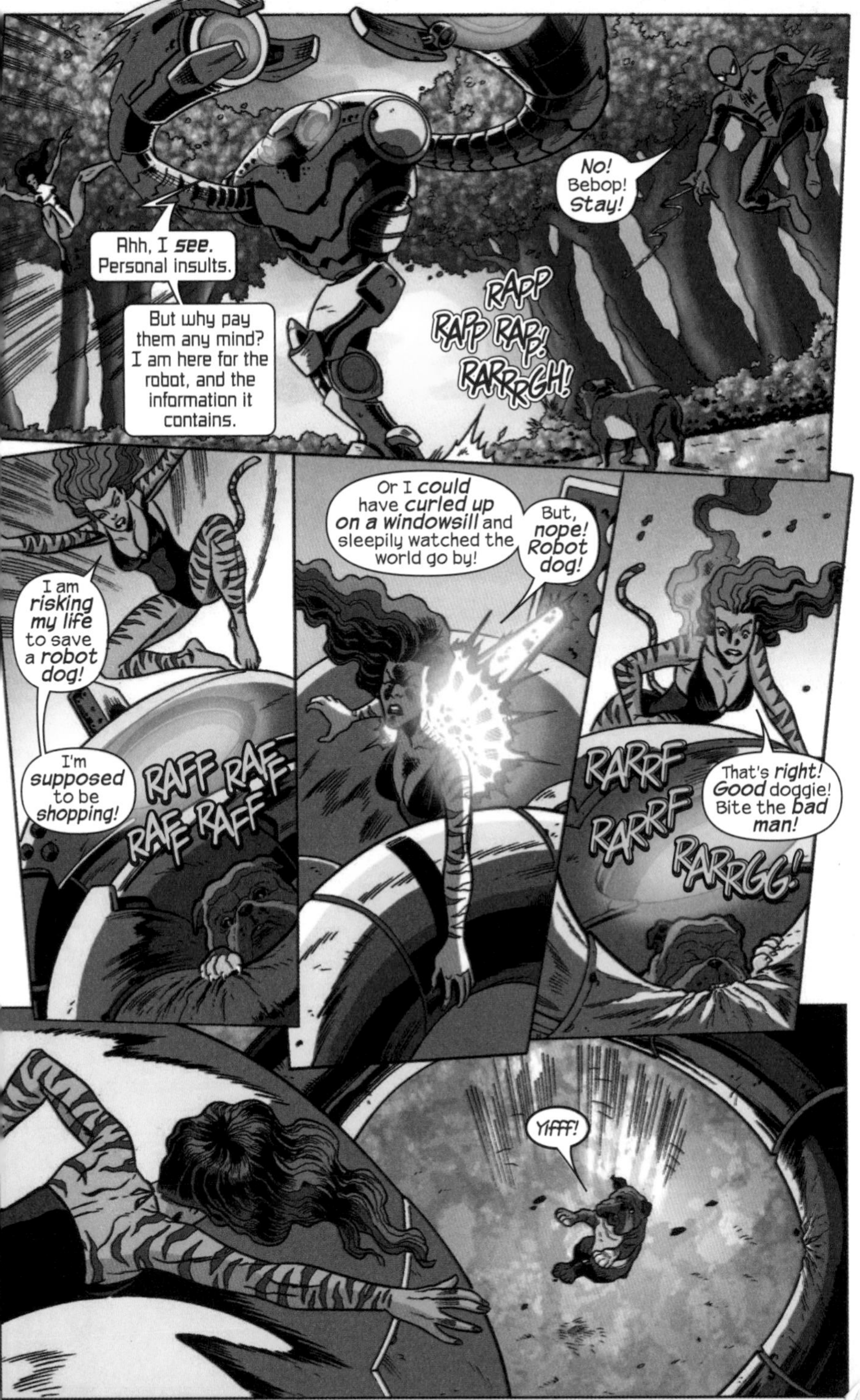
Ahh, I see. Personal insults.
But why pay them any mind? I am here for the robot, and the information it contains.
No! Bebop! Stay!
RAPP RAPP RAPP! RARRRGH!
I am risking my life to save a robot dog!
I'm supposed to be shopping!
RAFF RAFF RAFF RAFF
Or I could have curled up on a windowsill and sleepily watched the world go by!
But, nope! Robot dog!
RARRF RARRF RARRGG!
That's right! Good doggie! Bite the bad man!
YIFFF!

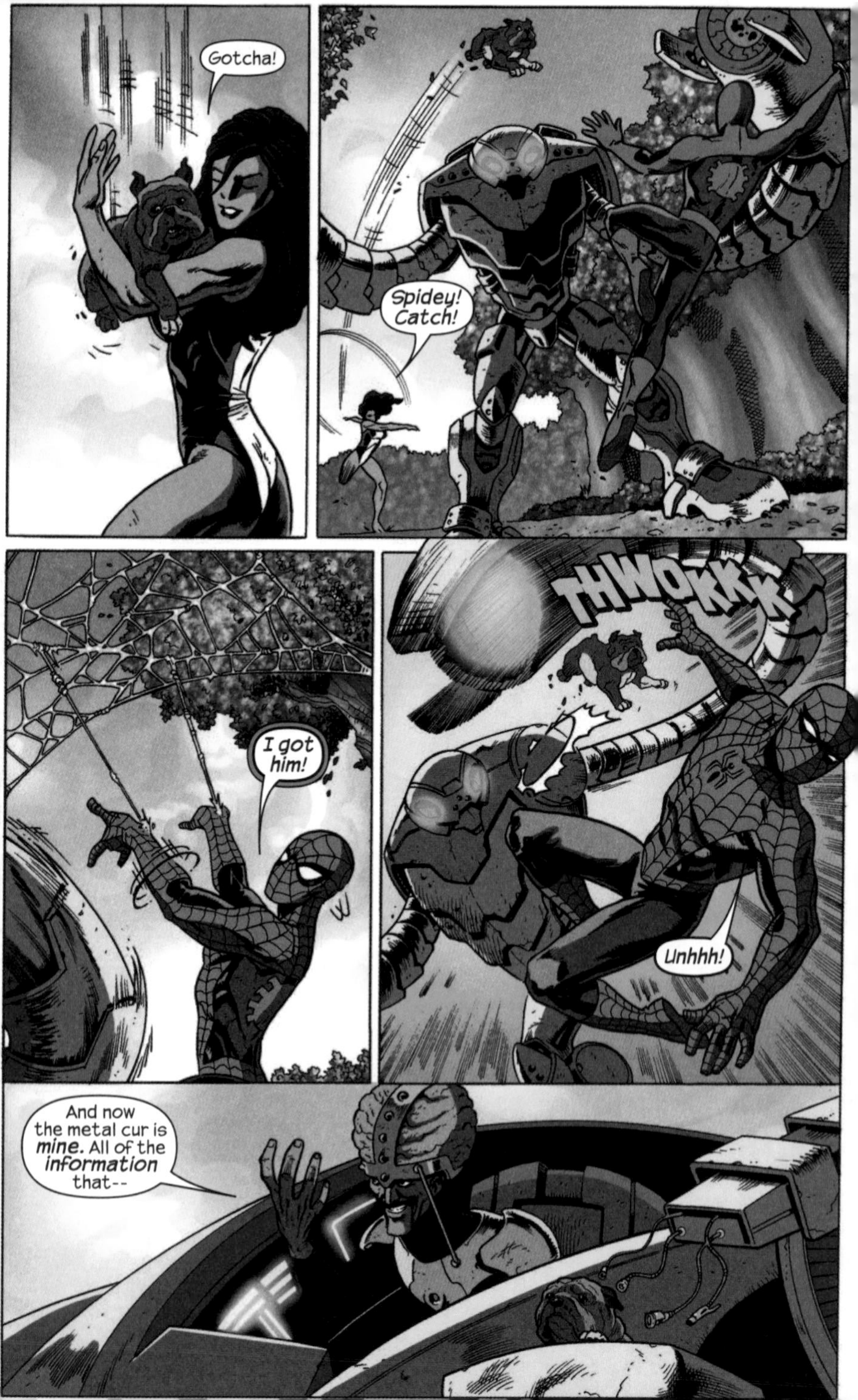
Gotcha!
Spidey! Catch!
I got him!
THWOKKK
Unhhh!
And now the metal cur is *mine.* All of the *information* that--

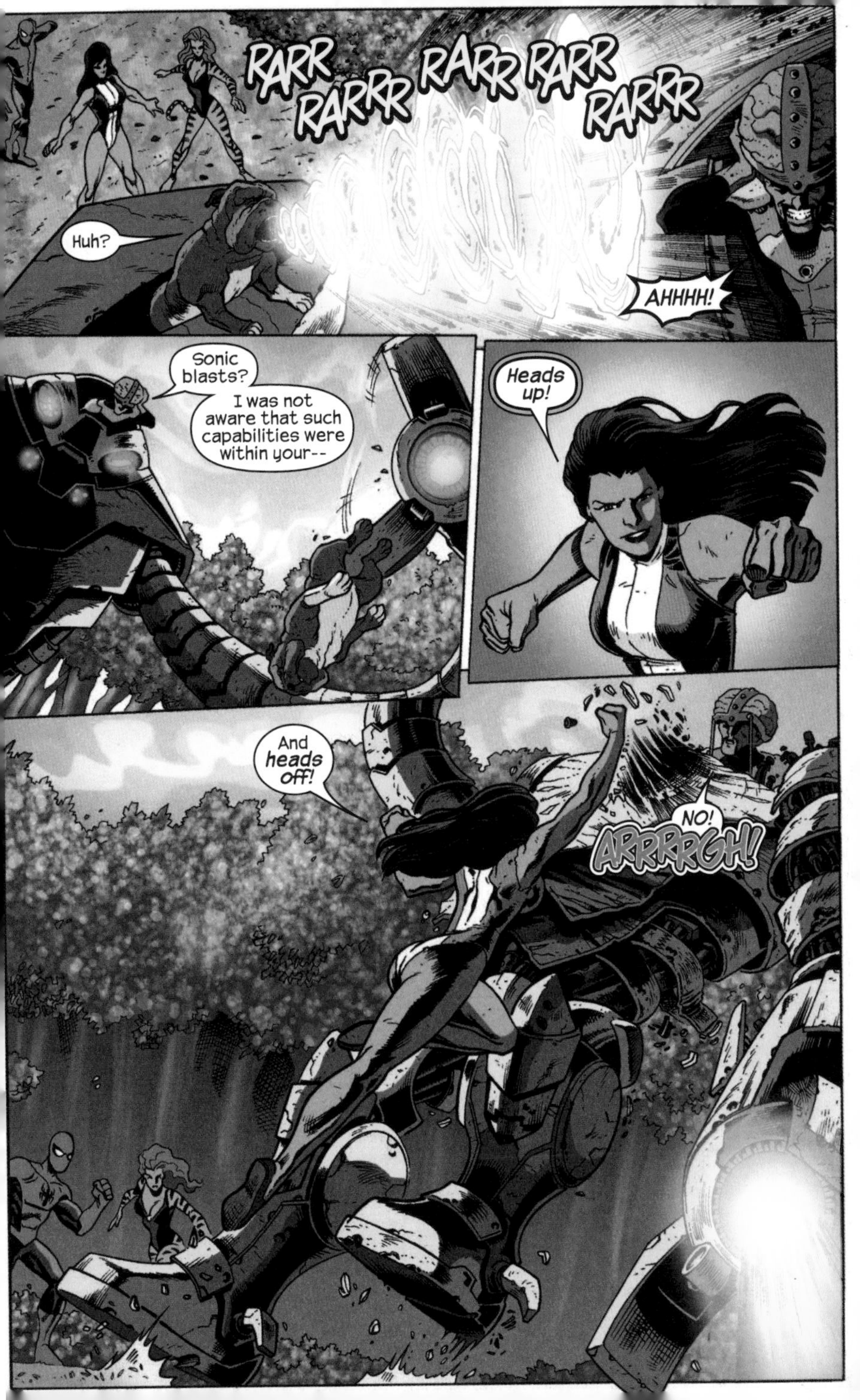
RARR RARRR RARR RARR RARRR
Huh?
AHHHH!
Sonic blasts?
I was not aware that such capabilities were within your--
Heads up!
And heads off!
NO!
ARRRRGH!

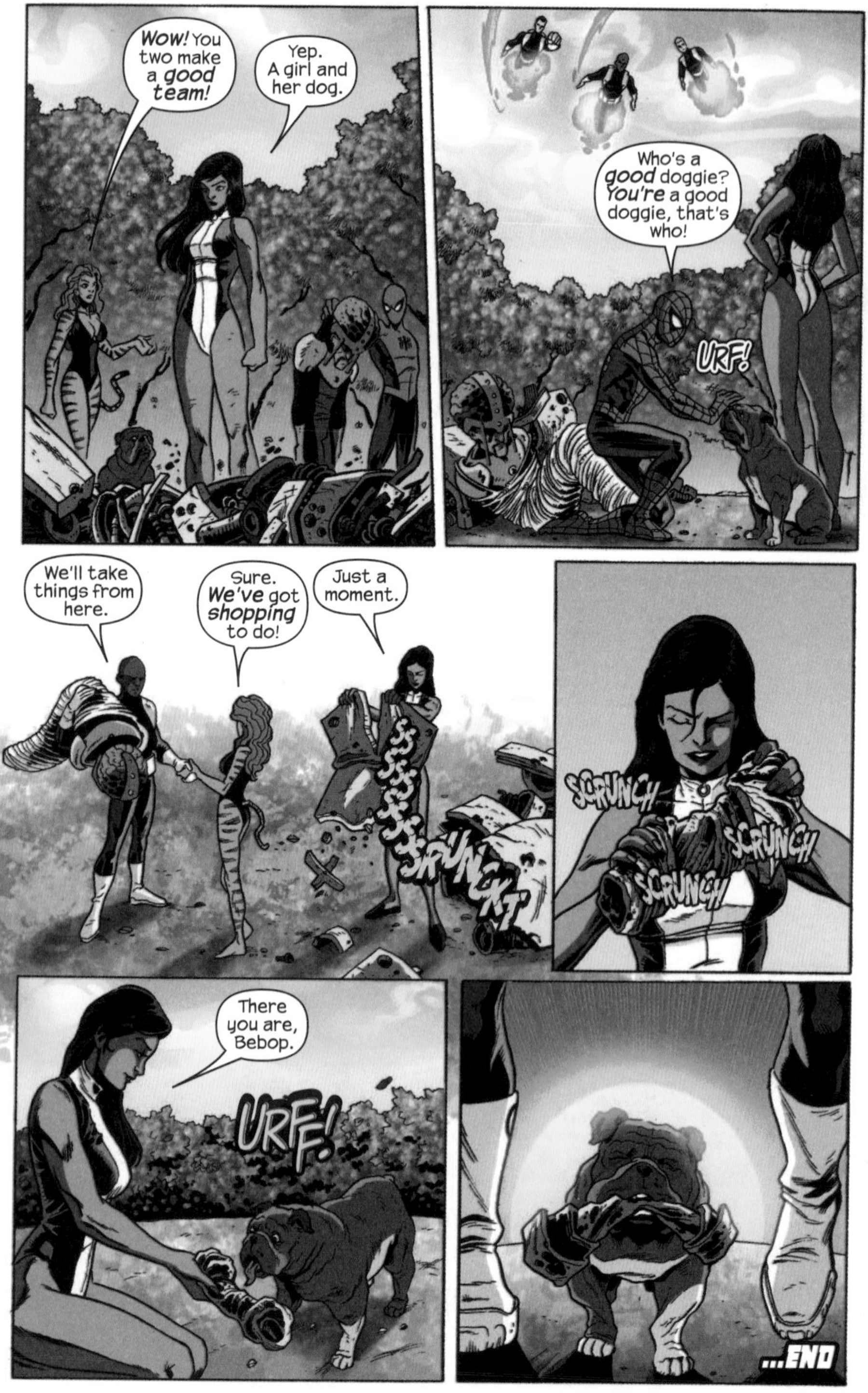
Wow! You two make a good team!
Yep. A girl and her dog.
Who's a good doggie? You're a good doggie, that's who!
URF!
We'll take things from here.
Sure. We've got shopping to do!
Just a moment.
SSSSSSSRUNCKT
SCRUNCH
SCRUNCH
SCRUNCH
There you are, Bebop.
URFF!
...END

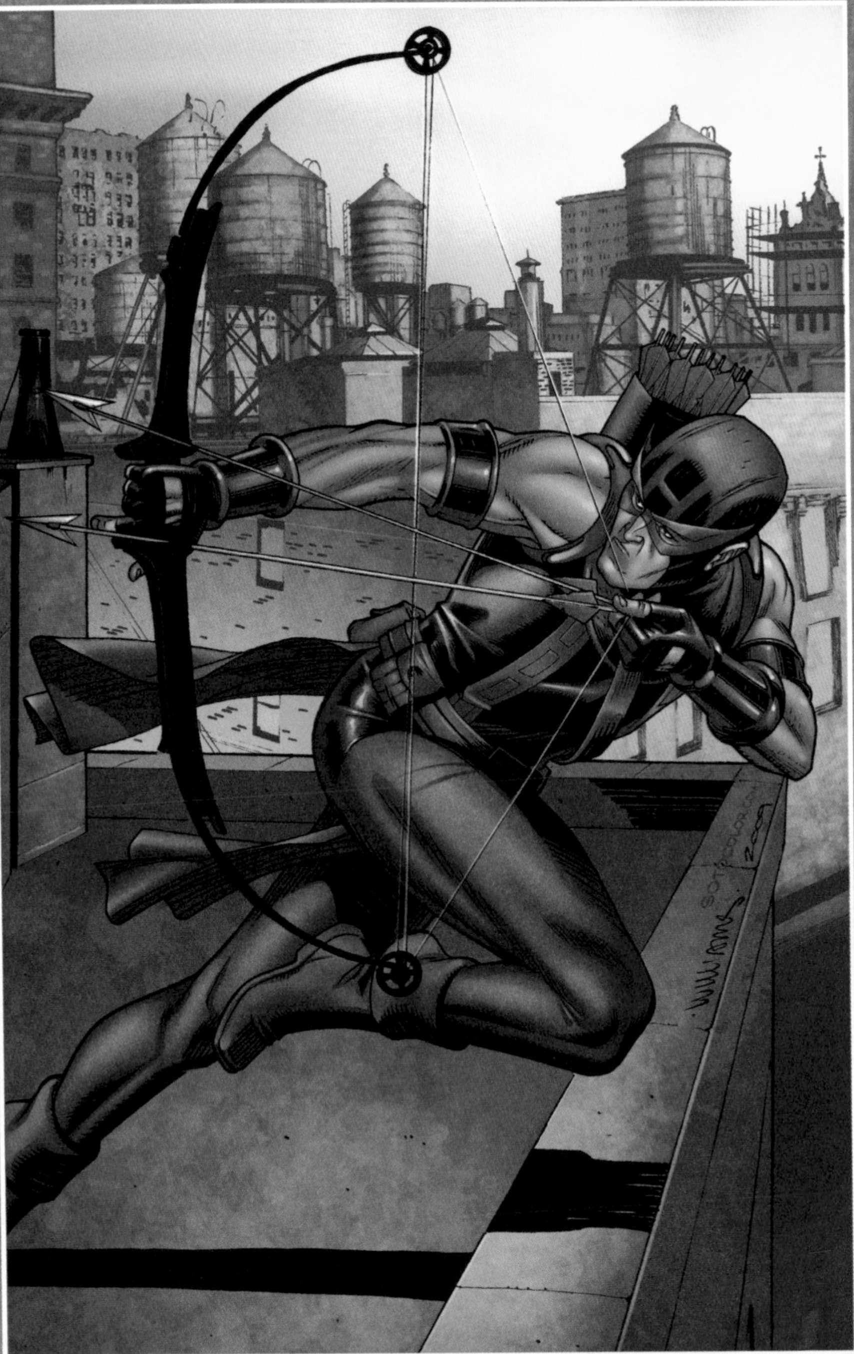

#14

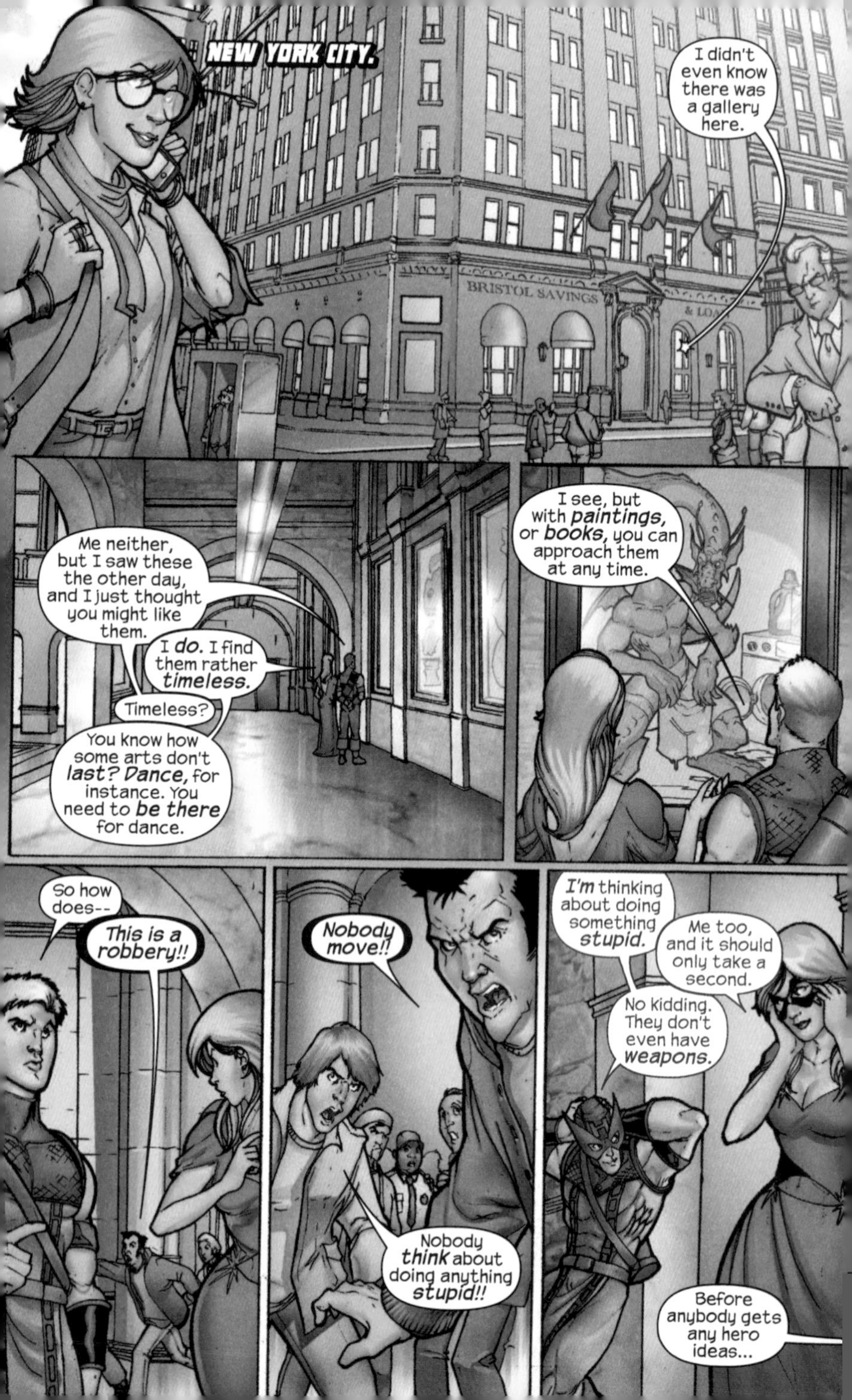
NEW YORK CITY.
I didn't even know there was a gallery here.
BRISTOL SAVINGS & LOA
Me neither, but I saw these the other day, and I just thought you might like them.
I do. I find them rather timeless.
Timeless?
You know how some arts don't last? Dance, for instance. You need to be there for dance.
I see, but with paintings, or books, you can approach them at any time.
So how does--
This is a robbery!!
Nobody move!!
Nobody think about doing anything stupid!!
I'm thinking about doing something stupid.
Me too, and it should only take a second.
No kidding. They don't even have weapons.
Before anybody gets any hero ideas...

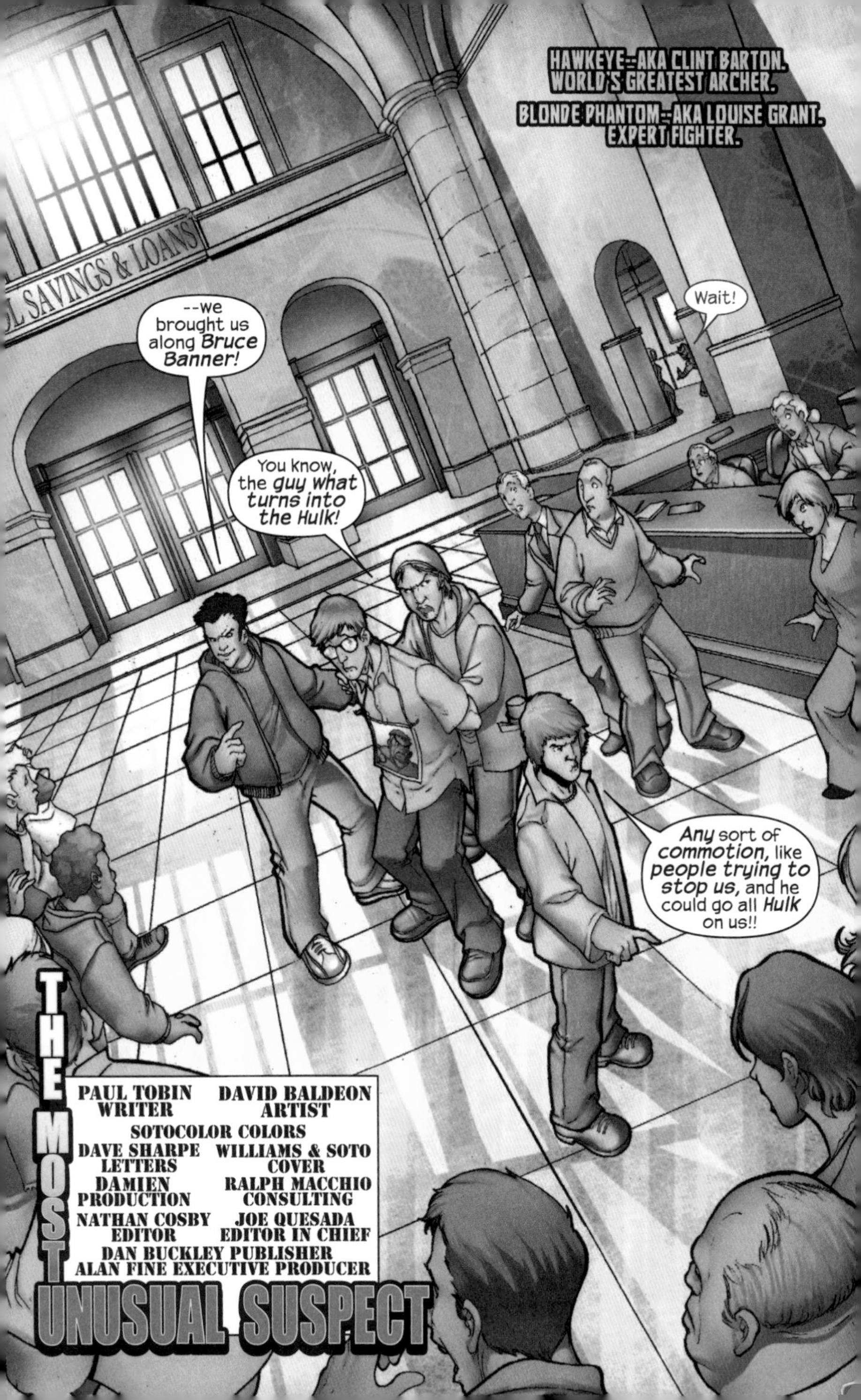

HAWKEYE--AKA CLINT BARTON. WORLD'S GREATEST ARCHER.
BLONDE PHANTOM--AKA LOUISE GRANT. EXPERT FIGHTER.
SAVINGS & LOANS
--we brought us along Bruce Banner!
You know, the guy what turns into the Hulk!
Wait!
Any sort of commotion, like people trying to stop us, and he could go all Hulk on us!!
THE MOST UNUSUAL SUSPECT
PAUL TOBIN WRITER
DAVID BALDEON ARTIST
SOTOCOLOR COLORS
DAVE SHARPE LETTERS
WILLIAMS & SOTO COVER
DAMIEN PRODUCTION
RALPH MACCHIO CONSULTING
NATHAN COSBY EDITOR
JOE QUESADA EDITOR IN CHIEF
DAN BUCKLEY PUBLISHER
ALAN FINE EXECUTIVE PRODUCER

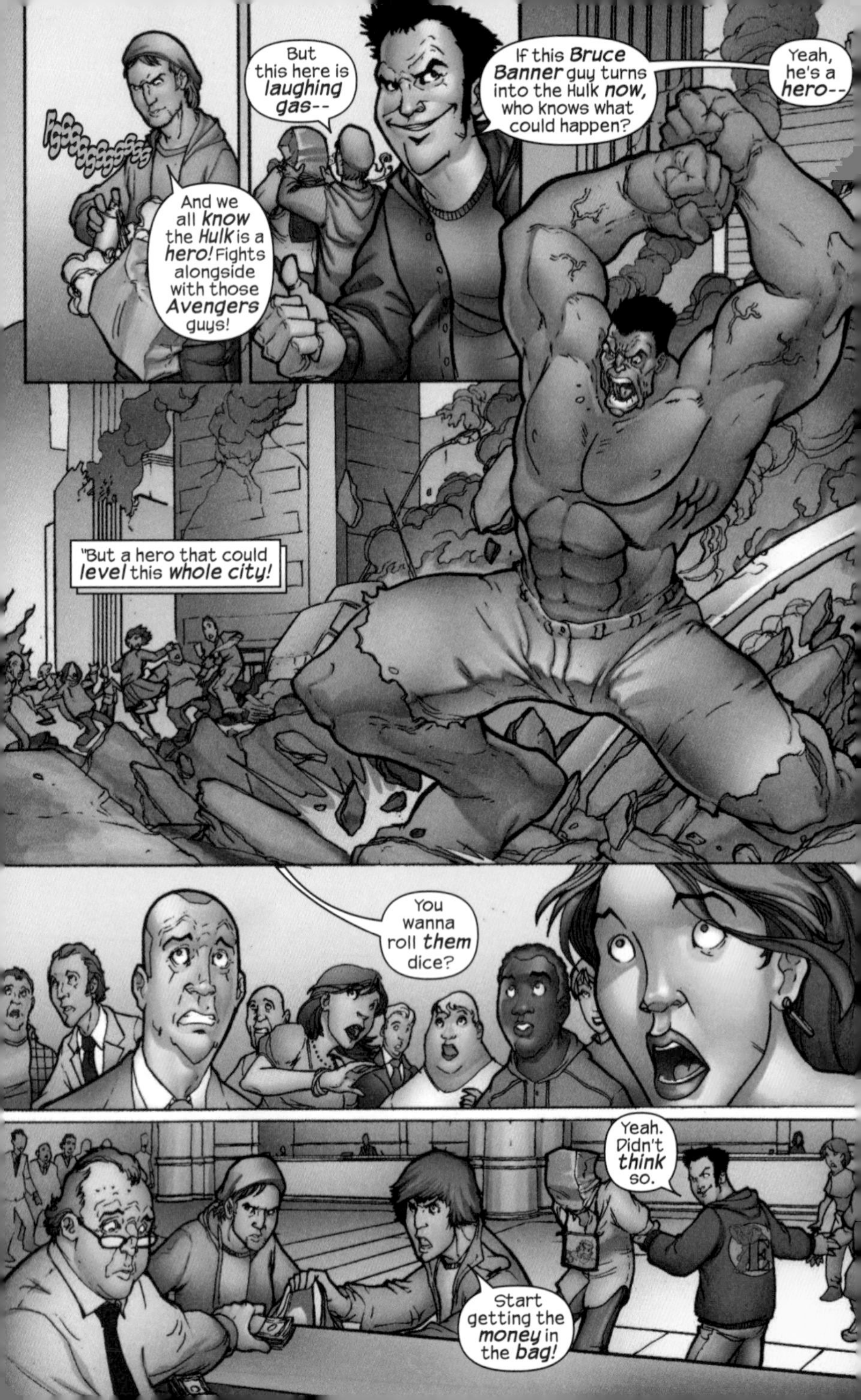
FSSSSSSSSSSS
But this here is laughing gas--
And we all know the Hulk is a hero! Fights alongside with those Avengers guys!
If this Bruce Banner guy turns into the Hulk now, who knows what could happen?
Yeah, he's a hero--
"But a hero that could level this whole city!
You wanna roll them dice?
Yeah. Didn't think so.
Start getting the money in the bag!

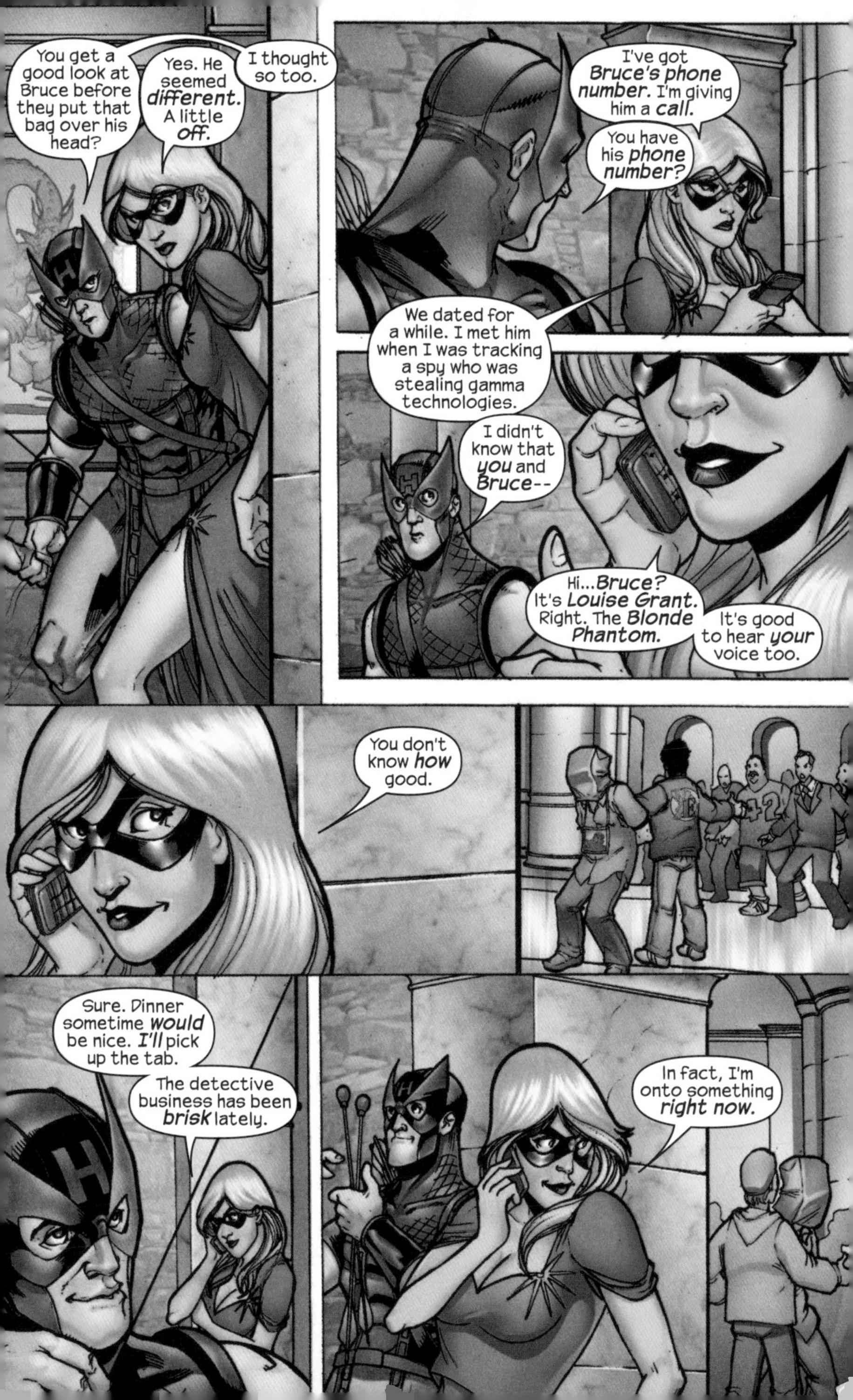
You get a good look at Bruce before they put that bag over his head?
Yes. He seemed *different.* A little *off.*
I thought so too.
I've got *Bruce's phone number.* I'm giving him a *call.*
You have his *phone number?*
We dated for a while. I met him when I was tracking a spy who was stealing gamma technologies.
I didn't know that *you* and *Bruce*--
Hi...*Bruce?* It's *Louise Grant.* Right. The *Blonde Phantom.*
It's good to hear *your* voice too.
You don't know *how* good.
Sure. Dinner sometime *would* be nice. *I'll* pick up the tab.
The detective business has been *brisk* lately.
In fact, I'm onto something *right now.*

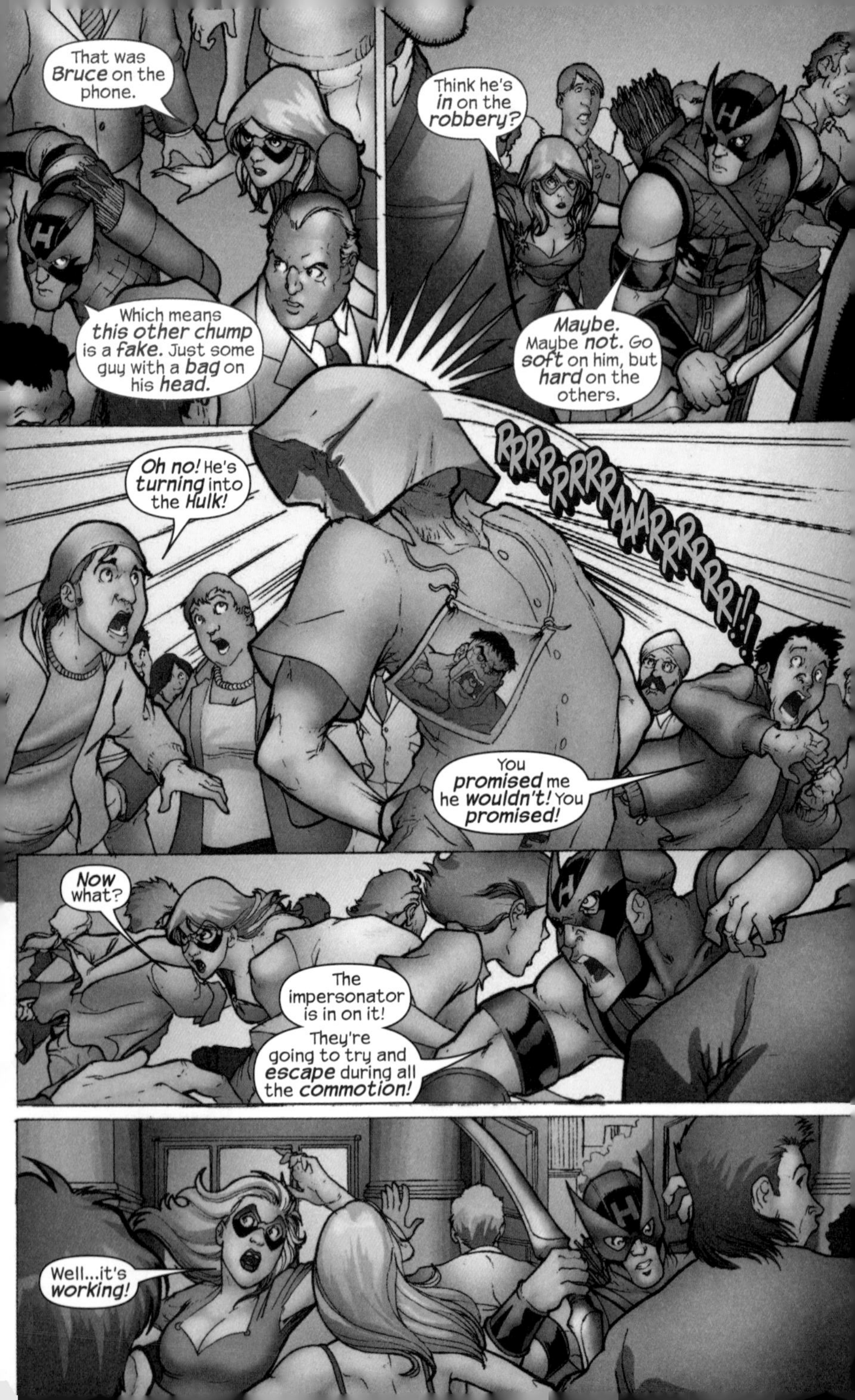
That was Bruce on the phone.
Which means this other chump is a fake. Just some guy with a bag on his head.
Think he's in on the robbery?
Maybe. Maybe not. Go soft on him, but hard on the others.
Oh no! He's turning into the Hulk!
RRRRRRRRAAARRRRRR!!!
You promised me he wouldn't! You promised!
Now what?
The impersonator is in on it!
They're going to try and escape during all the commotion!
Well...it's working!

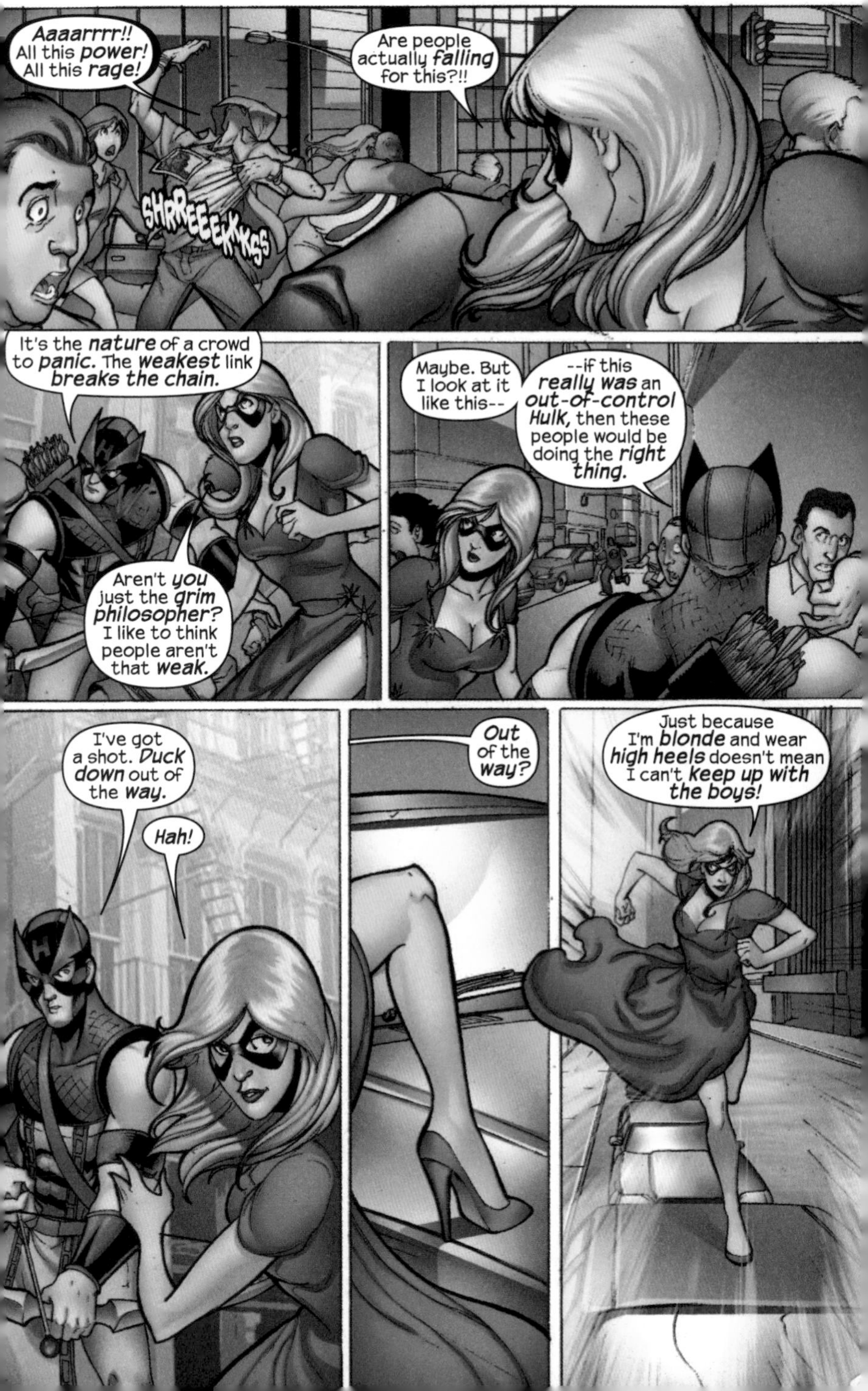
Aaaarrrr!! All this power! All this rage!
Are people actually falling for this?!!
SHRREEEKKKSS
It's the nature of a crowd to panic. The weakest link breaks the chain.
Aren't you just the grim philosopher? I like to think people aren't that weak.
Maybe. But I look at it like this--
--if this really was an out-of-control Hulk, then these people would be doing the right thing.
I've got a shot. Duck down out of the way.
Hah!
Out of the way?
Just because I'm blonde and wear high heels doesn't mean I can't keep up with the boys!

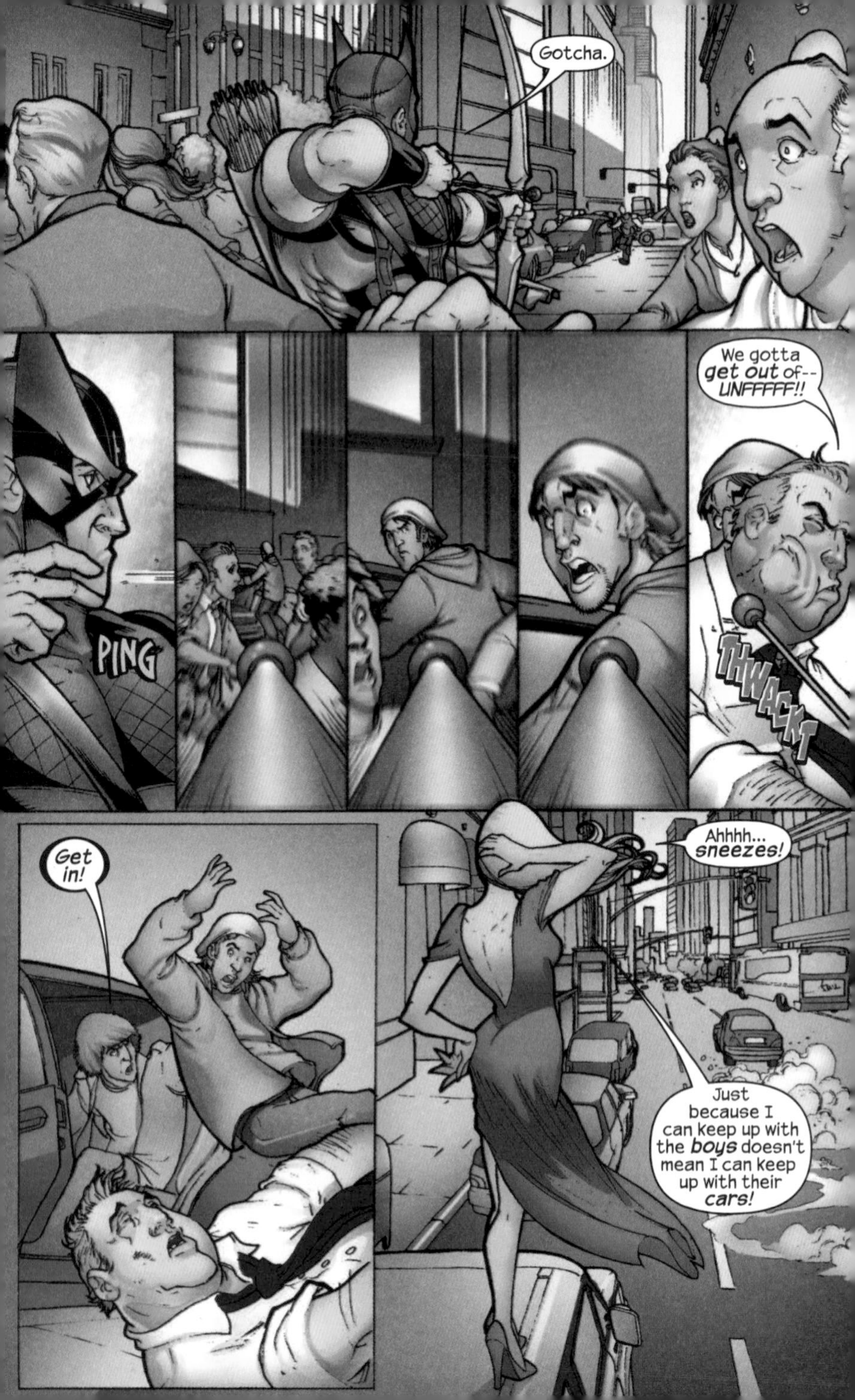
Gotcha.
PING
We gotta get out of-- UNFFFFF!!
THWACKT
Get in!
Ahhhh... sneezes!
Just because I can keep up with the boys doesn't mean I can keep up with their cars!

Fantastic. I feel really *proud* of letting *amateur bank robbers* get away.

What now?

We start with the *bank surveillance photos* and go from there.

11:43:34 MSG

I'm not matching these guys up with *any* database.

NO MATCH

NO MATCH   NO MATCH   NO MATCH

--several incidents of the so-called "Banner Bandit" within the past three days, with police assuring us that the culprit is an impersonator who--

Yeah. I seen 'em. Just on the news though, eh?

It's that Banner guy.

Nah, man. Didn't you hear the Avengers talking 'bout that?

Straight truth, man, it ain't Banner.

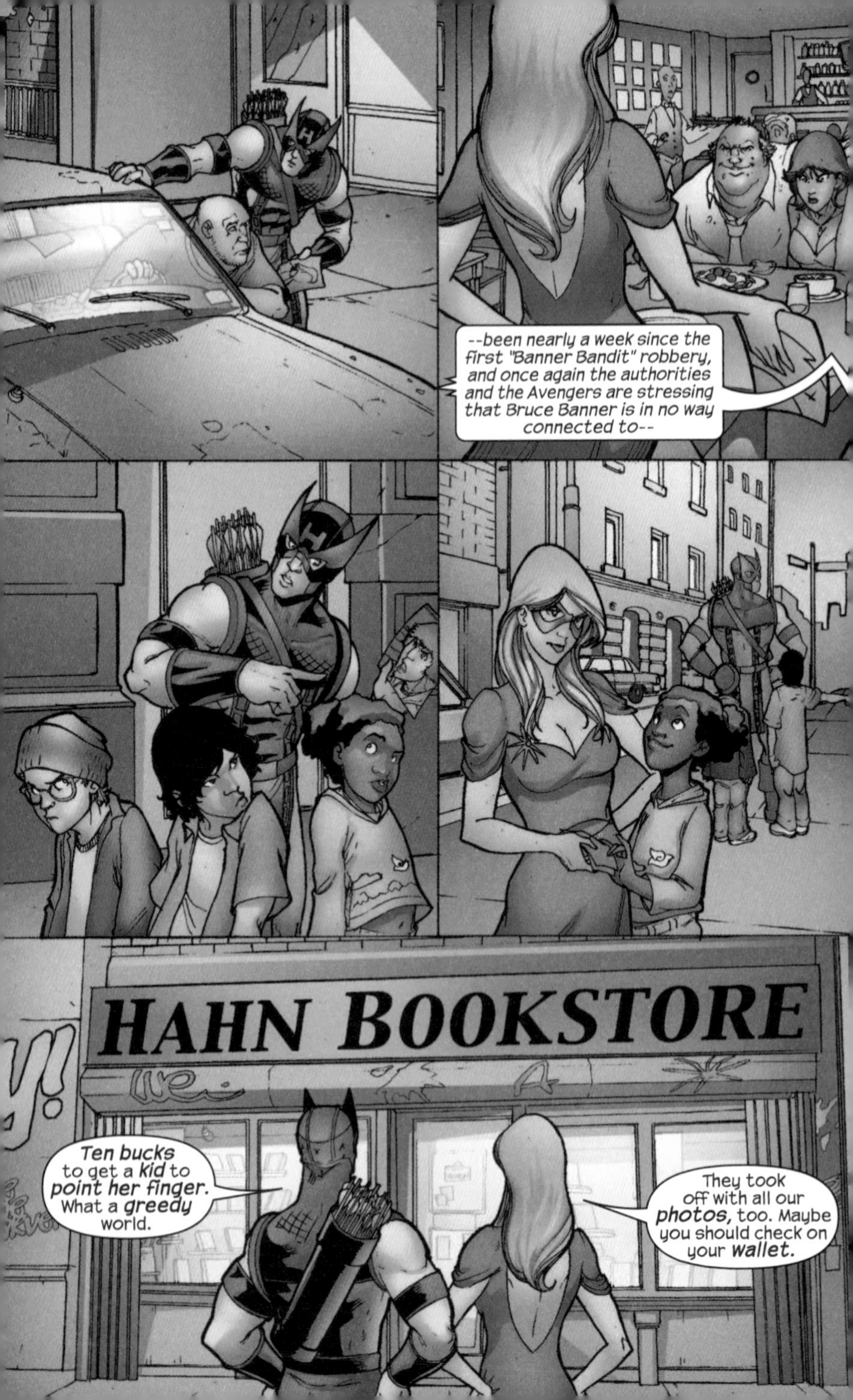
--been nearly a week since the first "Banner Bandit" robbery, and once again the authorities and the Avengers are stressing that Bruce Banner is in no way connected to--
HAHN BOOKSTORE
Ten bucks to get a kid to point her finger. What a greedy world.
They took off with all our photos, too. Maybe you should check on your wallet.

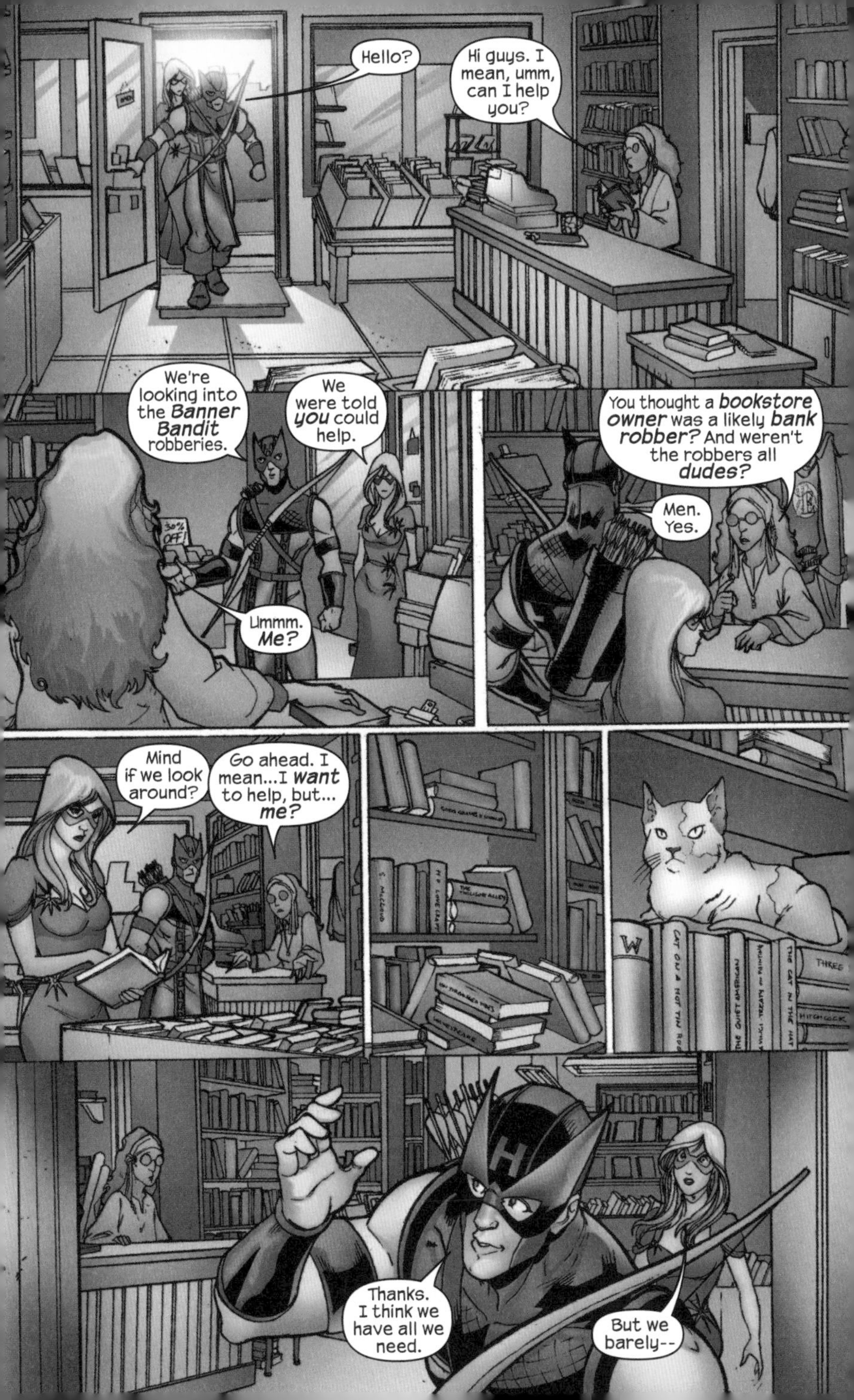
Hello?
Hi guys. I mean, umm, can I help you?
We're looking into the *Banner Bandit* robberies.
We were told *you* could help.
30% OFF!
Ummm. *Me?*
You thought a *bookstore owner* was a likely *bank robber?* And weren't the robbers all *dudes?*
Men. Yes.
Mind if we look around?
Go ahead. I mean...I *want* to help, but... *me?*
Thanks. I think we have all we need.
But we barely--

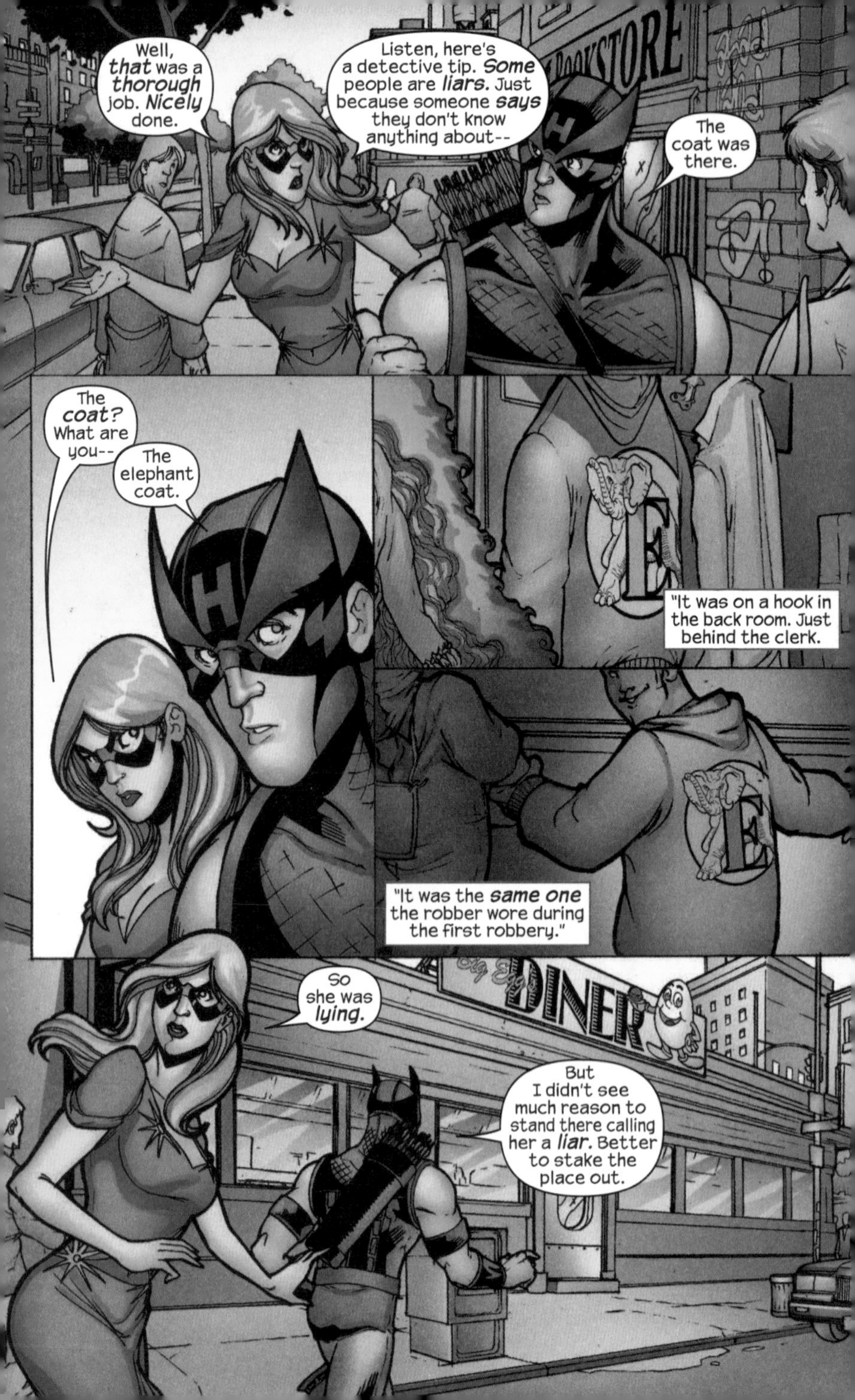

BOOKSTORE
Well, *that* was a *thorough* job. *Nicely* done.
Listen, here's a detective tip. *Some* people are *liars.* Just because someone *says* they don't know anything about--
The coat was there.
The *coat?* What are you--
The elephant coat.
"It was on a hook in the back room. Just behind the clerk.
"It was the *same one* the robber wore during the first robbery."
Big Egg's DINER
So she was *lying.*
But I didn't see much reason to stand there calling her a *liar.* Better to stake the place out.

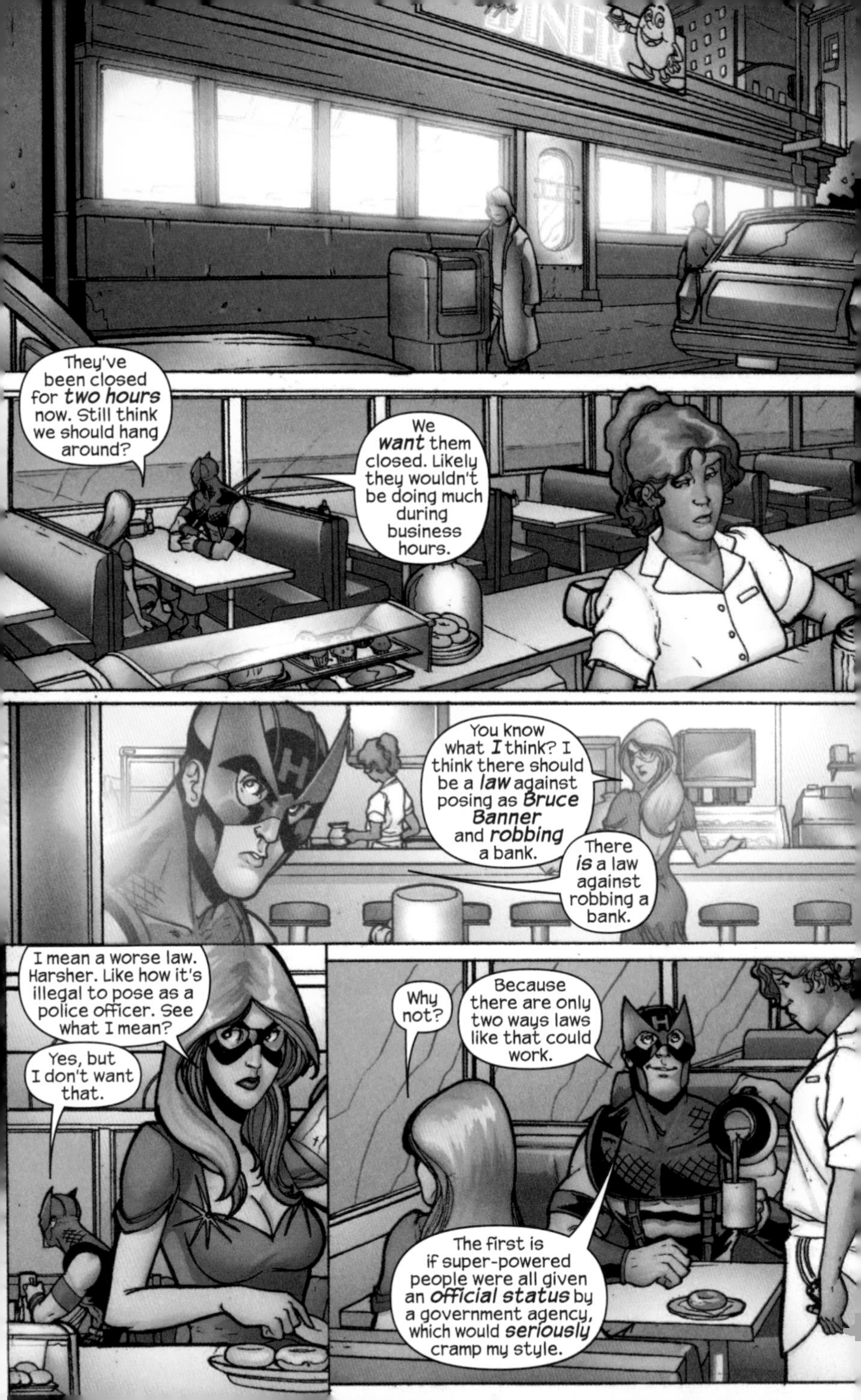

DINER
They've been closed for two hours now. Still think we should hang around?
We want them closed. Likely they wouldn't be doing much during business hours.
You know what I think? I think there should be a law against posing as Bruce Banner and robbing a bank.
There is a law against robbing a bank.
I mean a worse law. Harsher. Like how it's illegal to pose as a police officer. See what I mean?
Yes, but I don't want that.
Why not?
Because there are only two ways laws like that could work.
The first is if super-powered people were all given an official status by a government agency, which would seriously cramp my style.

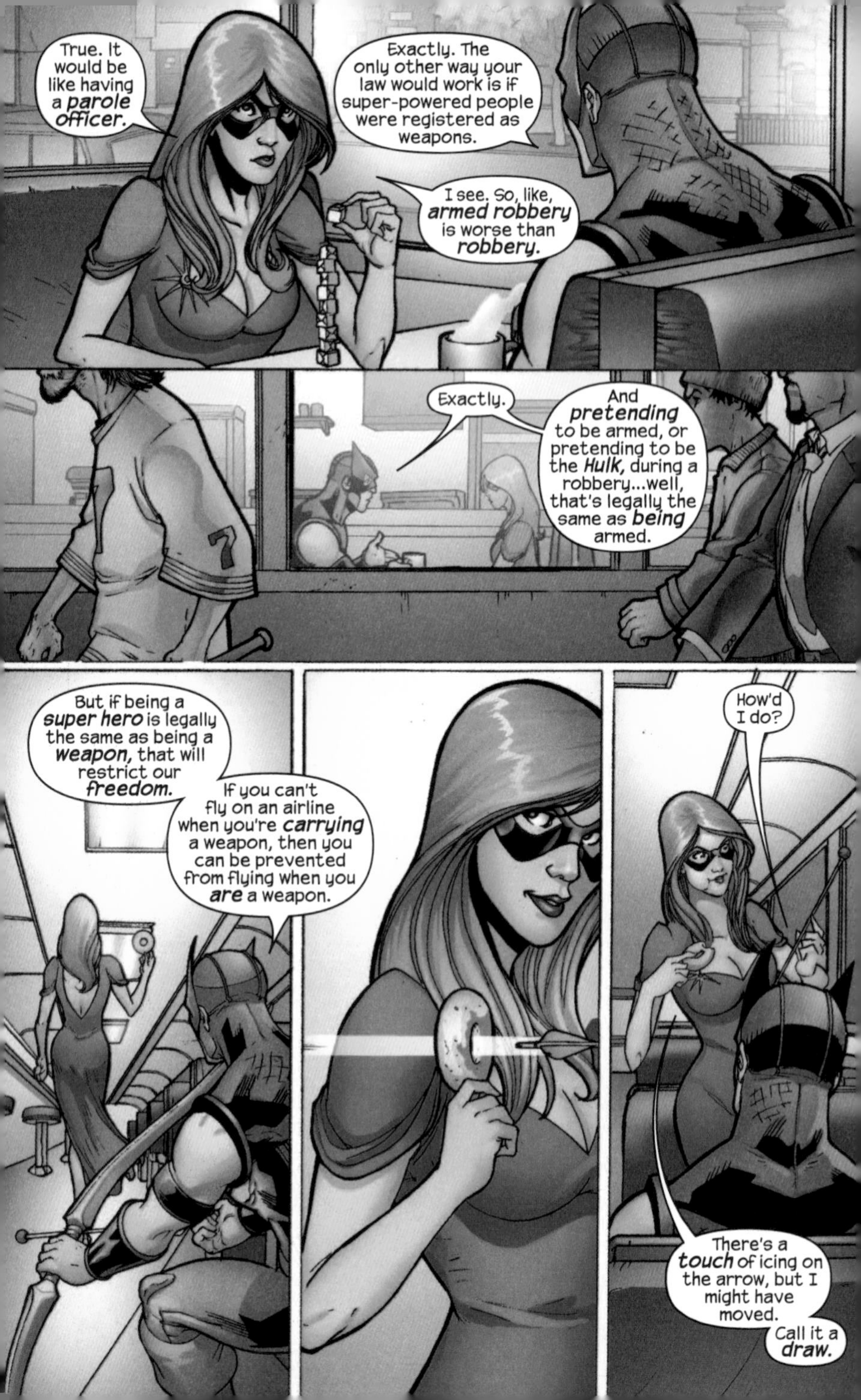

True. It would be like having a parole officer.
Exactly. The only other way your law would work is if super-powered people were registered as weapons.
I see. So, like, armed robbery is worse than robbery.
Exactly.
And pretending to be armed, or pretending to be the Hulk, during a robbery...well, that's legally the same as being armed.
But if being a super hero is legally the same as being a weapon, that will restrict our freedom.
If you can't fly on an airline when you're carrying a weapon, then you can be prevented from flying when you are a weapon.
How'd I do?
There's a touch of icing on the arrow, but I might have moved.
Call it a draw.

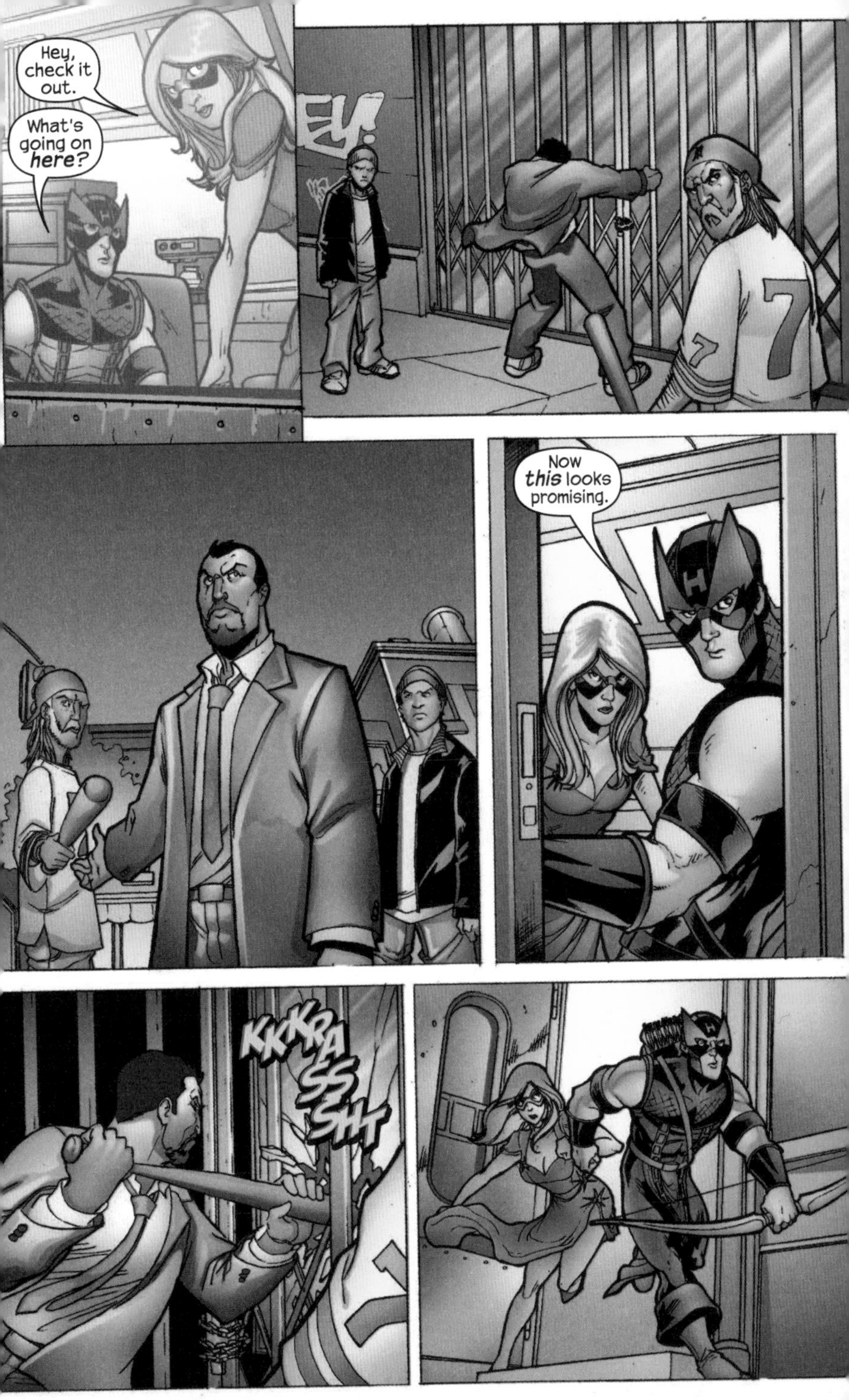
Hey, check it out.
What's going on *here*?
Now *this* looks promising.
KKKRASSSHT

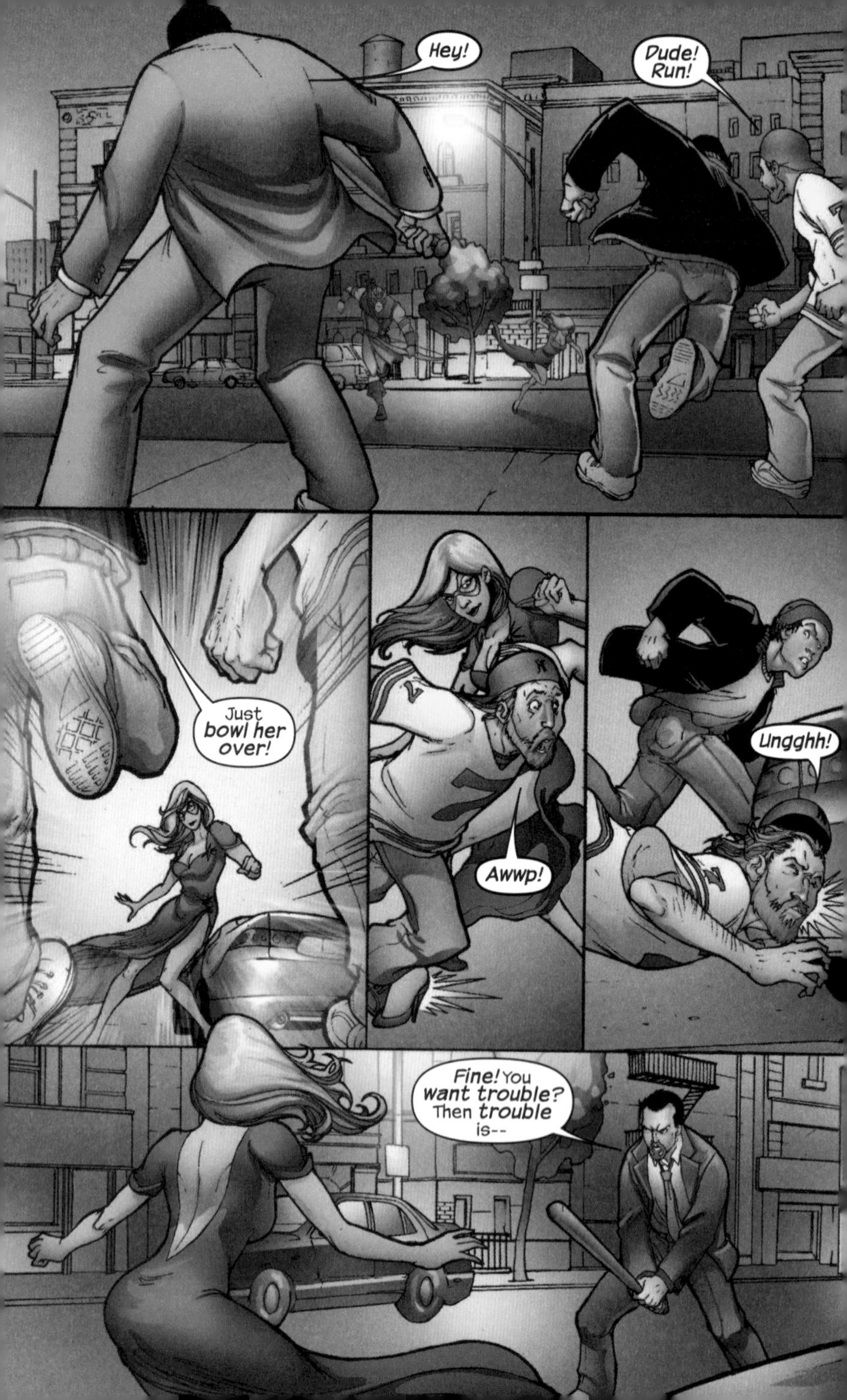

Hey!
Dude! Run!
Just bowl her over!
Awwp!
Ungghh!
Fine! You want trouble? Then trouble is--

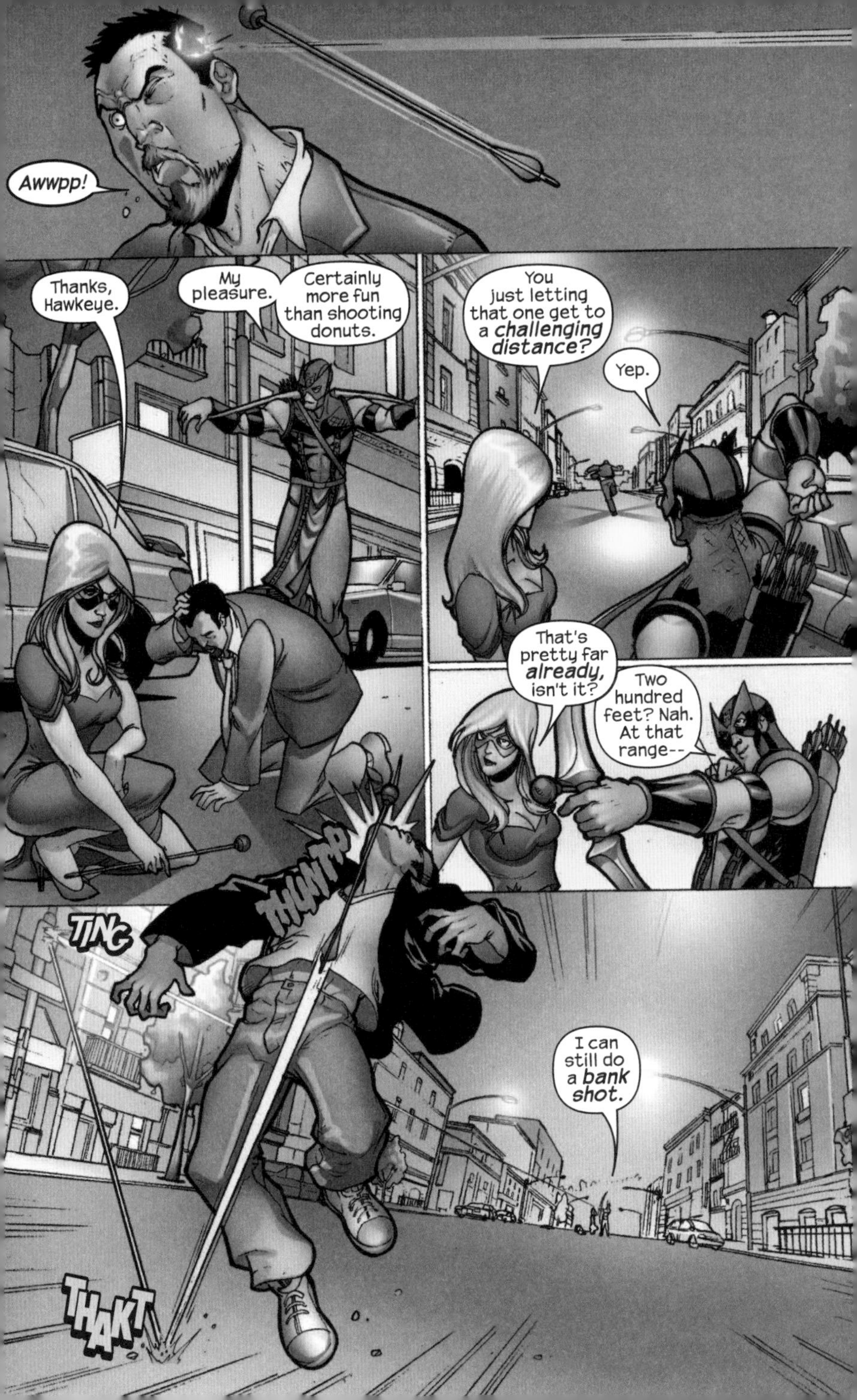

Awwpp!
Thanks, Hawkeye.
My pleasure.
Certainly more fun than shooting donuts.
You just letting that one get to a *challenging distance?*
Yep.
That's pretty far *already,* isn't it?
Two hundred feet? Nah. At that range--
TING
THUNK
THAKT
I can still do a *bank shot.*

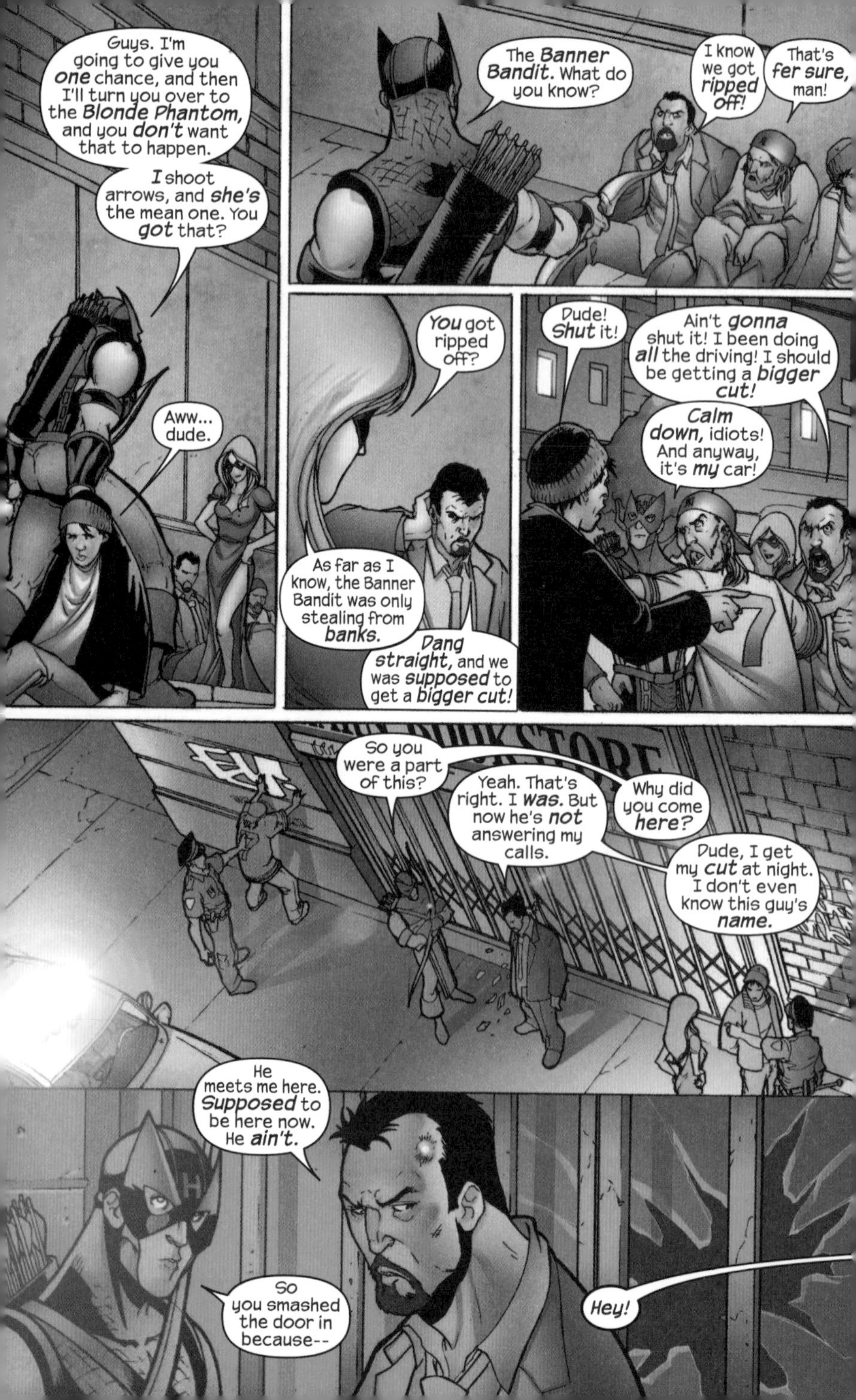
Guys. I'm going to give you one chance, and then I'll turn you over to the Blonde Phantom, and you don't want that to happen.
I shoot arrows, and she's the mean one. You got that?
Aww... dude.
The Banner Bandit. What do you know?
I know we got ripped off!
That's fer sure, man!
You got ripped off?
As far as I know, the Banner Bandit was only stealing from banks.
Dang straight, and we was supposed to get a bigger cut!
Dude! Shut it!
Ain't gonna shut it! I been doing all the driving! I should be getting a bigger cut!
Calm down, idiots! And anyway, it's my car!
So you were a part of this?
Yeah. That's right. I was. But now he's not answering my calls.
Why did you come here?
Dude, I get my cut at night. I don't even know this guy's name.
He meets me here. Supposed to be here now. He ain't.
So you smashed the door in because--
Hey!

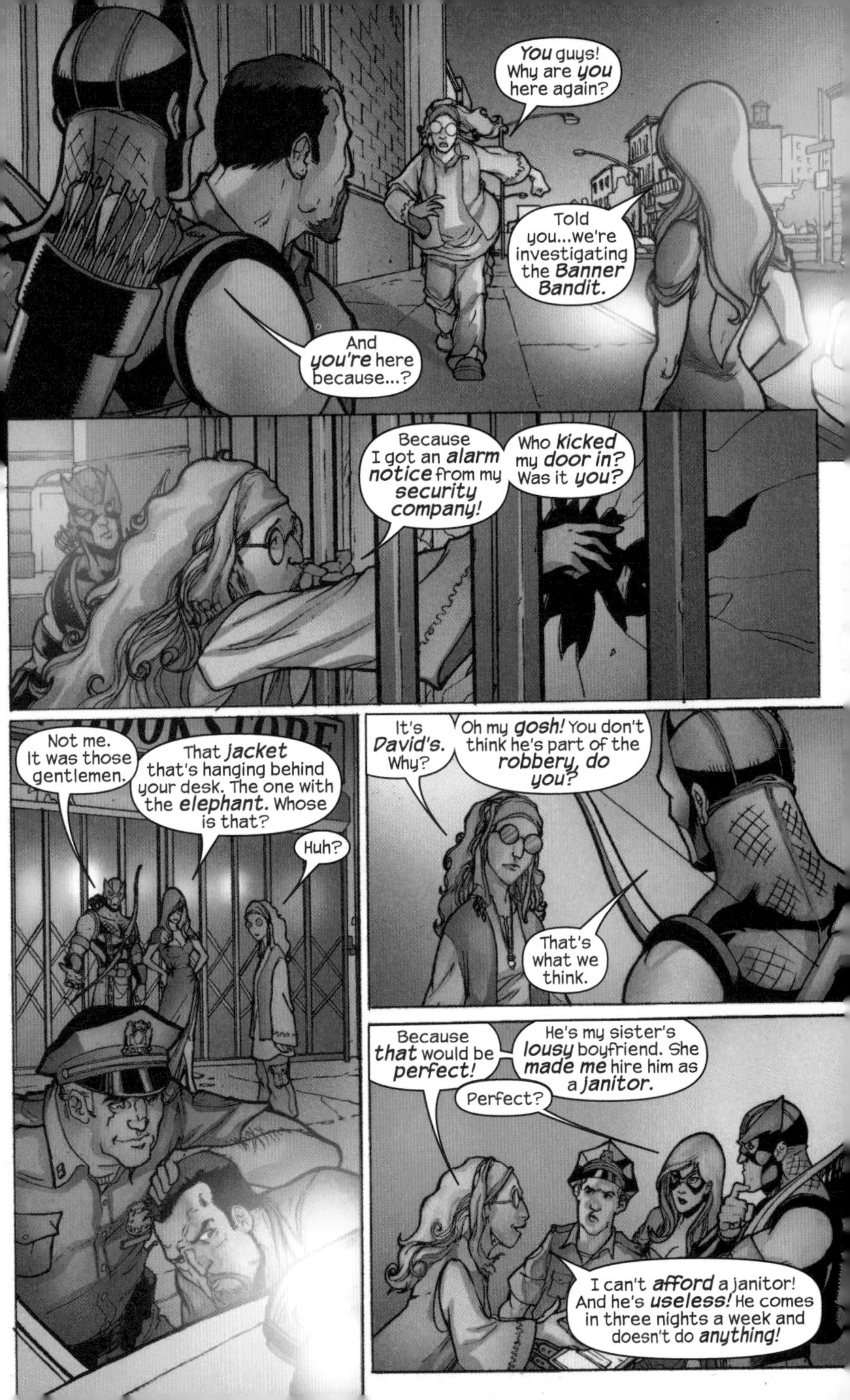
You guys! Why are you here again?
Told you...we're investigating the Banner Bandit.
And you're here because...?
Because I got an alarm notice from my security company!
Who kicked my door in? Was it you?
Not me. It was those gentlemen.
That jacket that's hanging behind your desk. The one with the elephant. Whose is that?
Huh?
It's David's. Why?
Oh my gosh! You don't think he's part of the robbery, do you?
That's what we think.
Because that would be perfect!
He's my sister's lousy boyfriend. She made me hire him as a janitor.
Perfect?
I can't afford a janitor! And he's useless! He comes in three nights a week and doesn't do anything!

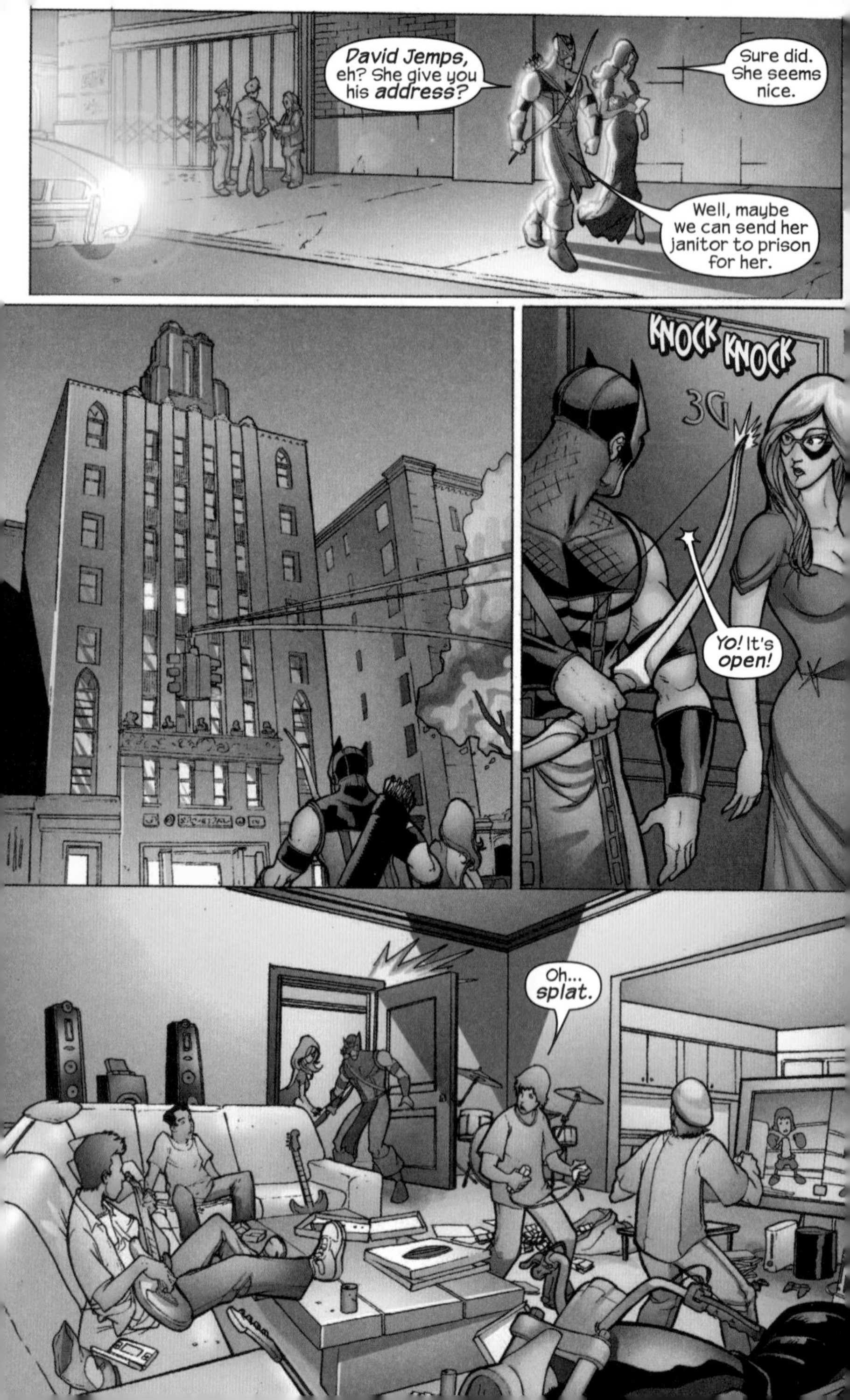
David Jemps, eh? She give you his address?
Sure did. She seems nice.
Well, maybe we can send her janitor to prison for her.
KNOCK KNOCK
3G
Yo! It's open!
Oh... splat.

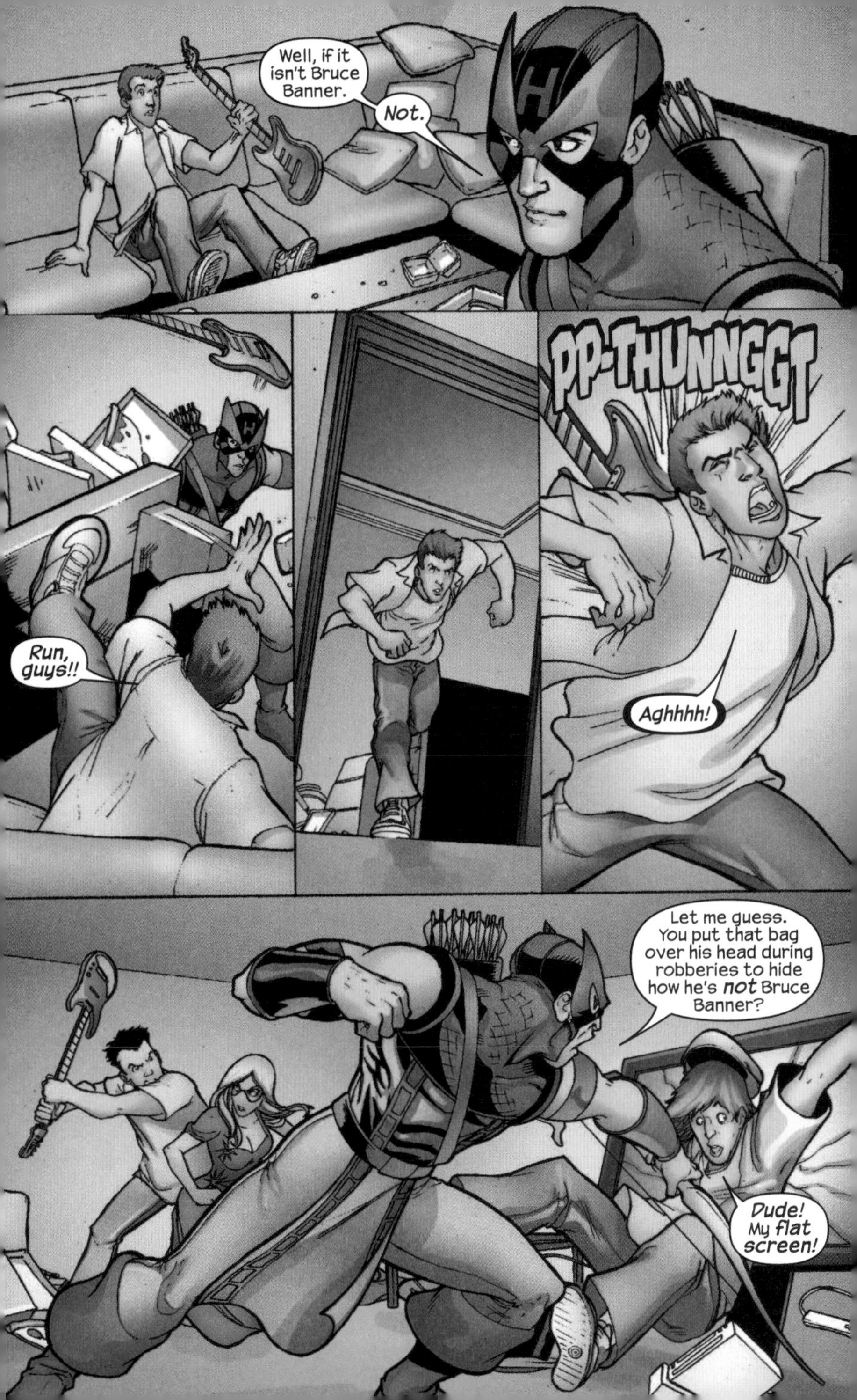
Well, if it isn't Bruce Banner.
Not.
Run, guys!!
PP-THUNNGGT
Aghhhh!
Let me guess. You put that bag over his head during robberies to hide how he's *not* Bruce Banner?
Dude! My *flat screen!*

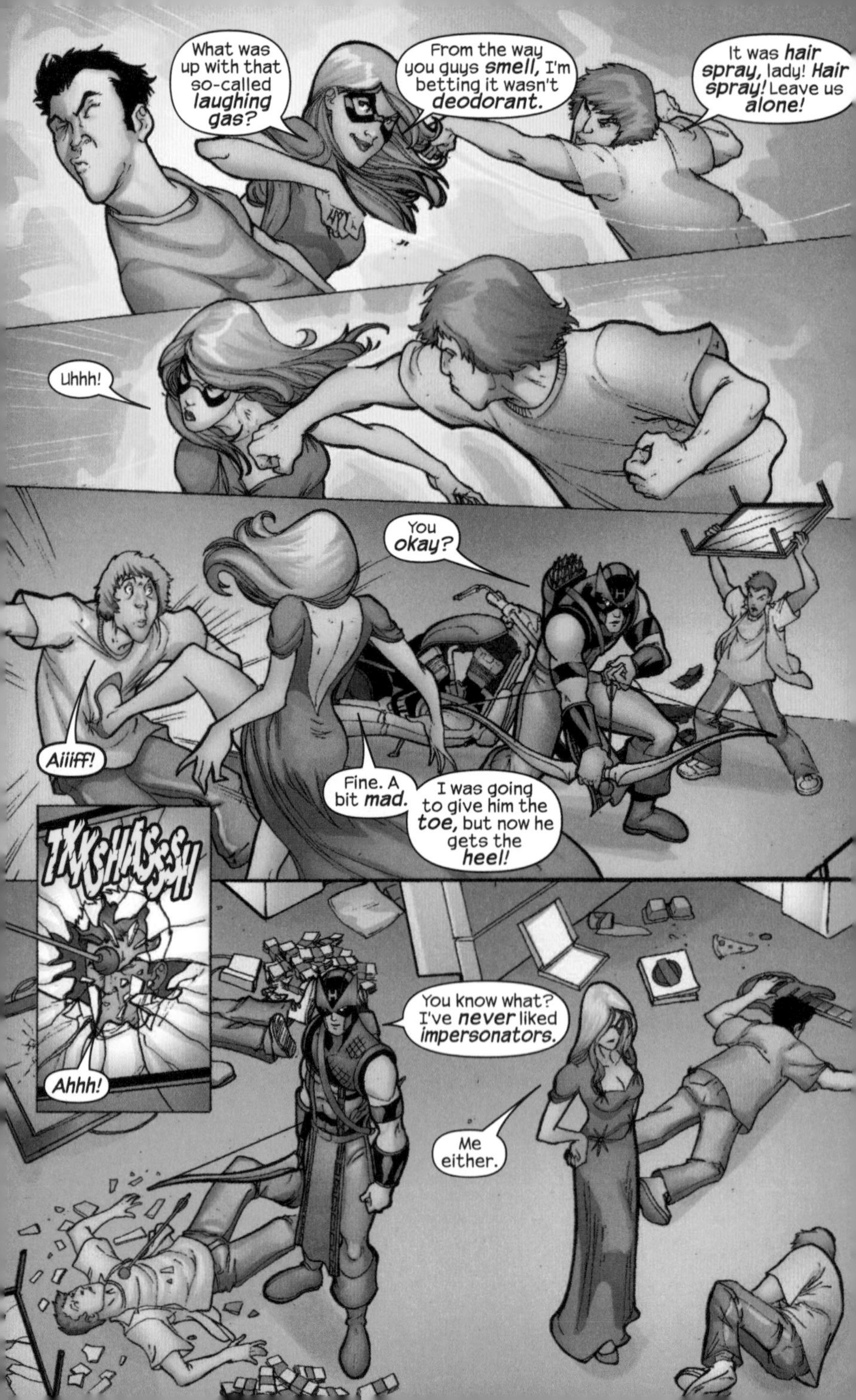

What was up with that so-called laughing gas?
From the way you guys smell, I'm betting it wasn't deodorant.
It was hair spray, lady! Hair spray! Leave us alone!
Uhhh!
You okay?
Aiiiff!
Fine. A bit mad.
I was going to give him the toe, but now he gets the heel!
TKKSHHASSSH
Ahhh!
You know what? I've never liked impersonators.
Me either.

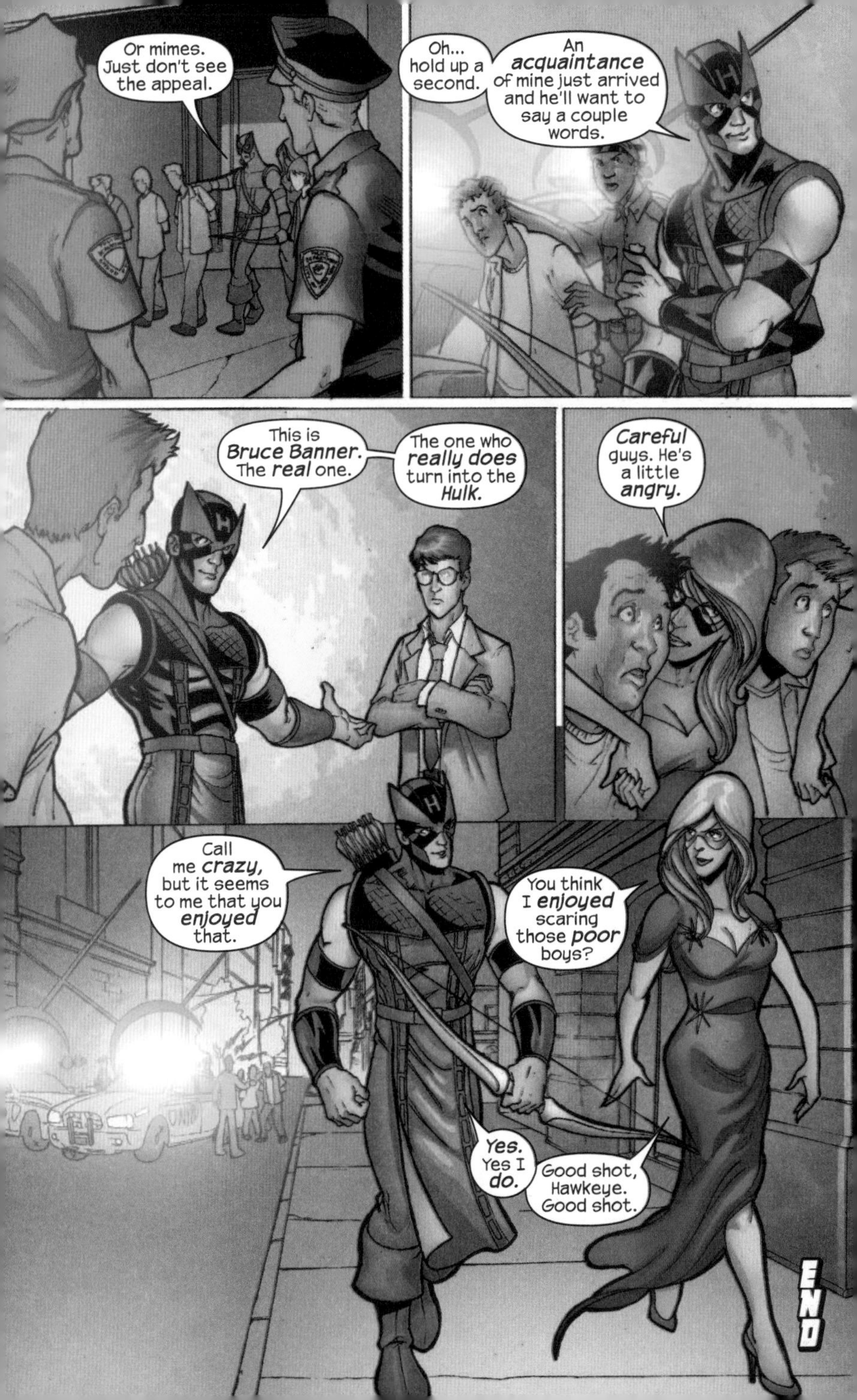

Or mimes. Just don't see the appeal.
Oh... hold up a second.
An acquaintance of mine just arrived and he'll want to say a couple words.
This is Bruce Banner. The real one.
The one who really does turn into the Hulk.
Careful guys. He's a little angry.
Call me crazy, but it seems to me that you enjoyed that.
You think I enjoyed scaring those poor boys?
Yes. Yes I do.
Good shot, Hawkeye. Good shot.
END

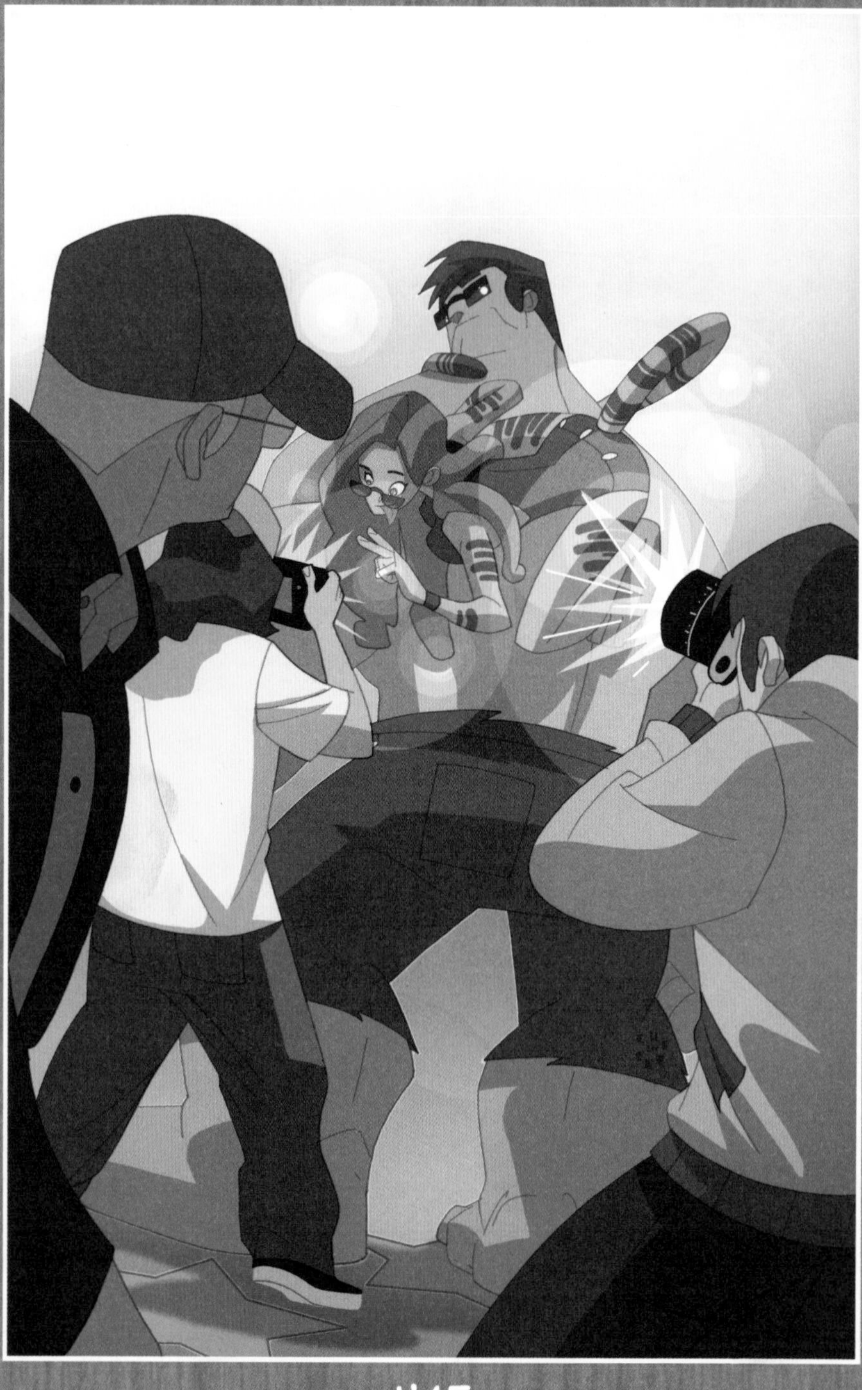

#15

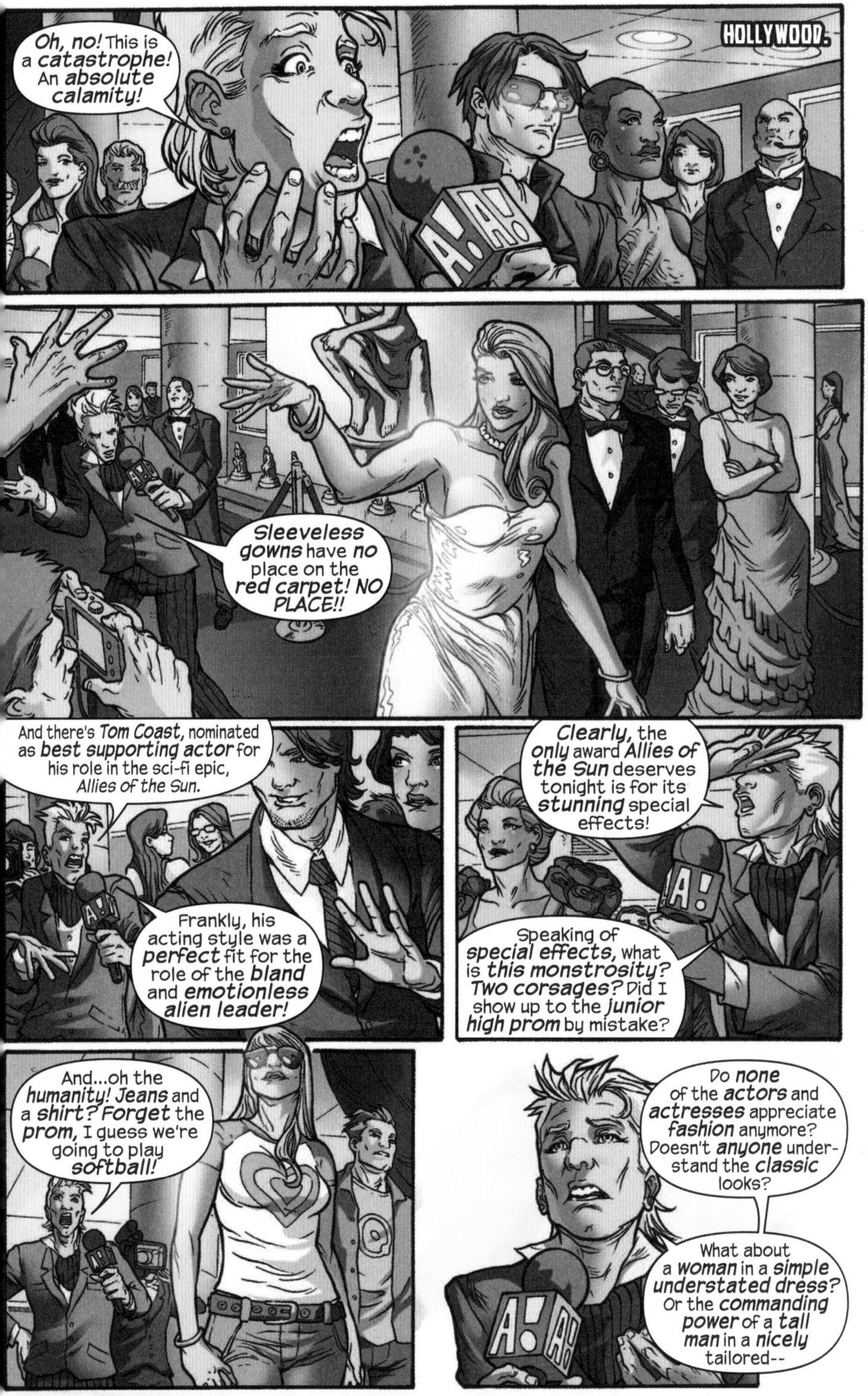
HOLLYWOOD.
Oh, no! This is a catastrophe! An absolute calamity!
Sleeveless gowns have no place on the red carpet! NO PLACE!!
And there's Tom Coast, nominated as best supporting actor for his role in the sci-fi epic, Allies of the Sun.
Frankly, his acting style was a perfect fit for the role of the bland and emotionless alien leader!
Clearly, the only award Allies of the Sun deserves tonight is for its stunning special effects!
Speaking of special effects, what is this monstrosity? Two corsages? Did I show up to the junior high prom by mistake?
And...oh the humanity! Jeans and a shirt? Forget the prom, I guess we're going to play softball!
Do none of the actors and actresses appreciate fashion anymore? Doesn't anyone under-stand the classic looks?
What about a woman in a simple understated dress? Or the commanding power of a tall man in a nicely tailored--

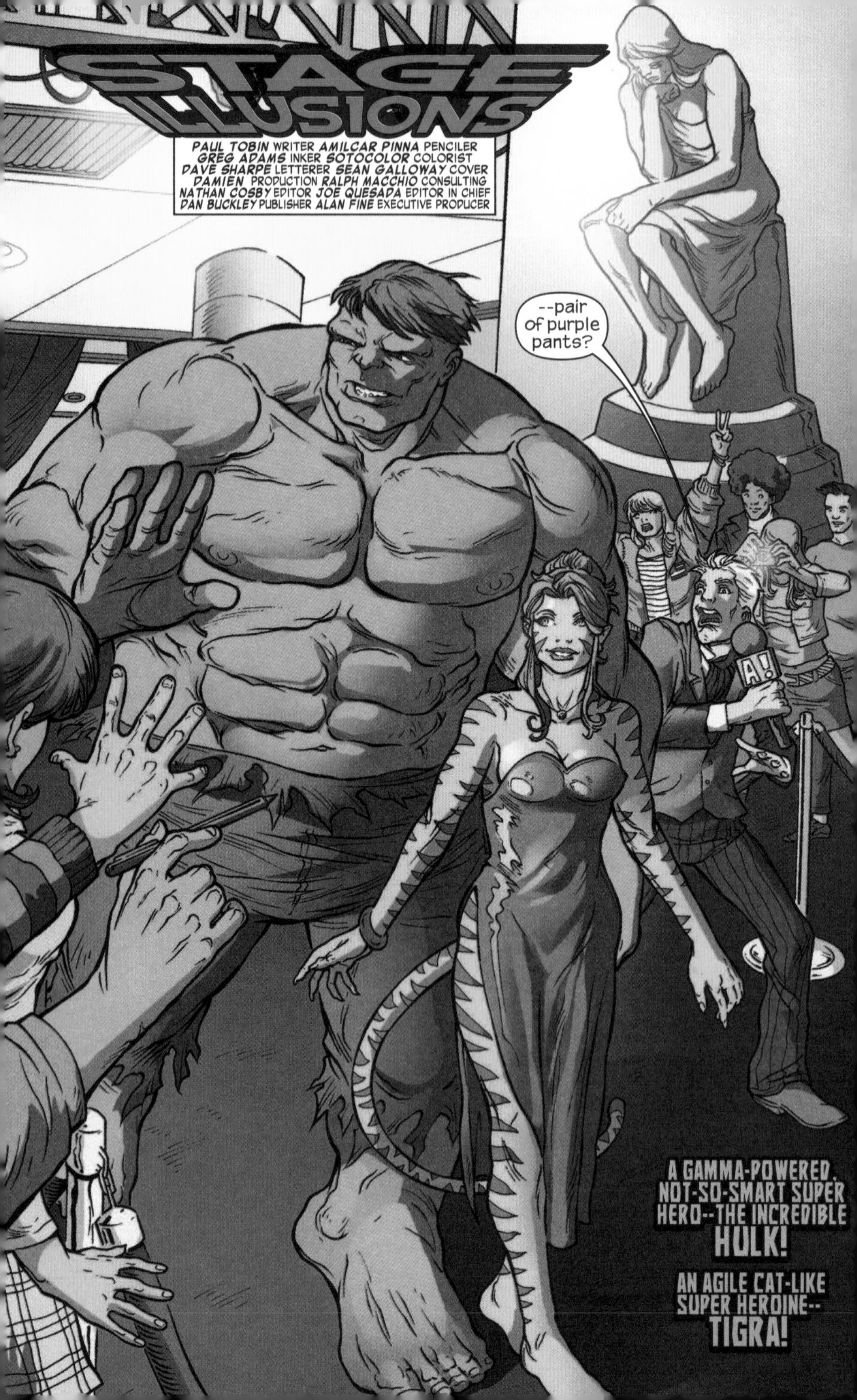
STAGE ILLUSIONS
PAUL TOBIN WRITER AMILCAR PINNA PENCILER
GREG ADAMS INKER SOTOCOLOR COLORIST
DAVE SHARPE LETTERER SEAN GALLOWAY COVER
DAMIEN PRODUCTION RALPH MACCHIO CONSULTING
NATHAN COSBY EDITOR JOE QUESADA EDITOR IN CHIEF
DAN BUCKLEY PUBLISHER ALAN FINE EXECUTIVE PRODUCER
--pair of purple pants?
A!
A GAMMA-POWERED, NOT-SO-SMART SUPER HERO--THE INCREDIBLE HULK!
AN AGILE CAT-LIKE SUPER HEROINE--TIGRA!

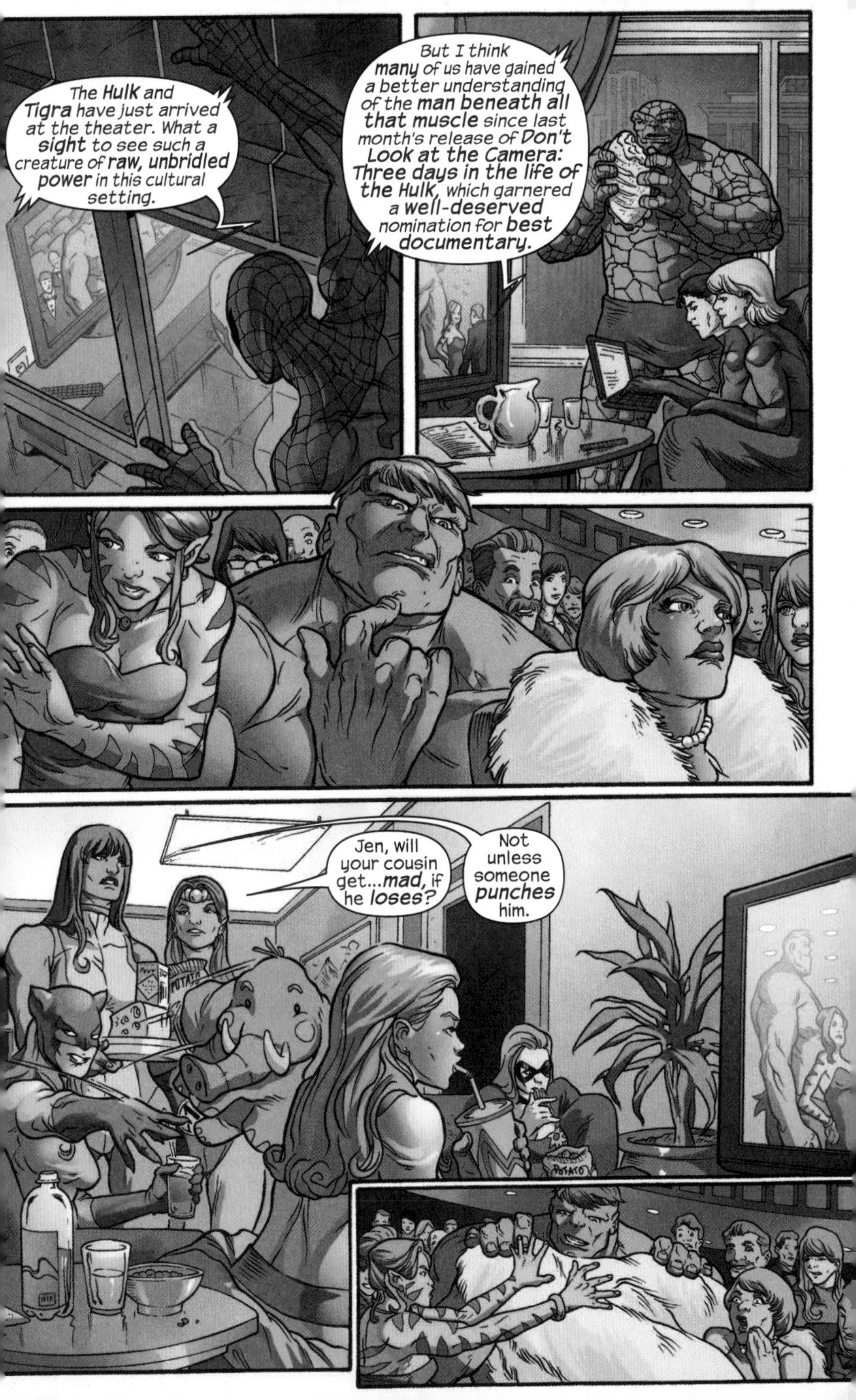
The Hulk and Tigra have just arrived at the theater. What a sight to see such a creature of raw, unbridled power in this cultural setting.
But I think many of us have gained a better understanding of the man beneath all that muscle since last month's release of Don't Look at the Camera: Three days in the life of the Hulk, which garnered a well-deserved nomination for best documentary.
Jen, will your cousin get...mad, if he loses?
Not unless someone punches him.
POTATO

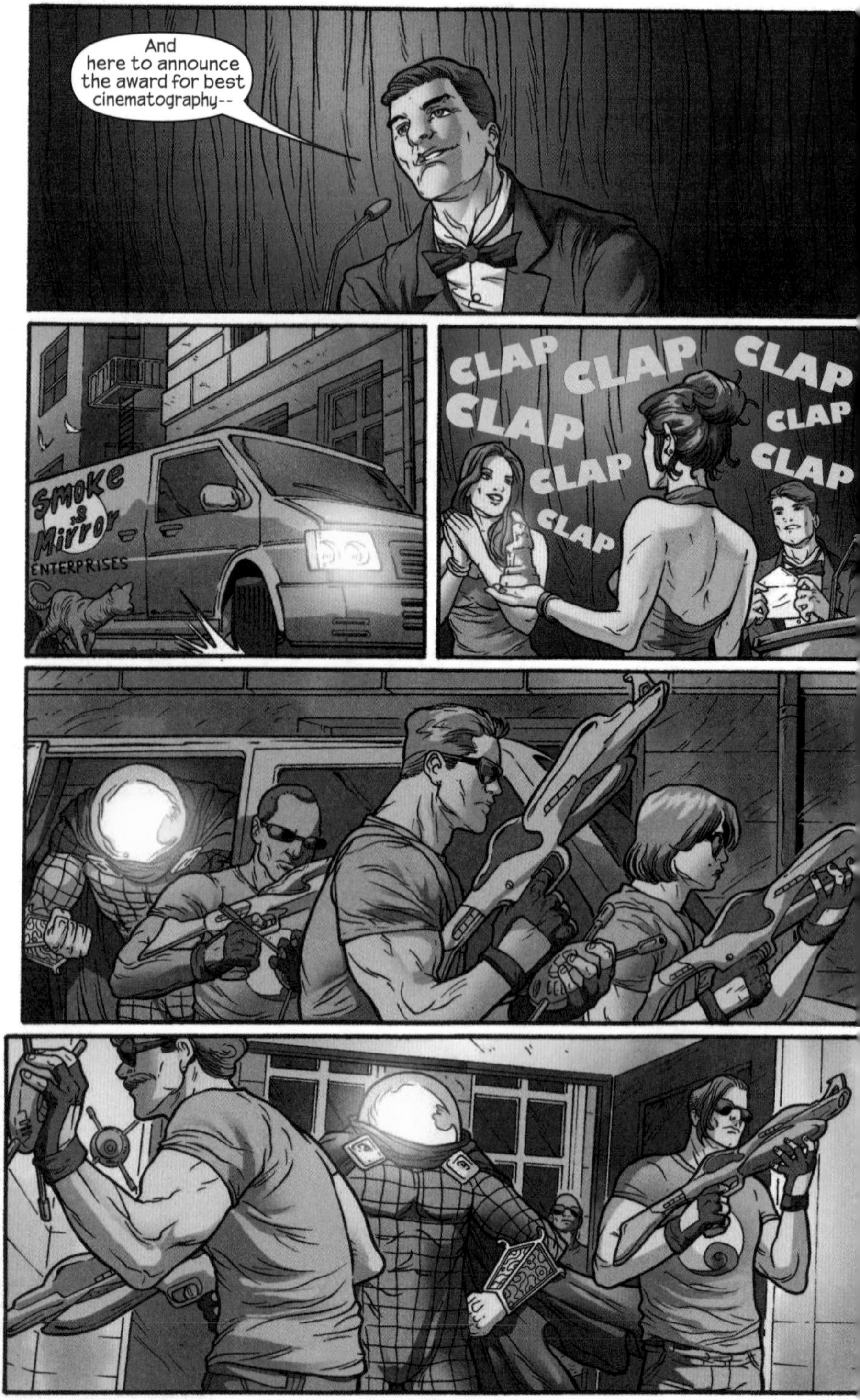
And here to announce the award for best cinematography--
Smoke & Mirror ENTERPRISES
CLAP CLAP CLAP CLAP CLAP CLAP CLAP CLAP

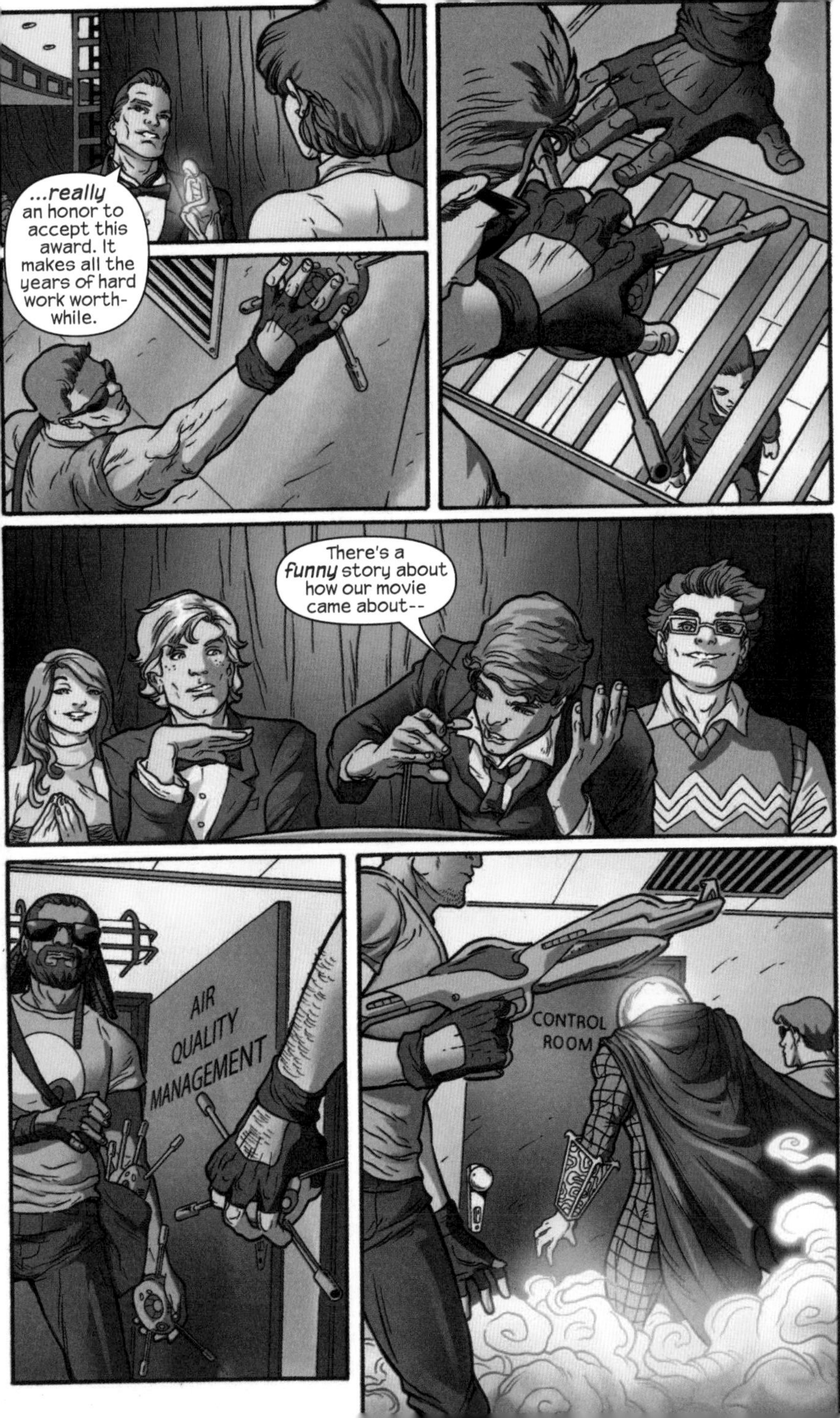
...really an honor to accept this award. It makes all the years of hard work worth-while.
There's a funny story about how our movie came about--
AIR QUALITY MANAGEMENT
CONTROL ROOM

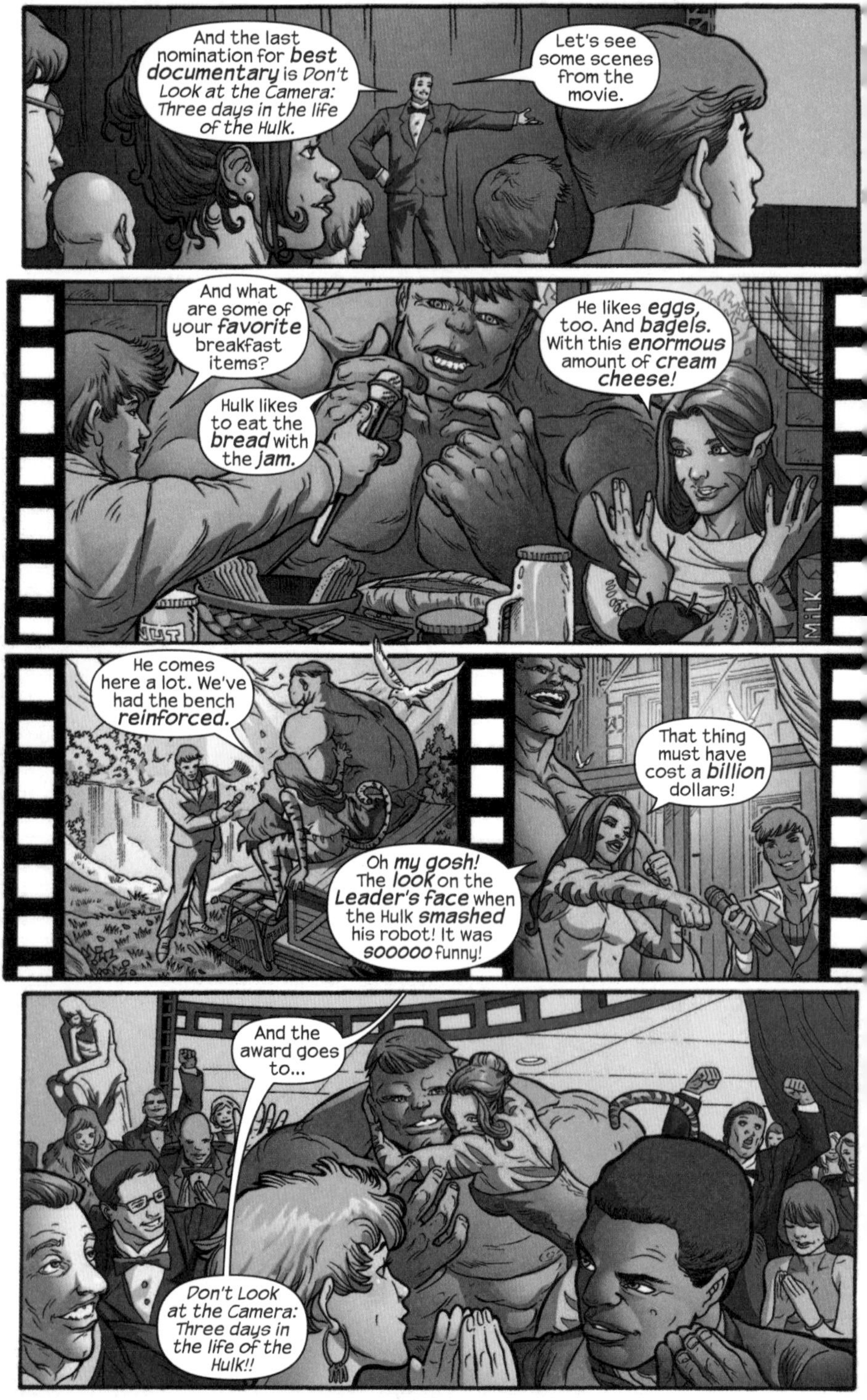
And the last nomination for best documentary is Don't Look at the Camera: Three days in the life of the Hulk.
Let's see some scenes from the movie.
And what are some of your favorite breakfast items?
Hulk likes to eat the bread with the jam.
He likes eggs, too. And bagels. With this enormous amount of cream cheese!
MILK
He comes here a lot. We've had the bench reinforced.
That thing must have cost a billion dollars!
Oh my gosh! The look on the Leader's face when the Hulk smashed his robot! It was sooooo funny!
And the award goes to...
Don't Look at the Camera: Three days in the life of the Hulk!!

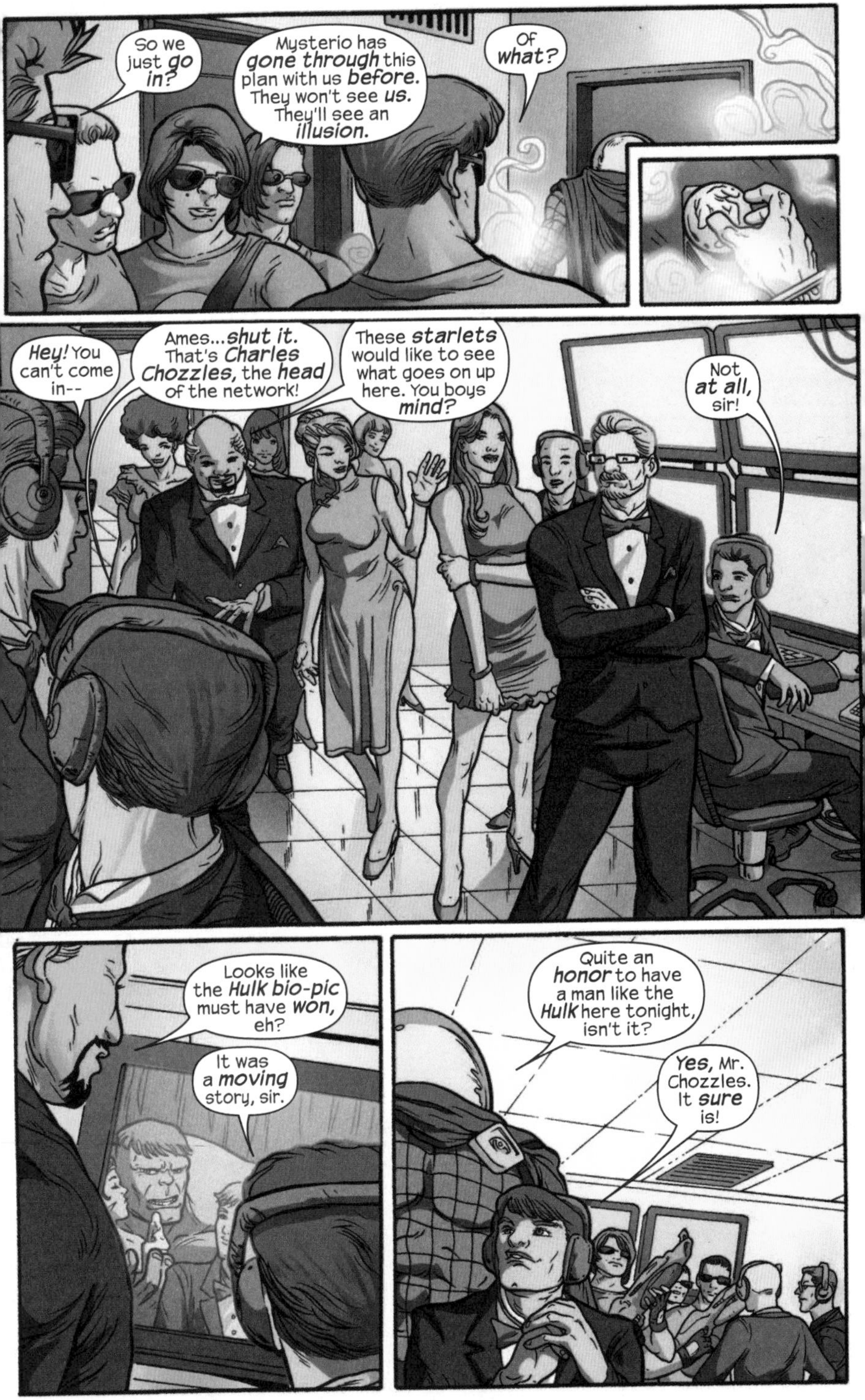
So we just go in?
Mysterio has gone through this plan with us before. They won't see us. They'll see an illusion.
Of what?
Hey! You can't come in--
Ames...shut it. That's Charles Chozzles, the head of the network!
These starlets would like to see what goes on up here. You boys mind?
Not at all, sir!
Looks like the Hulk bio-pic must have won, eh?
It was a moving story, sir.
Quite an honor to have a man like the Hulk here tonight, isn't it?
Yes, Mr. Chozzles. It sure is!

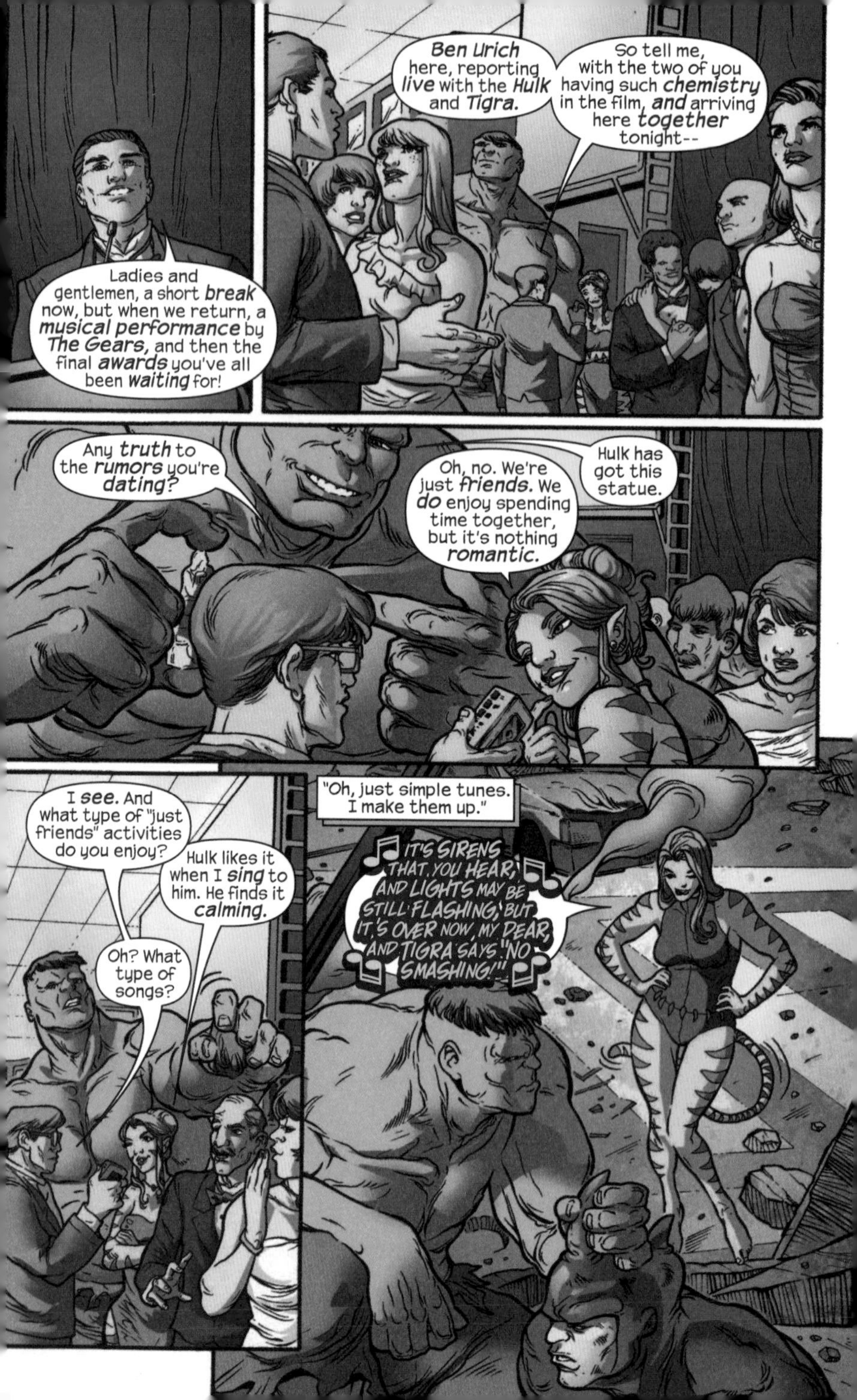
Ladies and gentlemen, a short break now, but when we return, a musical performance by The Gears, and then the final awards you've all been waiting for!
Ben Urich here, reporting live with the Hulk and Tigra.
So tell me, with the two of you having such chemistry in the film, and arriving here together tonight--
Any truth to the rumors you're dating?
Oh, no. We're just friends. We do enjoy spending time together, but it's nothing romantic.
Hulk has got this statue.
I see. And what type of "just friends" activities do you enjoy?
Hulk likes it when I sing to him. He finds it calming.
Oh? What type of songs?
"Oh, just simple tunes. I make them up."
IT'S SIRENS THAT YOU HEAR, AND LIGHTS MAY BE STILL FLASHING, BUT IT'S OVER NOW, MY DEAR, AND TIGRA SAYS "NO SMASHING!"

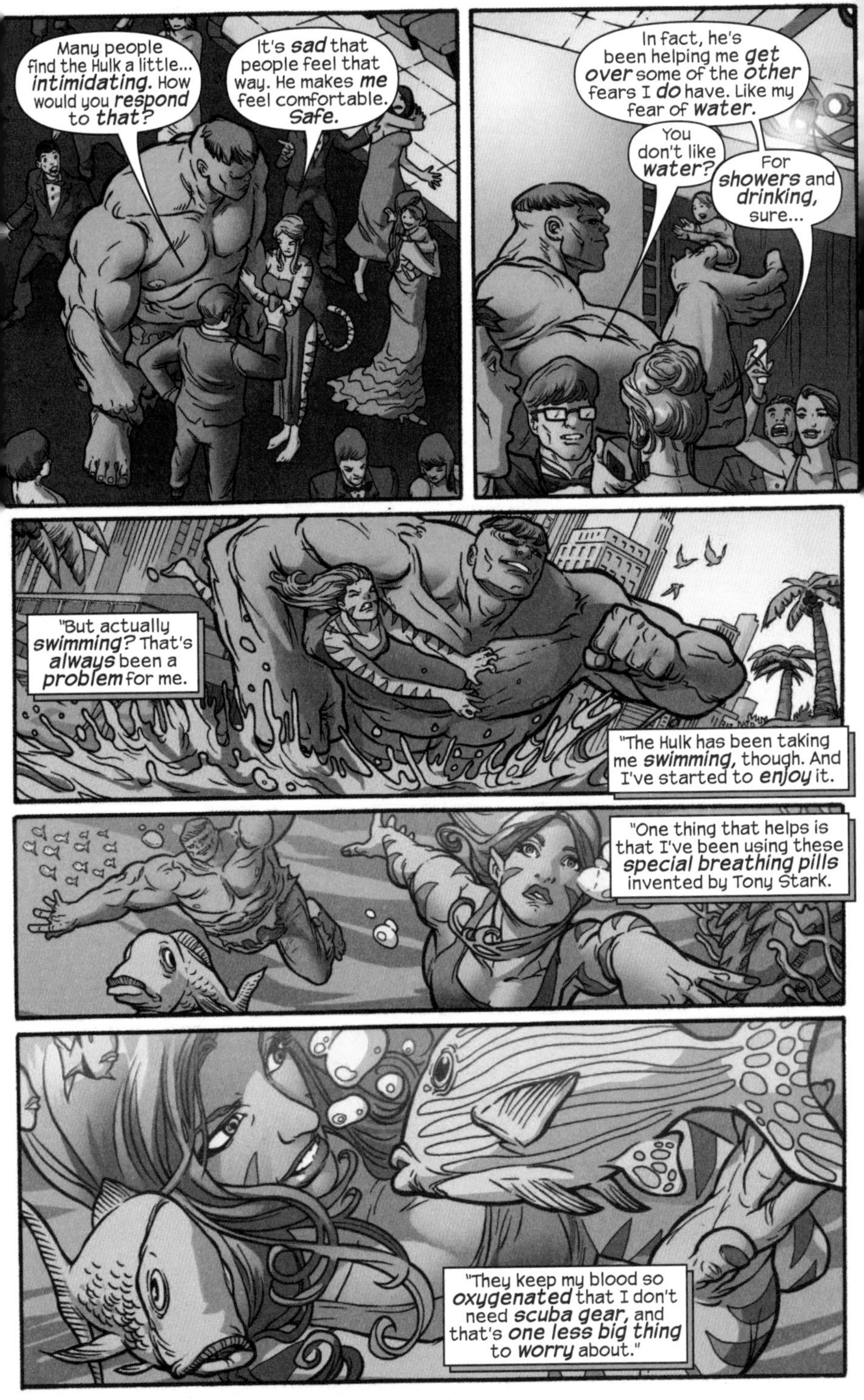
Many people find the Hulk a little... intimidating. How would you respond to that?
It's sad that people feel that way. He makes me feel comfortable. Safe.
In fact, he's been helping me get over some of the other fears I do have. Like my fear of water.
You don't like water?
For showers and drinking, sure...
"But actually swimming? That's always been a problem for me.
"The Hulk has been taking me swimming, though. And I've started to enjoy it.
"One thing that helps is that I've been using these special breathing pills invented by Tony Stark.
"They keep my blood so oxygenated that I don't need scuba gear, and that's one less big thing to worry about."

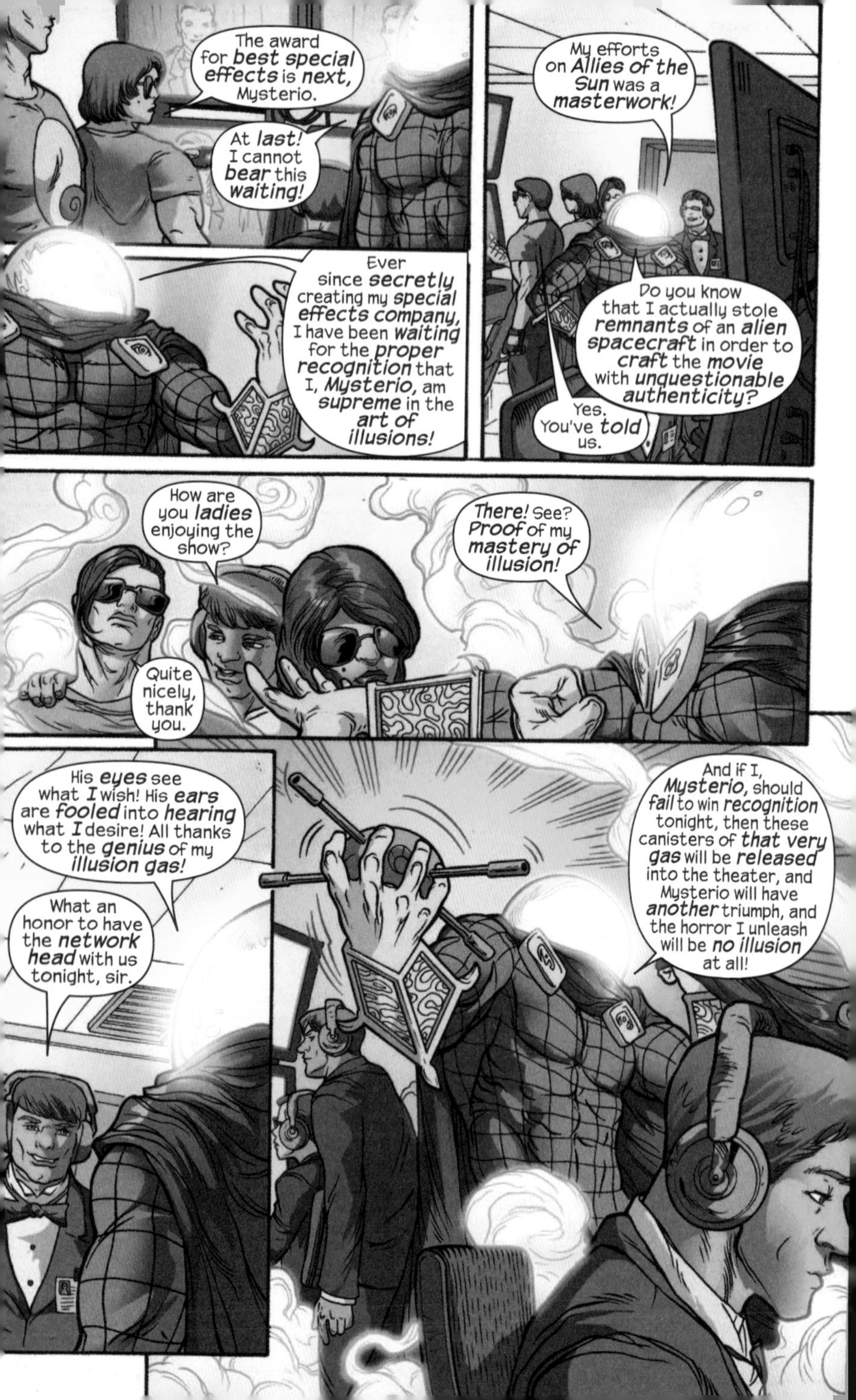
The award for best special effects is next, Mysterio.
At last! I cannot bear this waiting!
Ever since secretly creating my special effects company, I have been waiting for the proper recognition that I, Mysterio, am supreme in the art of illusions!
My efforts on Allies of the Sun was a masterwork!
Do you know that I actually stole remnants of an alien spacecraft in order to craft the movie with unquestionable authenticity?
Yes. You've told us.
How are you ladies enjoying the show?
There! See? Proof of my mastery of illusion!
Quite nicely, thank you.
His eyes see what I wish! His ears are fooled into hearing what I desire! All thanks to the genius of my illusion gas!
What an honor to have the network head with us tonight, sir.
And if I, Mysterio, should fail to win recognition tonight, then these canisters of that very gas will be released into the theater, and Mysterio will have another triumph, and the horror I unleash will be no illusion at all!

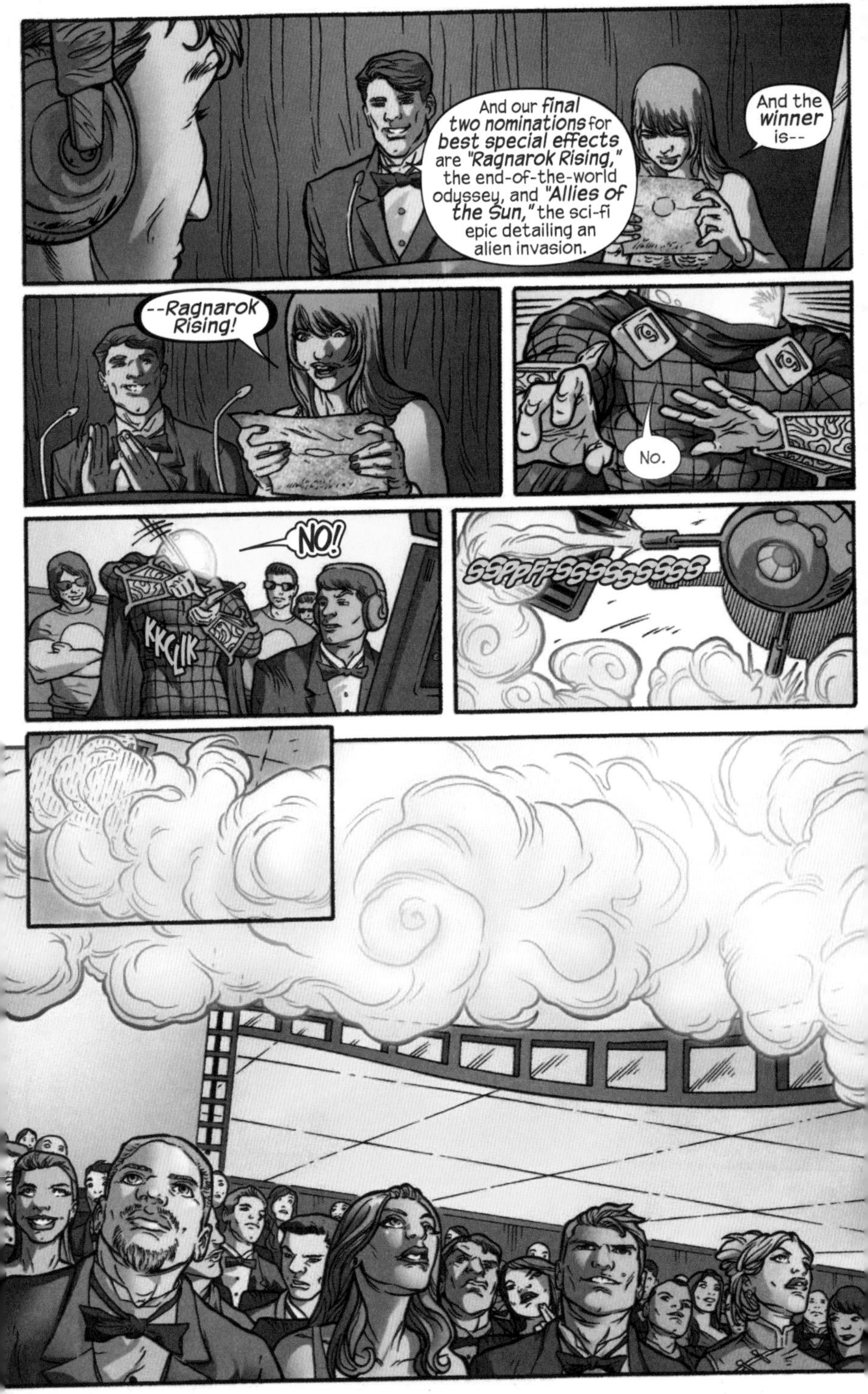
And our final two nominations for best special effects are "Ragnarok Rising," the end-of-the-world odyssey, and "Allies of the Sun," the sci-fi epic detailing an alien invasion.
And the winner is--
--Ragnarok Rising!
No.
NO!
KKCLIK
SSPPFFSSSSSSSSSS

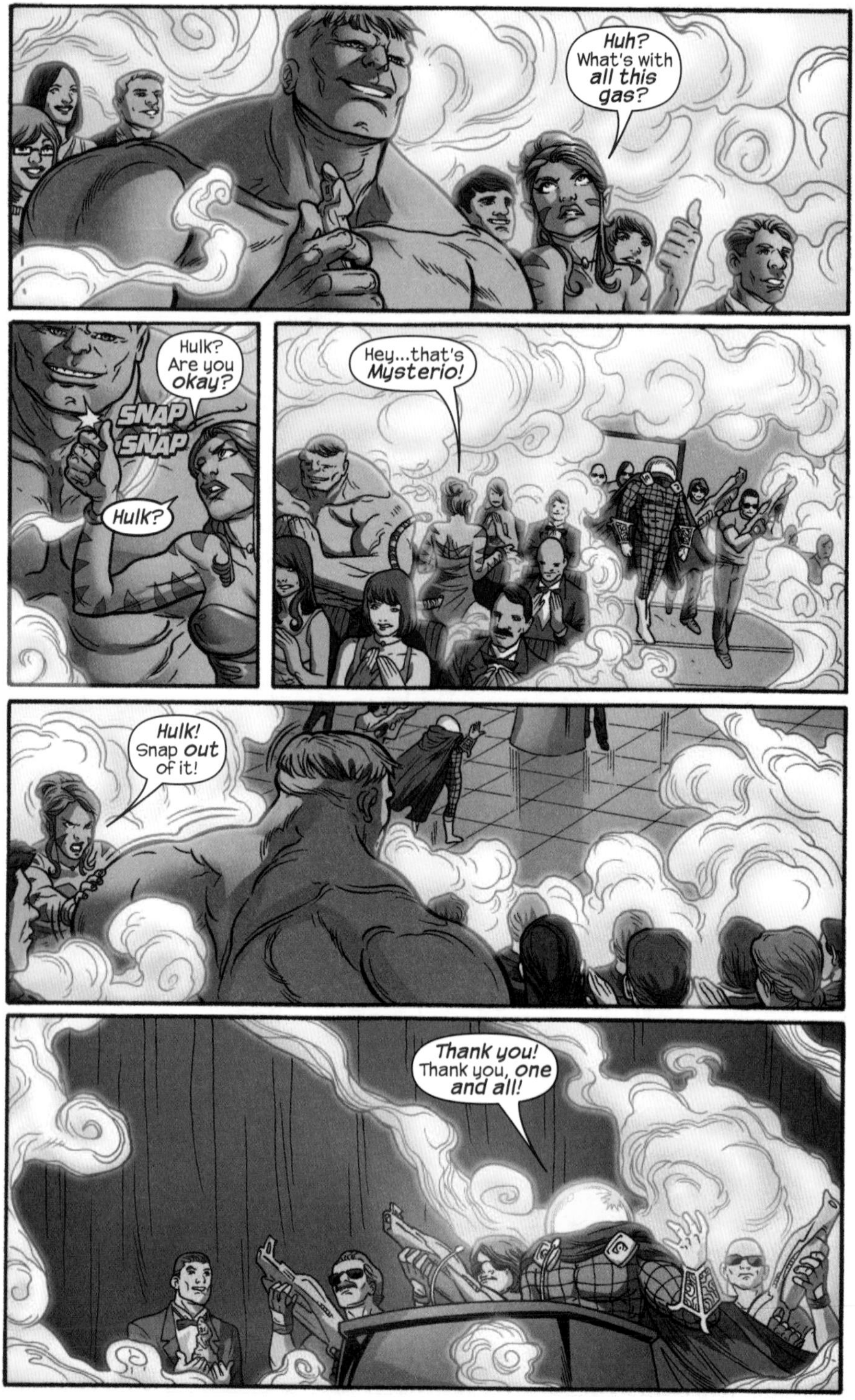
Huh? What's with all this gas?
Hulk? Are you okay?
SNAP
SNAP
Hulk?
Hey...that's Mysterio!
Hulk! Snap out of it!
Thank you! Thank you, one and all!

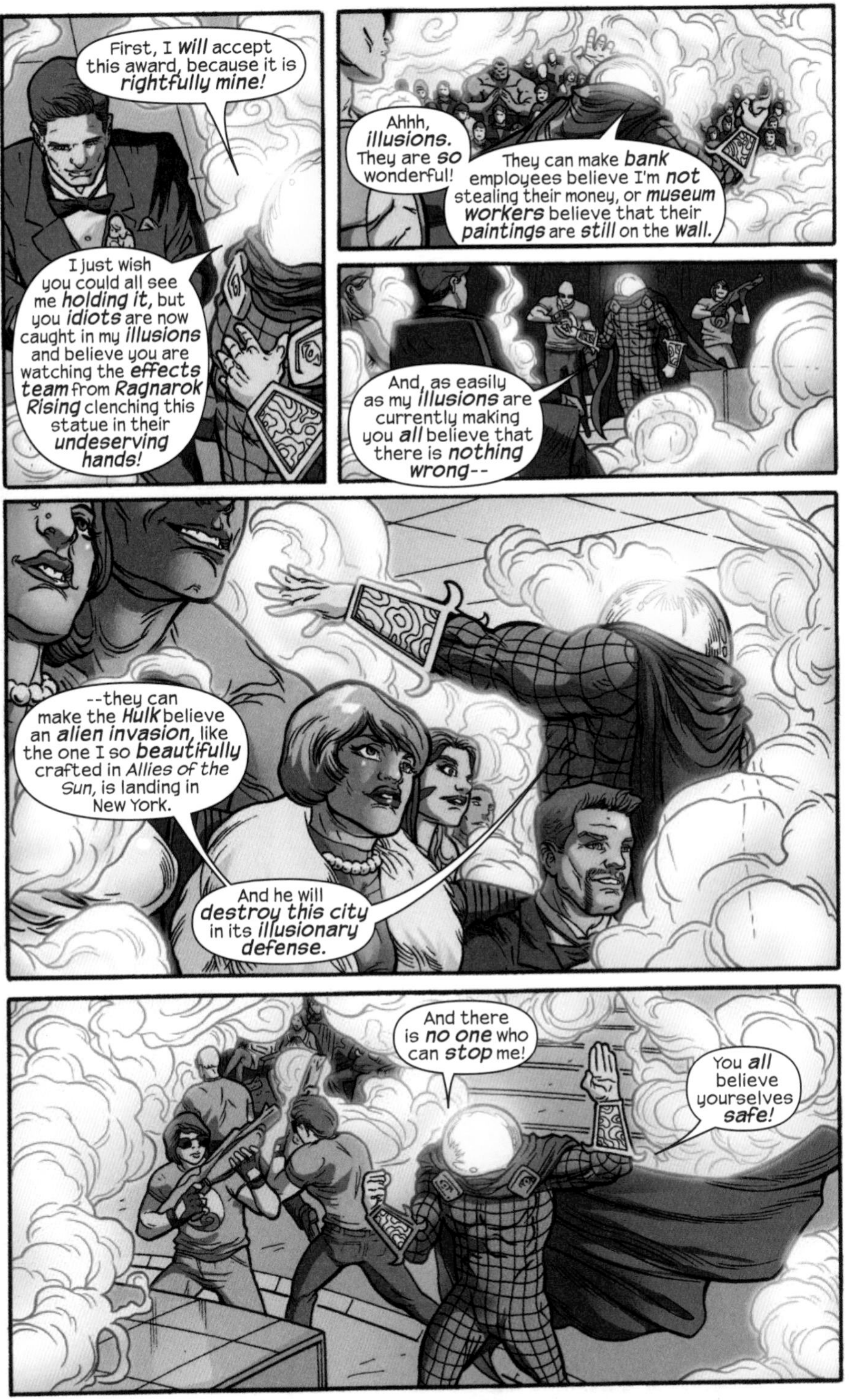
First, I will accept this award, because it is rightfully mine!
I just wish you could all see me holding it, but you idiots are now caught in my illusions and believe you are watching the effects team from Ragnarok Rising clenching this statue in their undeserving hands!
Ahhh, illusions. They are so wonderful!
They can make bank employees believe I'm not stealing their money, or museum workers believe that their paintings are still on the wall.
And, as easily as my illusions are currently making you all believe that there is nothing wrong--
--they can make the Hulk believe an alien invasion, like the one I so beautifully crafted in Allies of the Sun, is landing in New York.
And he will destroy this city in its illusionary defense.
And there is no one who can stop me!
You all believe yourselves safe!

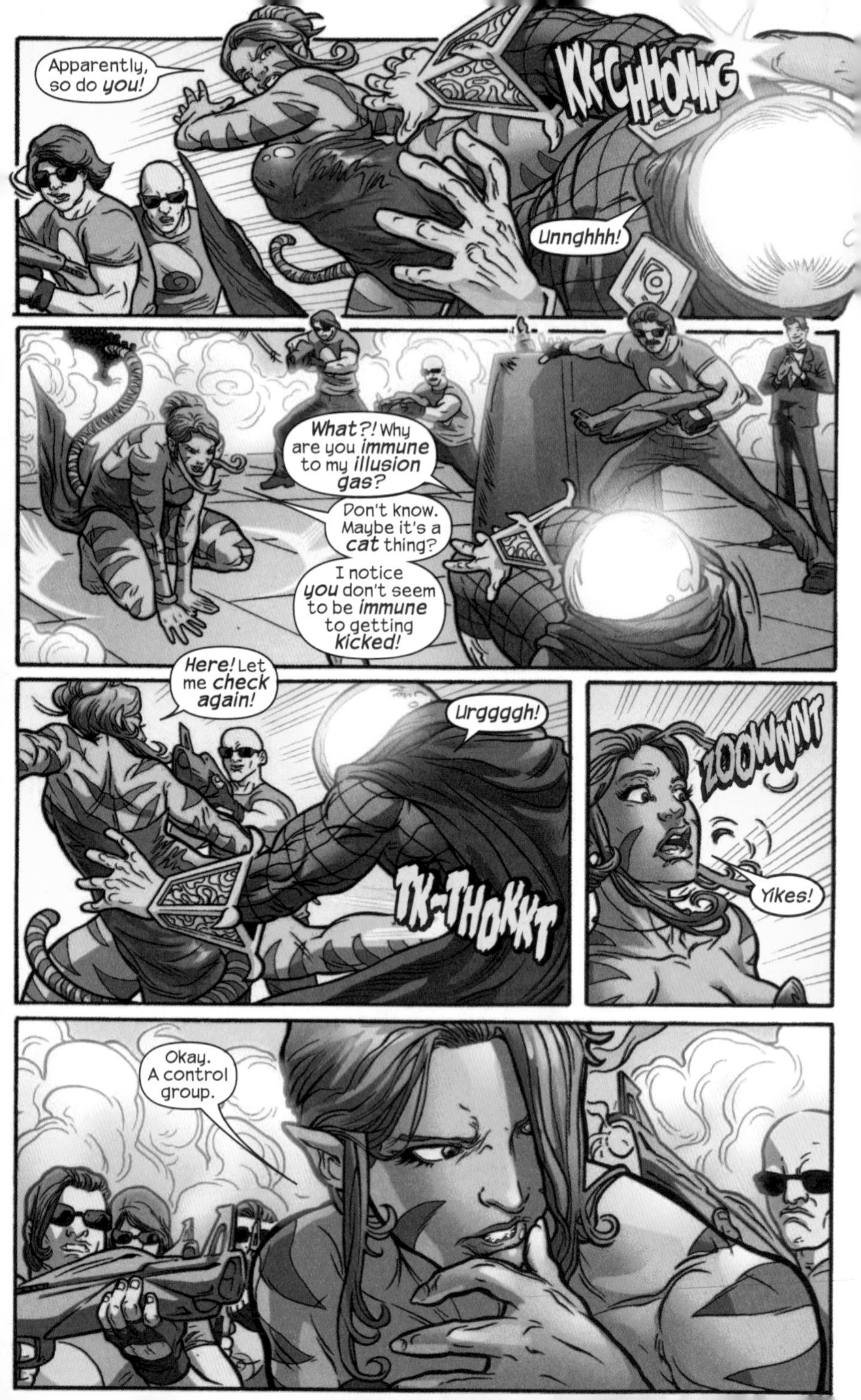
Apparently, so do you!
KK-CHHONNG
Unnghhh!
What?! Why are you immune to my illusion gas?
Don't know. Maybe it's a cat thing?
I notice you don't seem to be immune to getting kicked!
Here! Let me check again!
Urggggh!
TK-THOKKT
ZOOWNNT
Yikes!
Okay. A control group.

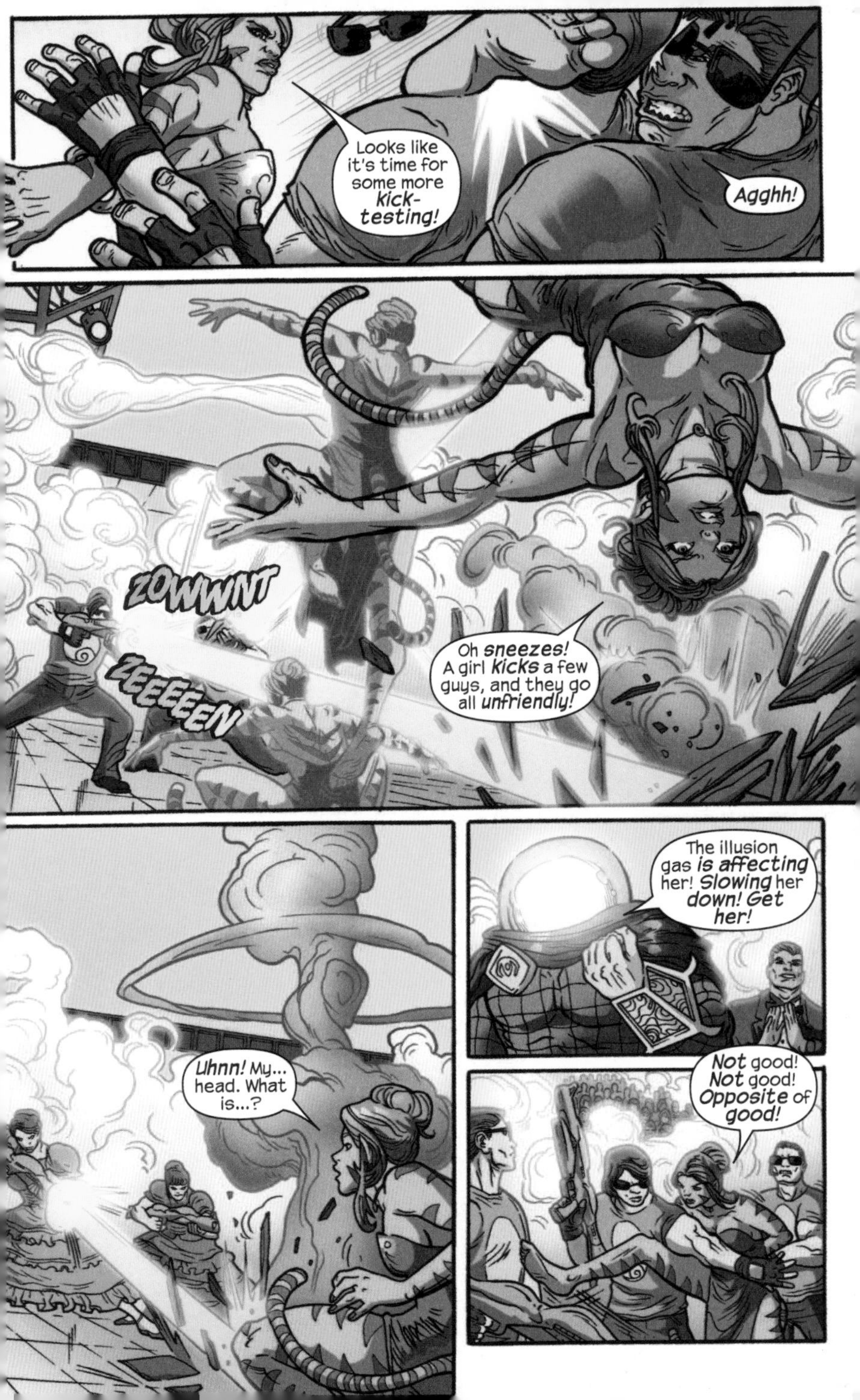
Looks like it's time for some more *kick-testing!*
Agghh!
ZOWWNT
ZEEEEEEN
Oh *sneezes!* A girl *kicks* a few guys, and they go all *unfriendly!*
Uhnn! My... head. What is...?
The illusion gas *is affecting* her! *Slowing* her *down! Get her!*
Not good! *Not* good! *Opposite* of *good!*

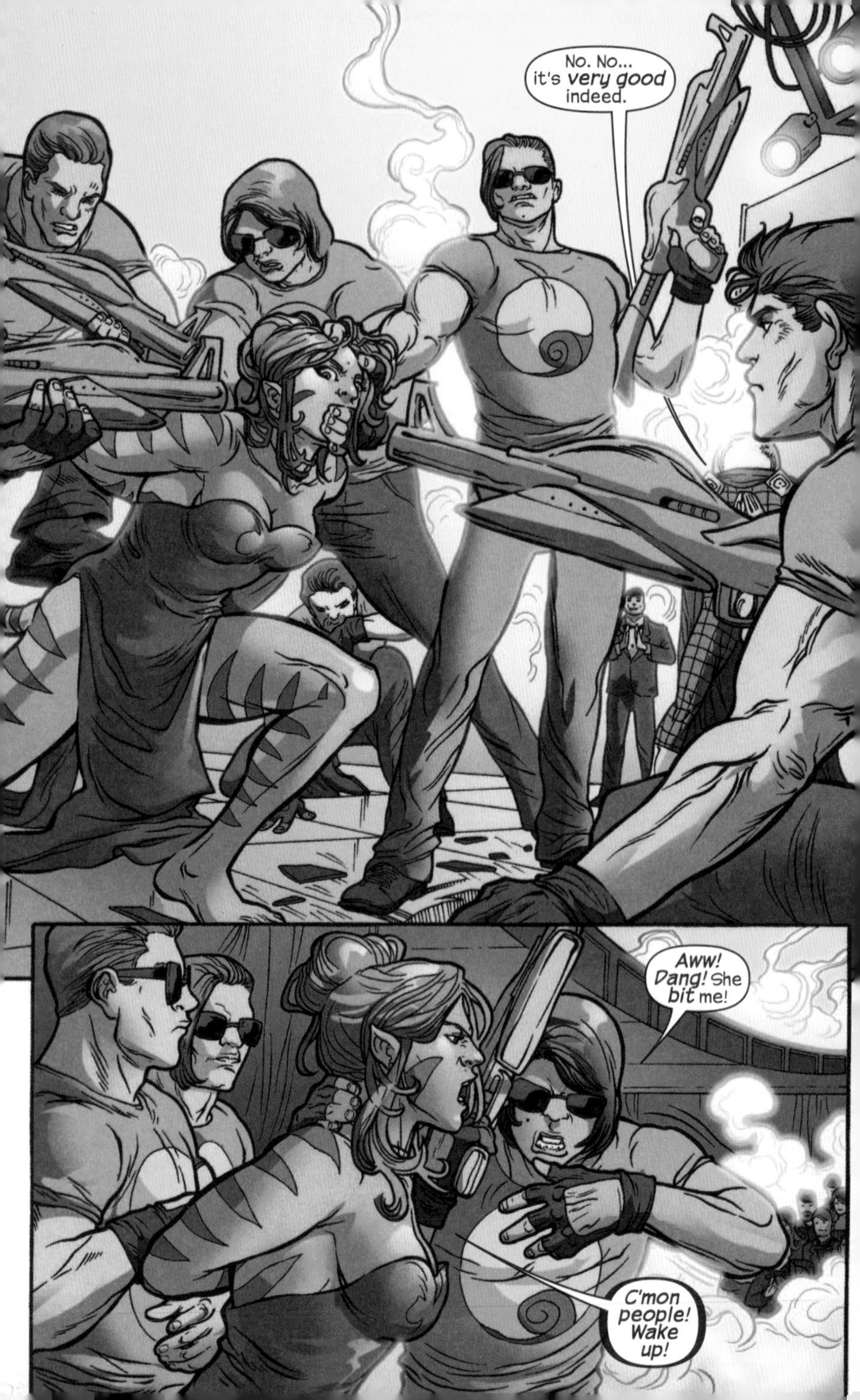
No. No... it's very good indeed.
Aww! Dang! She bit me!
C'mon people! Wake up!

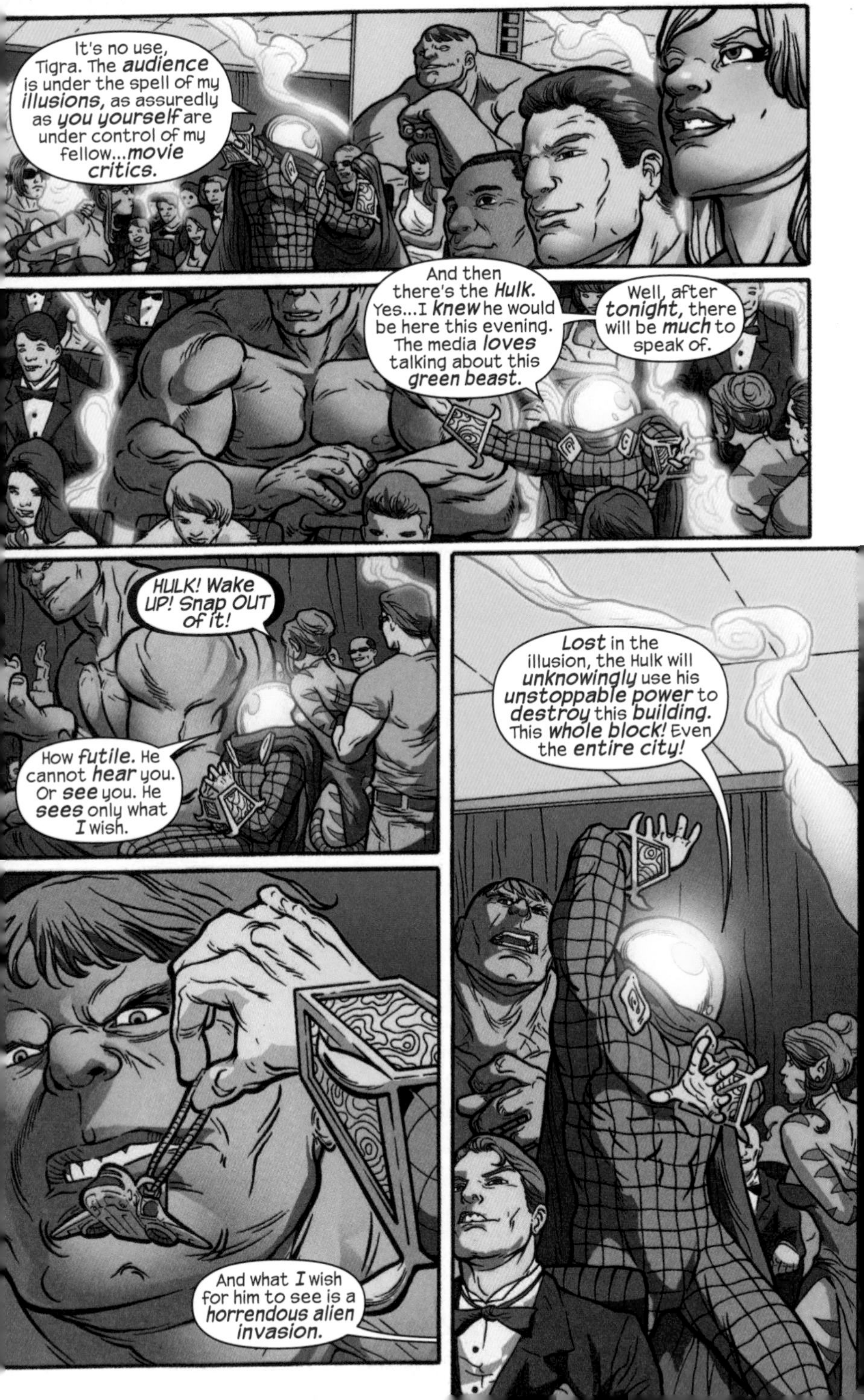

It's no use, Tigra. The audience is under the spell of my illusions, as assuredly as you yourself are under control of my fellow...movie critics.
And then there's the Hulk. Yes...I knew he would be here this evening. The media loves talking about this green beast.
Well, after tonight, there will be much to speak of.
HULK! Wake UP! Snap OUT of it!
How futile. He cannot hear you. Or see you. He sees only what I wish.
And what I wish for him to see is a horrendous alien invasion.
Lost in the illusion, the Hulk will unknowingly use his unstoppable power to destroy this building. This whole block! Even the entire city!

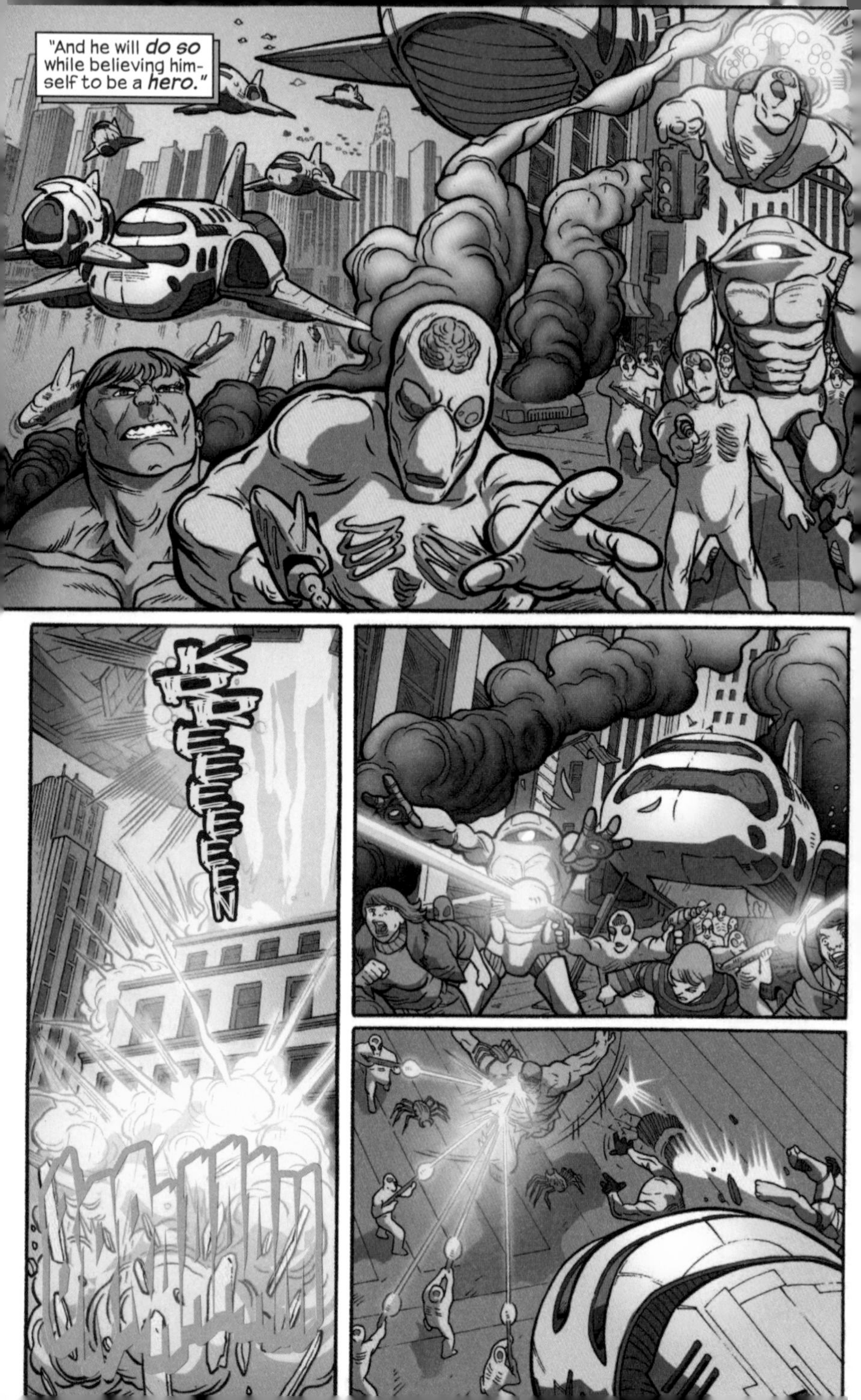
"And he will *do so* while believing him-self to be a *hero.*"
KRREEEEEN

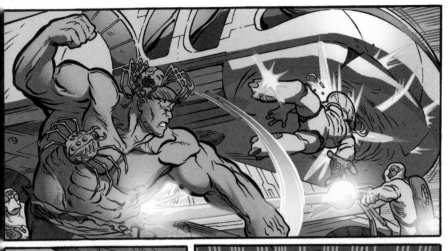

♪ IT'S SIRENS THAT YOU HEAR-- ♪

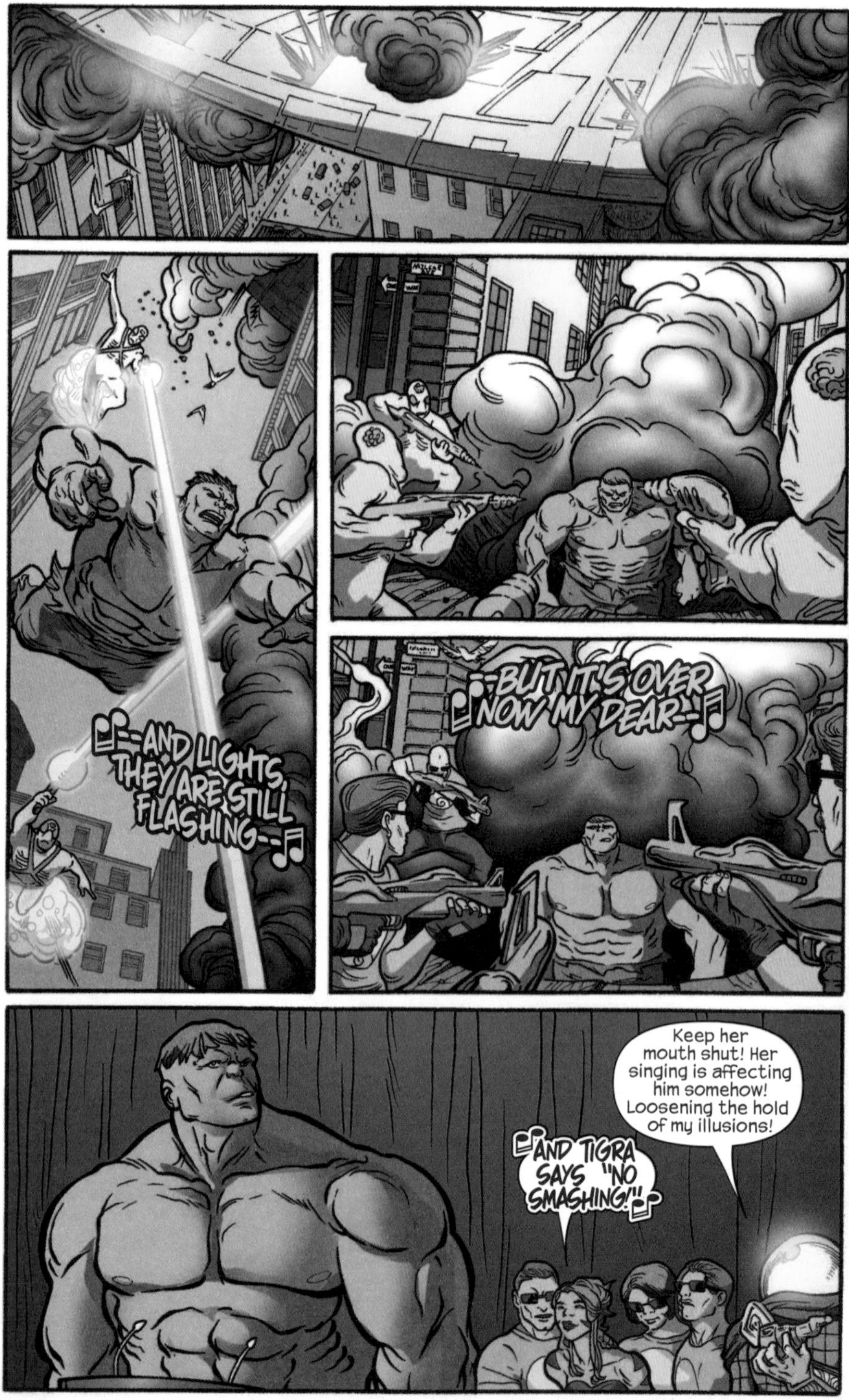
--AND LIGHTS, THEY ARE STILL FLASHING--
--BUT IT'S OVER NOW MY DEAR--
Keep her mouth shut! Her singing is affecting him somehow! Loosening the hold of my illusions!
AND TIGRA SAYS "NO SMASHING!"

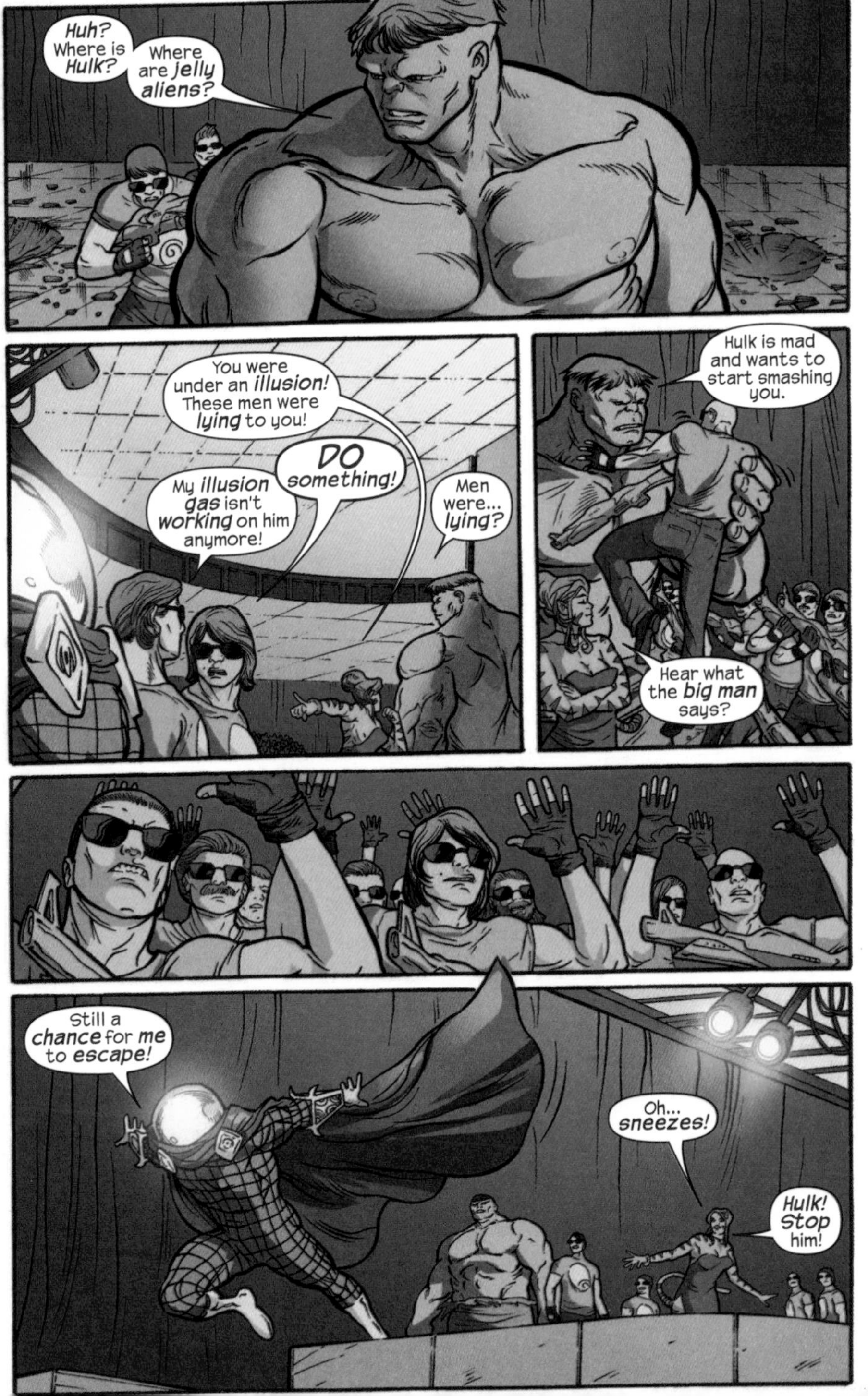
Huh? Where is Hulk?
Where are jelly aliens?
You were under an illusion! These men were lying to you!
My illusion gas isn't working on him anymore!
DO something!
Men were... lying?
Hulk is mad and wants to start smashing you.
Hear what the big man says?
Still a chance for me to escape!
Oh... sneezes!
Hulk! Stop him!

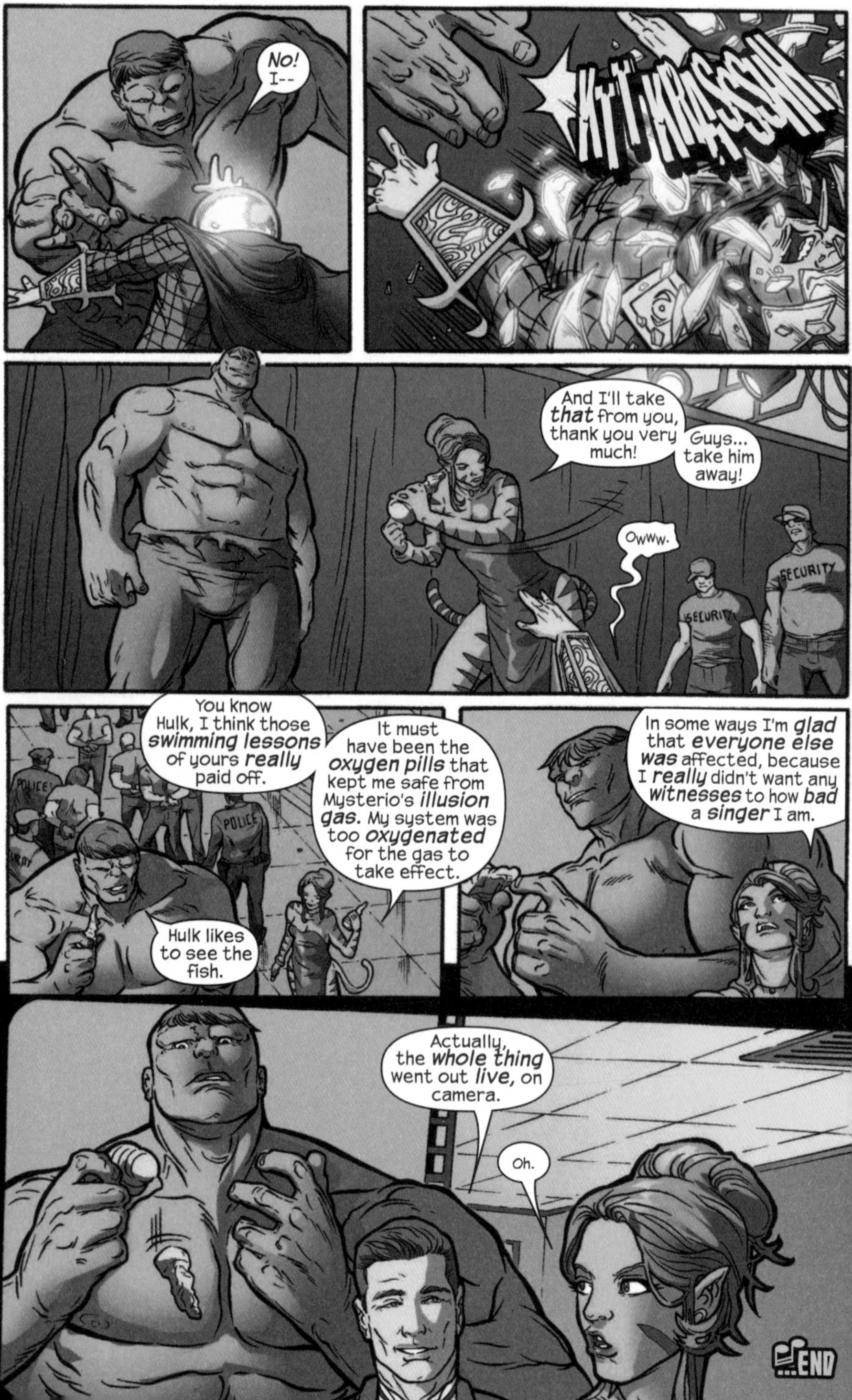
No! I--
KT'T-KRASSSH
And I'll take *that* from you, thank you very much!
Guys... take him away!
Owww.
SECURITY
SECURITY
You know Hulk, I think those *swimming lessons* of yours *really* paid off.
Hulk likes to see the fish.
It must have been the *oxygen pills* that kept me safe from Mysterio's *illusion gas.* My system was too *oxygenated* for the gas to take effect.
POLICE
POLICE
In some ways I'm *glad* that *everyone else was* affected, because I *really* didn't want any *witnesses* to how *bad* a *singer* I am.
Actually, the *whole thing* went out *live,* on camera.
Oh.
...END

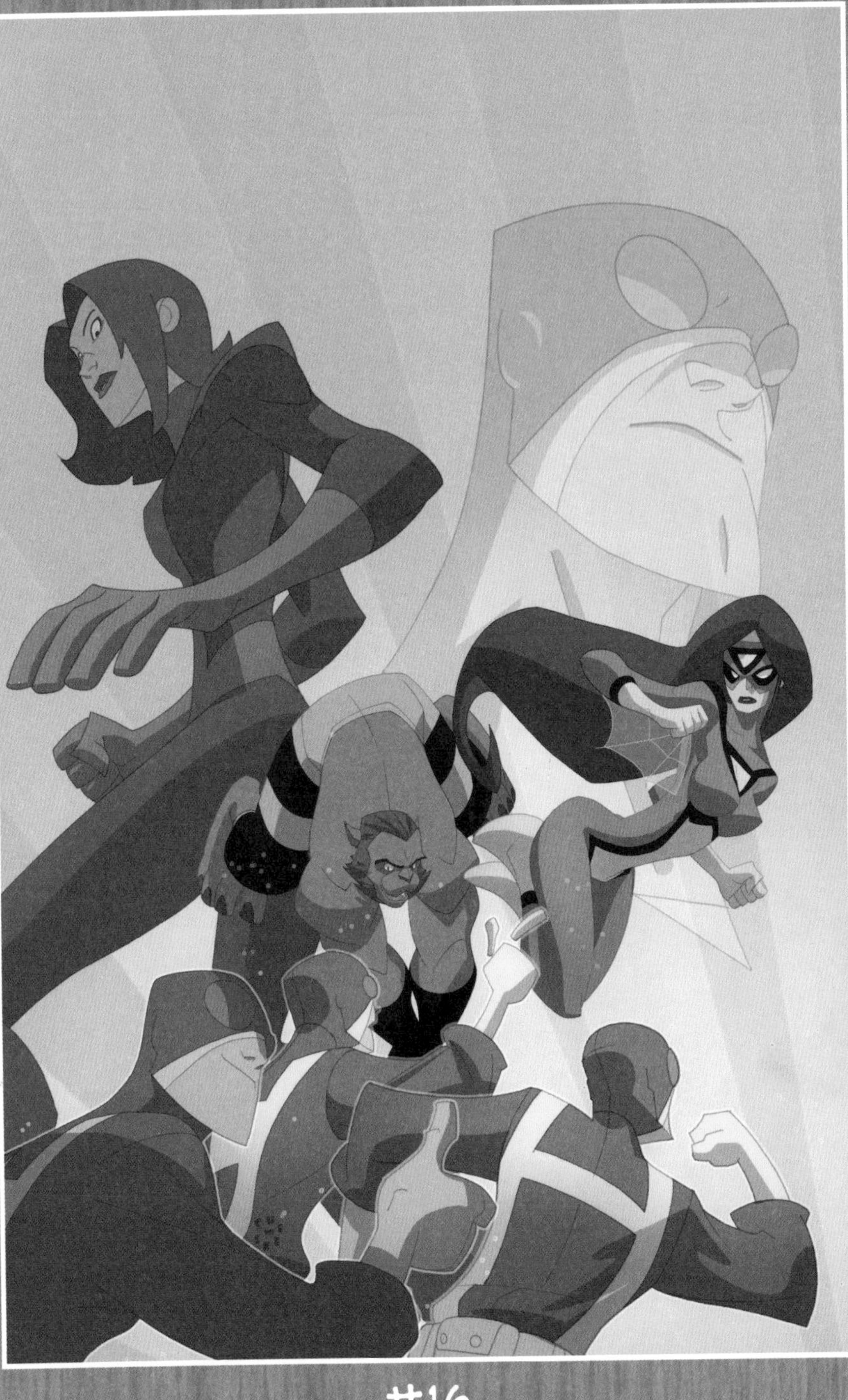

#16

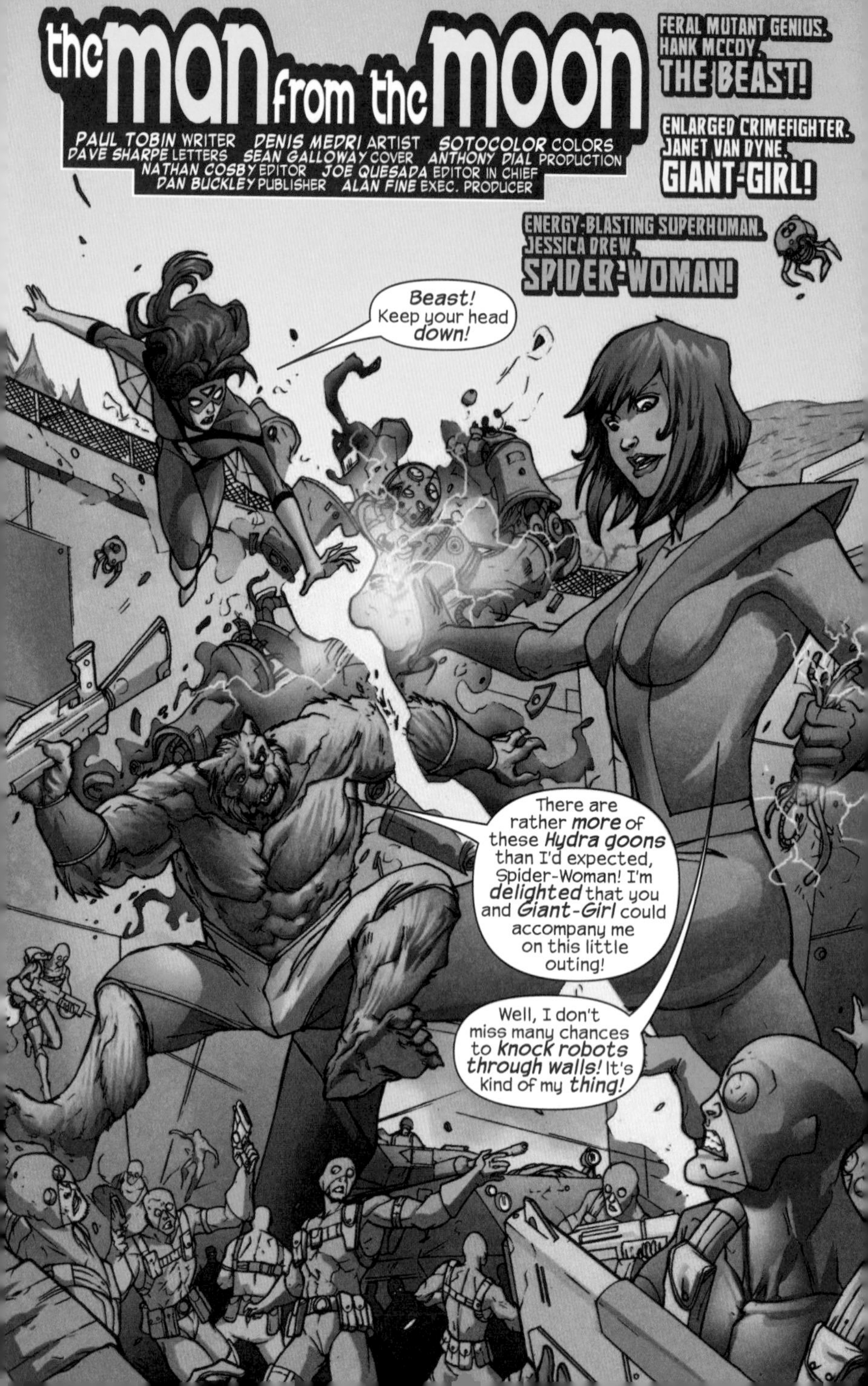
the MAN from the MOON
PAUL TOBIN WRITER DENIS MEDRI ARTIST SOTOCOLOR COLORS
DAVE SHARPE LETTERS SEAN GALLOWAY COVER ANTHONY DIAL PRODUCTION
NATHAN COSBY EDITOR JOE QUESADA EDITOR IN CHIEF
DAN BUCKLEY PUBLISHER ALAN FINE EXEC. PRODUCER
FERAL MUTANT GENIUS. HANK MCCOY. THE BEAST!
ENLARGED CRIMEFIGHTER. JANET VAN DYNE. GIANT-GIRL!
ENERGY-BLASTING SUPERHUMAN. JESSICA DREW. SPIDER-WOMAN!
Beast! Keep your head down!
There are rather more of these Hydra goons than I'd expected, Spider-Woman! I'm delighted that you and Giant-Girl could accompany me on this little outing!
Well, I don't miss many chances to knock robots through walls! It's kind of my thing!

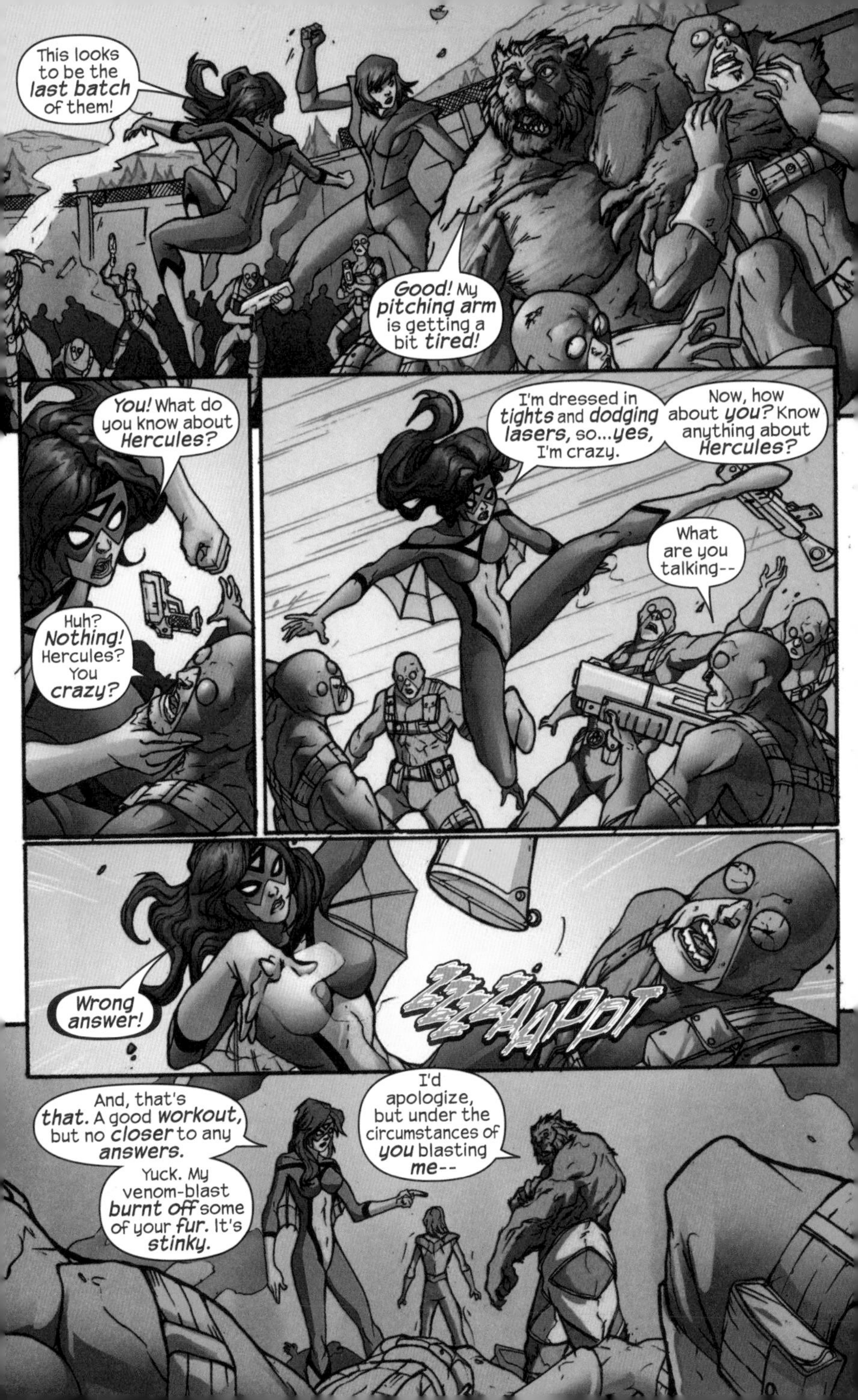
This looks to be the last batch of them!
Good! My pitching arm is getting a bit tired!
You! What do you know about Hercules?
Huh? Nothing! Hercules? You crazy?
I'm dressed in tights and dodging lasers, so...yes, I'm crazy.
Now, how about you? Know anything about Hercules?
What are you talking--
Wrong answer!
ZZZZAAPPPT
And, that's that. A good workout, but no closer to any answers.
Yuck. My venom-blast burnt off some of your fur. It's stinky.
I'd apologize, but under the circumstances of you blasting me--

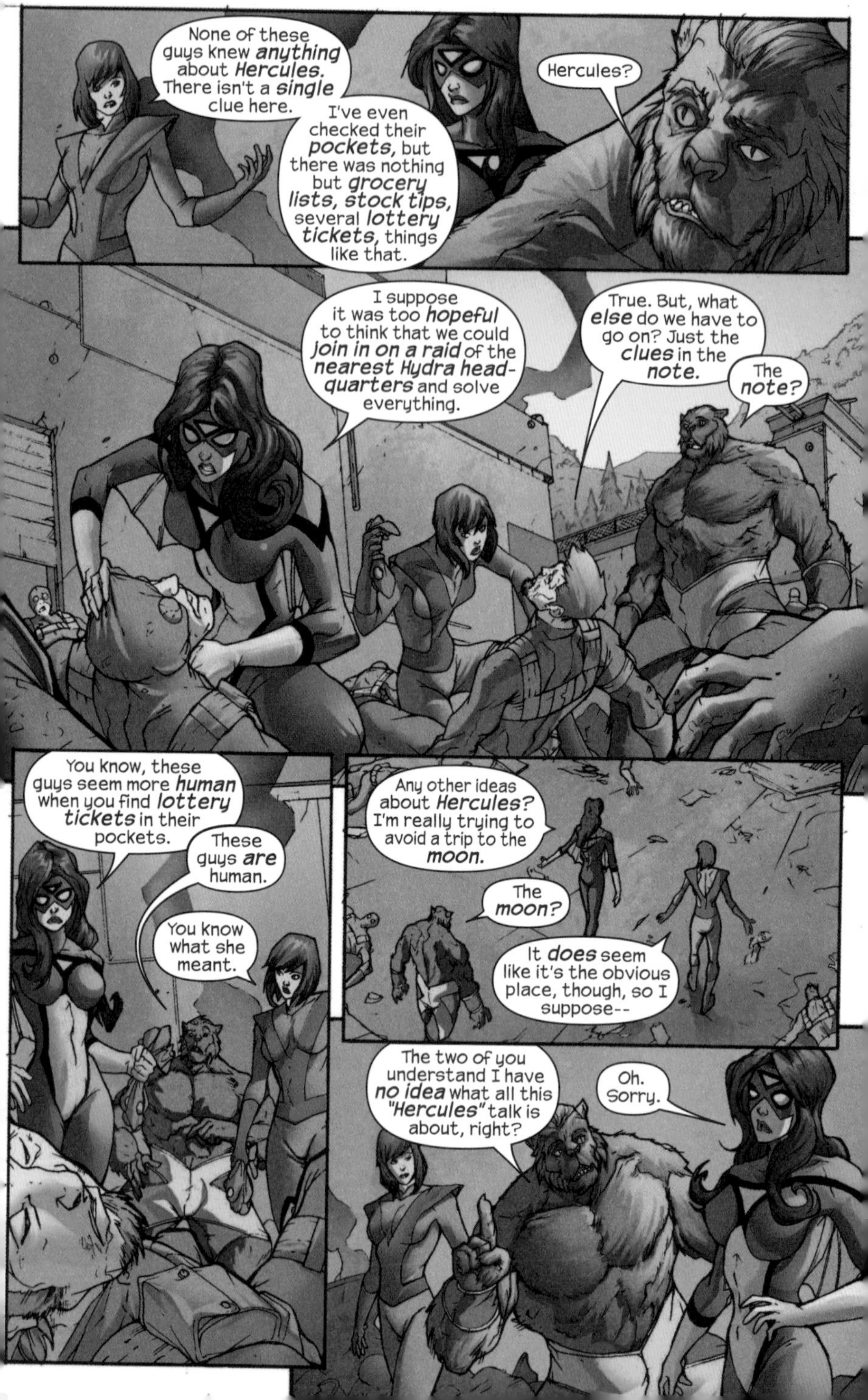
None of these guys knew anything about Hercules. There isn't a single clue here.
I've even checked their pockets, but there was nothing but grocery lists, stock tips, several lottery tickets, things like that.
Hercules?
I suppose it was too hopeful to think that we could join in on a raid of the nearest Hydra head-quarters and solve everything.
True. But, what else do we have to go on? Just the clues in the note.
The note?
You know, these guys seem more human when you find lottery tickets in their pockets.
These guys are human.
You know what she meant.
Any other ideas about Hercules? I'm really trying to avoid a trip to the moon.
The moon?
It does seem like it's the obvious place, though, so I suppose--
The two of you understand I have no idea what all this "Hercules" talk is about, right?
Oh. Sorry.

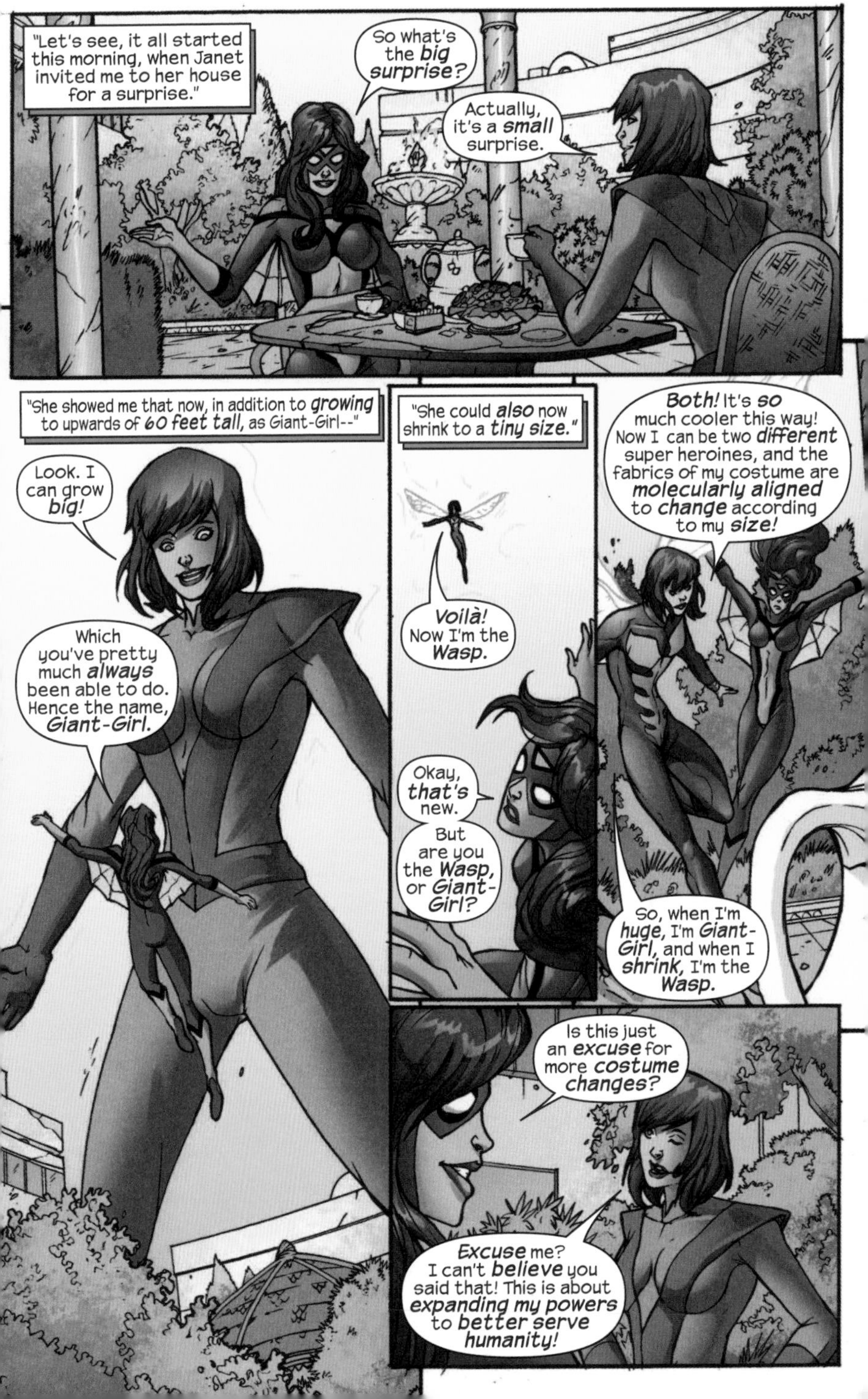
"Let's see, it all started this morning, when Janet invited me to her house for a surprise."
So what's the big surprise?
Actually, it's a small surprise.
"She showed me that now, in addition to growing to upwards of 60 feet tall, as Giant-Girl--"
Look. I can grow big!
Which you've pretty much always been able to do. Hence the name, Giant-Girl.
"She could also now shrink to a tiny size."
Voilà! Now I'm the Wasp.
Okay, that's new.
But are you the Wasp, or Giant-Girl?
Both! It's so much cooler this way! Now I can be two different super heroines, and the fabrics of my costume are molecularly aligned to change according to my size!
So, when I'm huge, I'm Giant-Girl, and when I shrink, I'm the Wasp.
Is this just an excuse for more costume changes?
Excuse me? I can't believe you said that! This is about expanding my powers to better serve humanity!

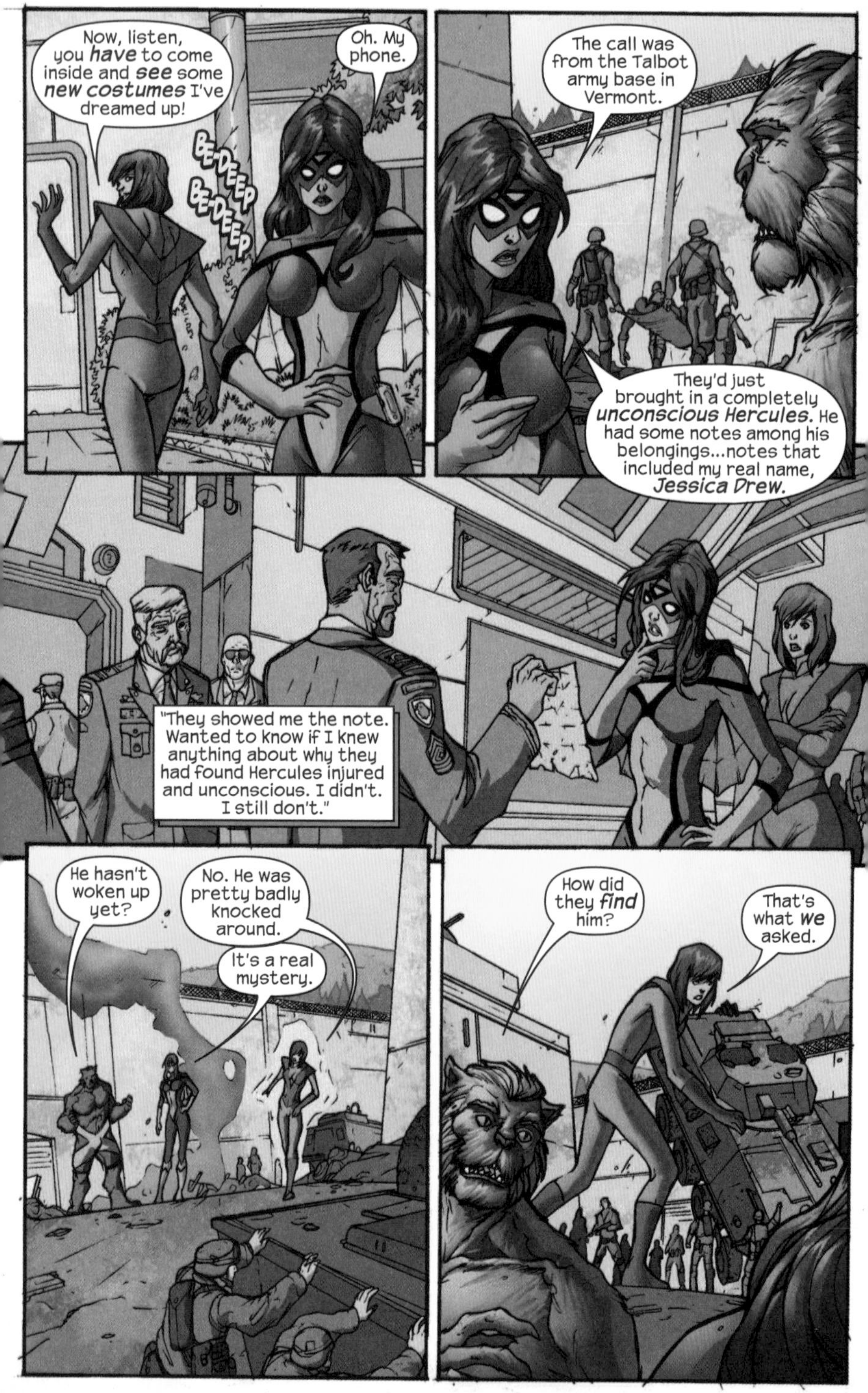

Now, listen, you have to come inside and see some new costumes I've dreamed up!
Oh. My phone.
BE-DEEP BE-DEEP
The call was from the Talbot army base in Vermont.
They'd just brought in a completely unconscious Hercules. He had some notes among his belongings...notes that included my real name, Jessica Drew.
"They showed me the note. Wanted to know if I knew anything about why they had found Hercules injured and unconscious. I didn't. I still don't."
He hasn't woken up yet?
No. He was pretty badly knocked around.
It's a real mystery.
How did they find him?
That's what we asked.

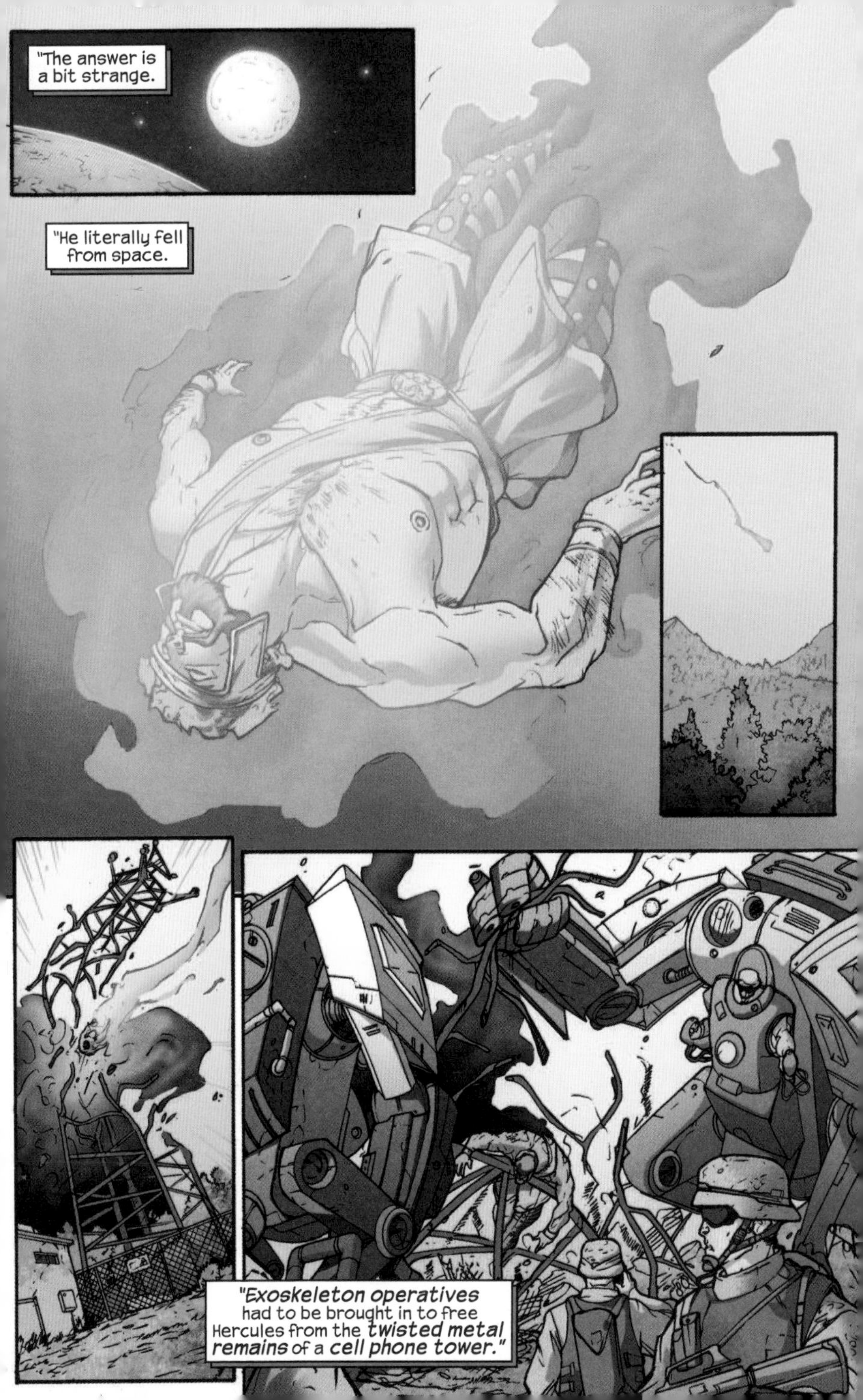
"The answer is a bit strange.
"He literally fell from space.
"Exoskeleton operatives had to be brought in to free Hercules from the twisted metal remains of a cell phone tower."

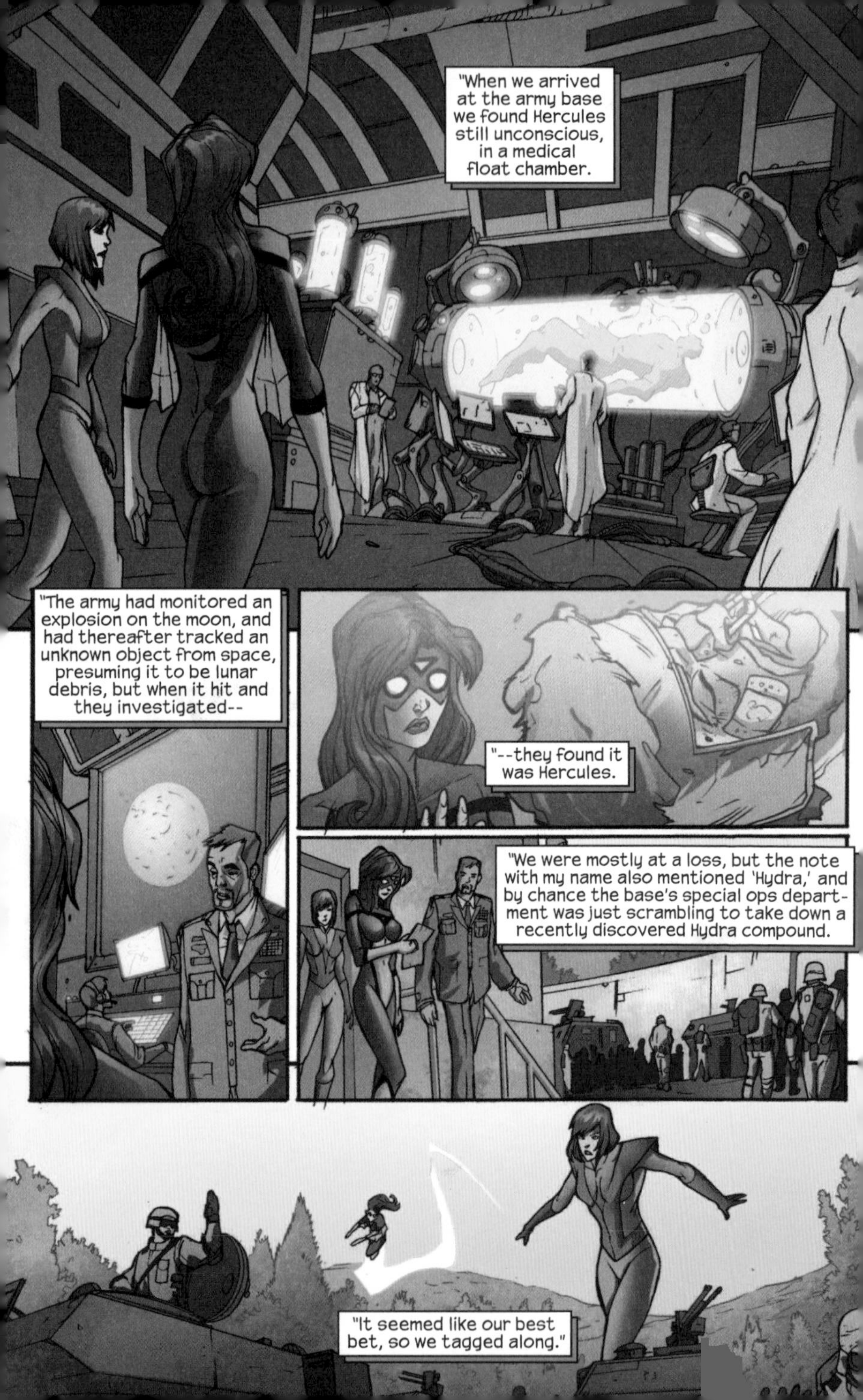
"When we arrived at the army base we found Hercules still unconscious, in a medical float chamber.
"The army had monitored an explosion on the moon, and had thereafter tracked an unknown object from space, presuming it to be lunar debris, but when it hit and they investigated--
"--they found it was Hercules.
"We were mostly at a loss, but the note with my name also mentioned 'Hydra,' and by chance the base's special ops department was just scrambling to take down a recently discovered Hydra compound.
"It seemed like our best bet, so we tagged along."

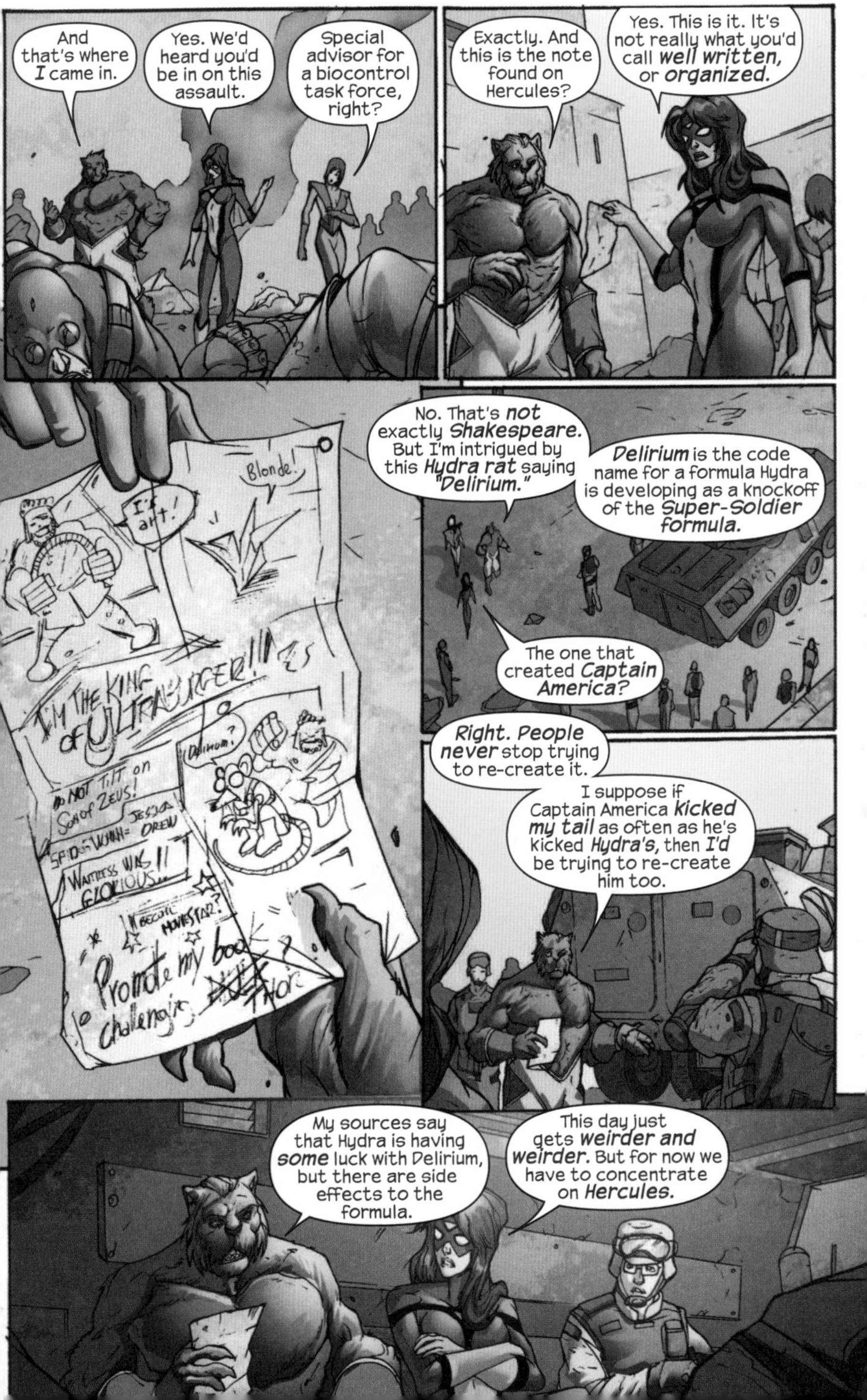

And that's where I came in.
Yes. We'd heard you'd be in on this assault.
Special advisor for a biocontrol task force, right?
Exactly. And this is the note found on Hercules?
Yes. This is it. It's not really what you'd call well written, or organized.
Blonde!
It's art!
I'M THE KING OF ULTRABURGER!!!
Delirium?
DO NOT TILT on Son of Zeus!
SPIDER-WOMAN= JESSICA DREW
WAITRESS WAS!! GLORIOUS!!
BECOME MOVIESTAR?
Promote my book
No. That's not exactly Shakespeare. But I'm intrigued by this Hydra rat saying "Delirium."
Delirium is the code name for a formula Hydra is developing as a knockoff of the Super-Soldier formula.
The one that created Captain America?
Right. People never stop trying to re-create it.
I suppose if Captain America kicked my tail as often as he's kicked Hydra's, then I'd be trying to re-create him too.
My sources say that Hydra is having some luck with Delirium, but there are side effects to the formula.
This day just gets weirder and weirder. But for now we have to concentrate on Hercules.

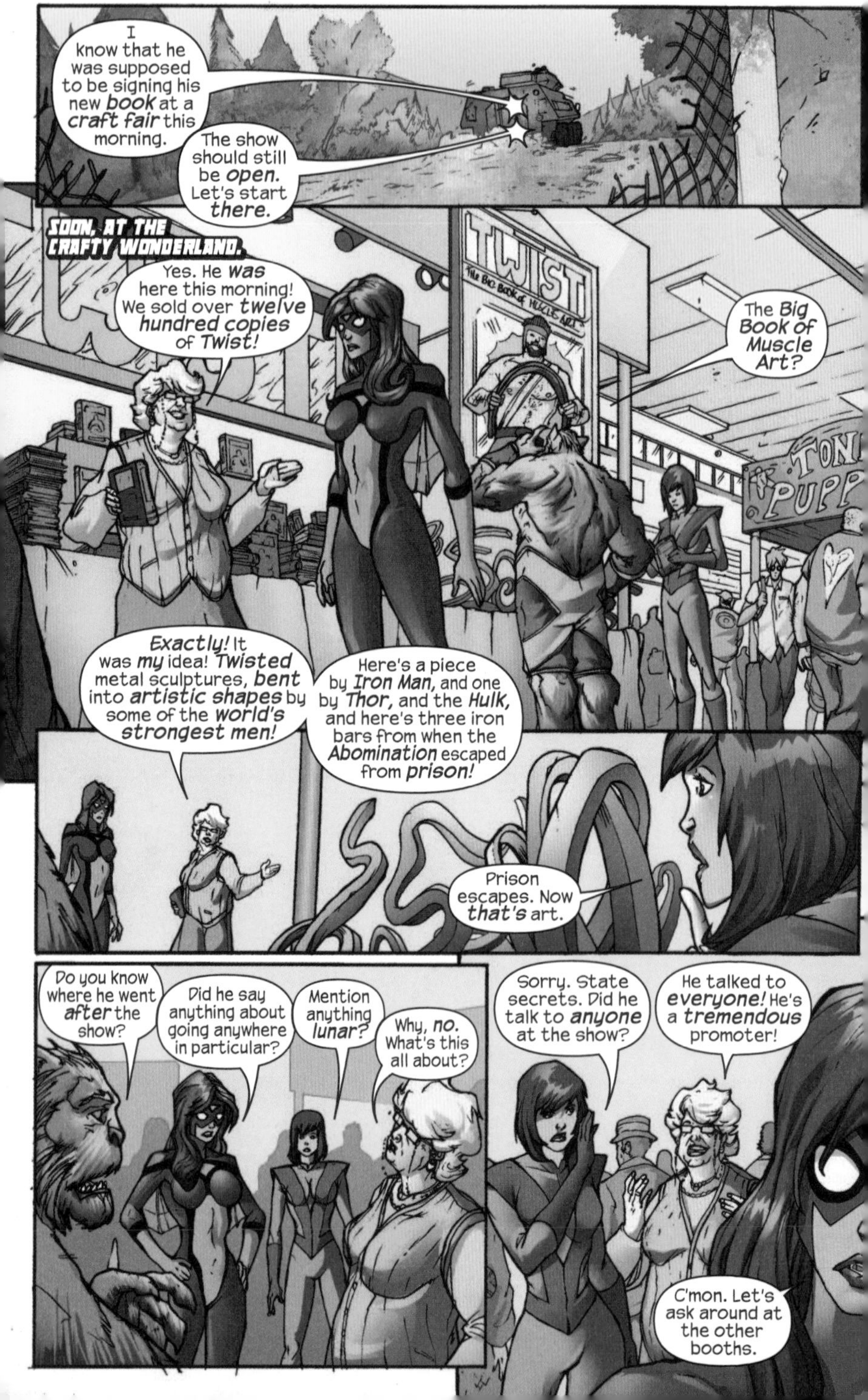
I know that he was supposed to be signing his new book at a craft fair this morning.
The show should still be open. Let's start there.
SOON, AT THE CRAFTY WONDERLAND.
Yes. He was here this morning! We sold over twelve hundred copies of Twist!
TWIST
THE BIG BOOK of MUSCLE ART
The Big Book of Muscle Art?
Exactly! It was my idea! Twisted metal sculptures, bent into artistic shapes by some of the world's strongest men!
Here's a piece by Iron Man, and one by Thor, and the Hulk, and here's three iron bars from when the Abomination escaped from prison!
Prison escapes. Now that's art.
Do you know where he went after the show?
Did he say anything about going anywhere in particular?
Mention anything lunar?
Why, no. What's this all about?
Sorry. State secrets. Did he talk to anyone at the show?
He talked to everyone! He's a tremendous promoter!
C'mon. Let's ask around at the other booths.

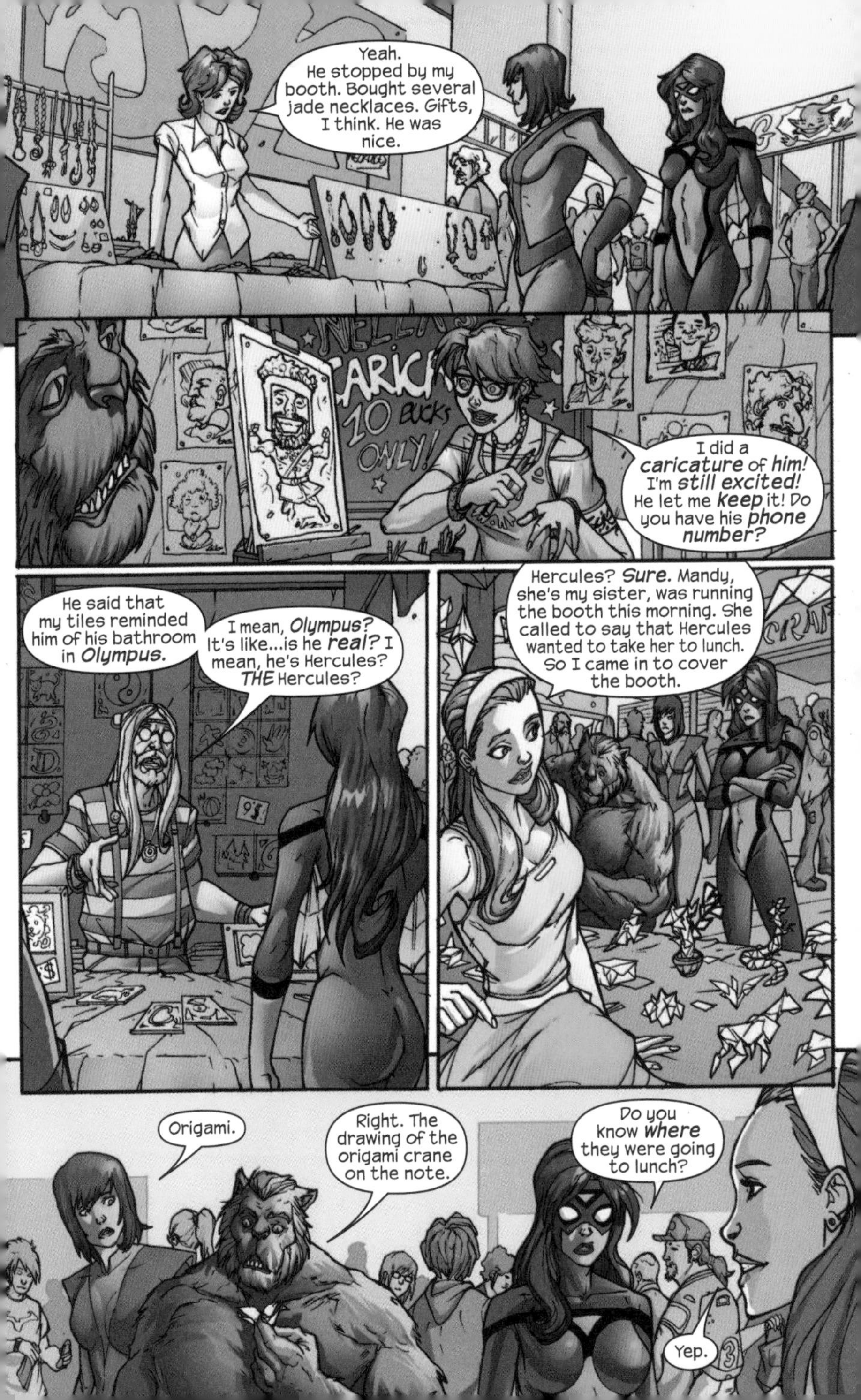
Yeah. He stopped by my booth. Bought several jade necklaces. Gifts, I think. He was nice.
I did a caricature of him! I'm still excited! He let me keep it! Do you have his phone number?
He said that my tiles reminded him of his bathroom in Olympus.
I mean, Olympus? It's like...is he real? I mean, he's Hercules? THE Hercules?
Hercules? Sure. Mandy, she's my sister, was running the booth this morning. She called to say that Hercules wanted to take her to lunch. So I came in to cover the booth.
Origami.
Right. The drawing of the origami crane on the note.
Do you know where they were going to lunch?
Yep.

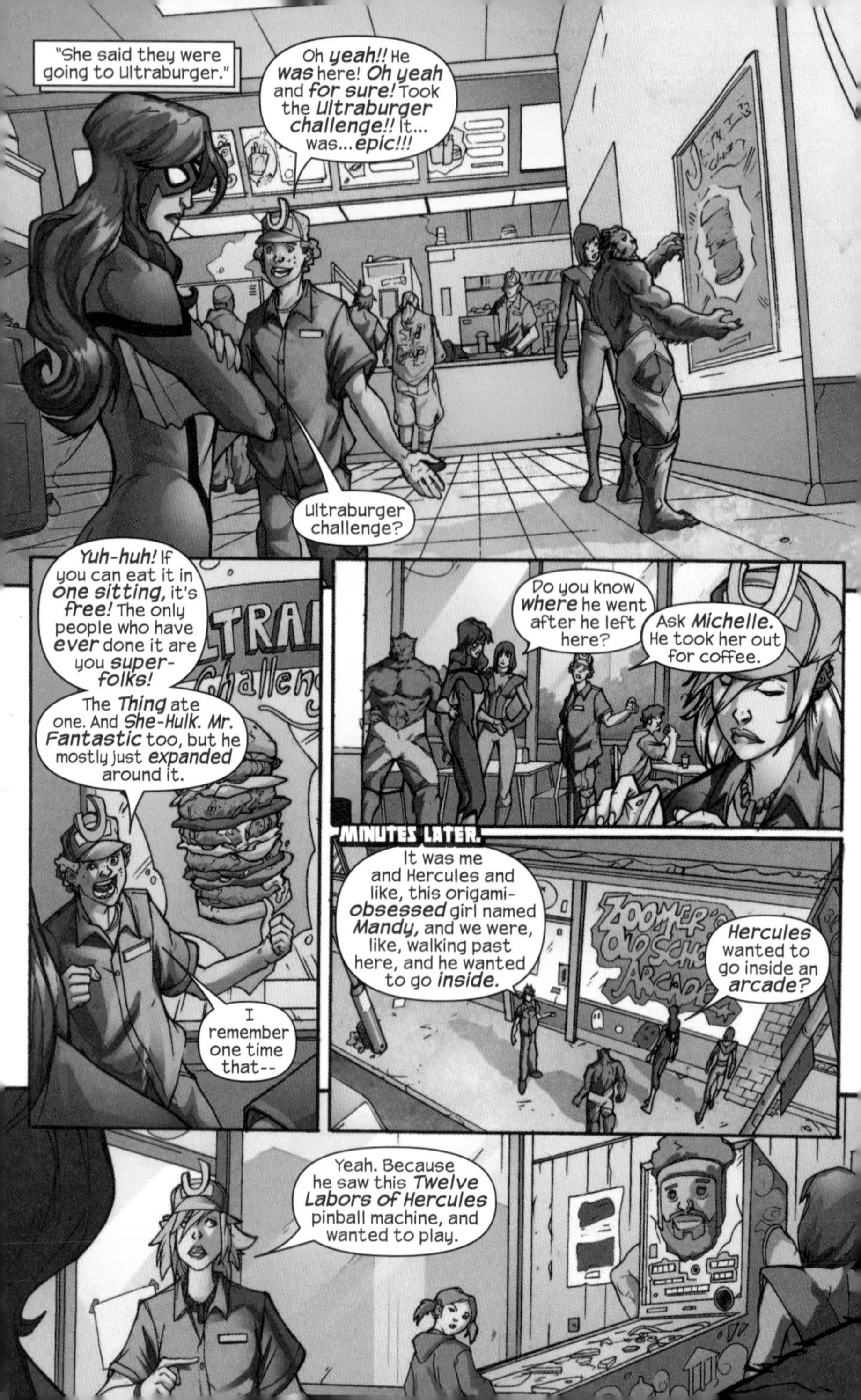
"She said they were going to Ultraburger."
Oh yeah!! He was here! Oh yeah and for sure! Took the Ultraburger challenge!! It... was... epic!!!
Ultraburger challenge?
Yuh-huh! If you can eat it in one sitting, it's free! The only people who have ever done it are you super-folks!
The Thing ate one. And She-Hulk. Mr. Fantastic too, but he mostly just expanded around it.
I remember one time that--
Do you know where he went after he left here?
Ask Michelle. He took her out for coffee.
MINUTES LATER.
It was me and Hercules and like, this origami-obsessed girl named Mandy, and we were, like, walking past here, and he wanted to go inside.
Hercules wanted to go inside an arcade?
Yeah. Because he saw this Twelve Labors of Hercules pinball machine, and wanted to play.

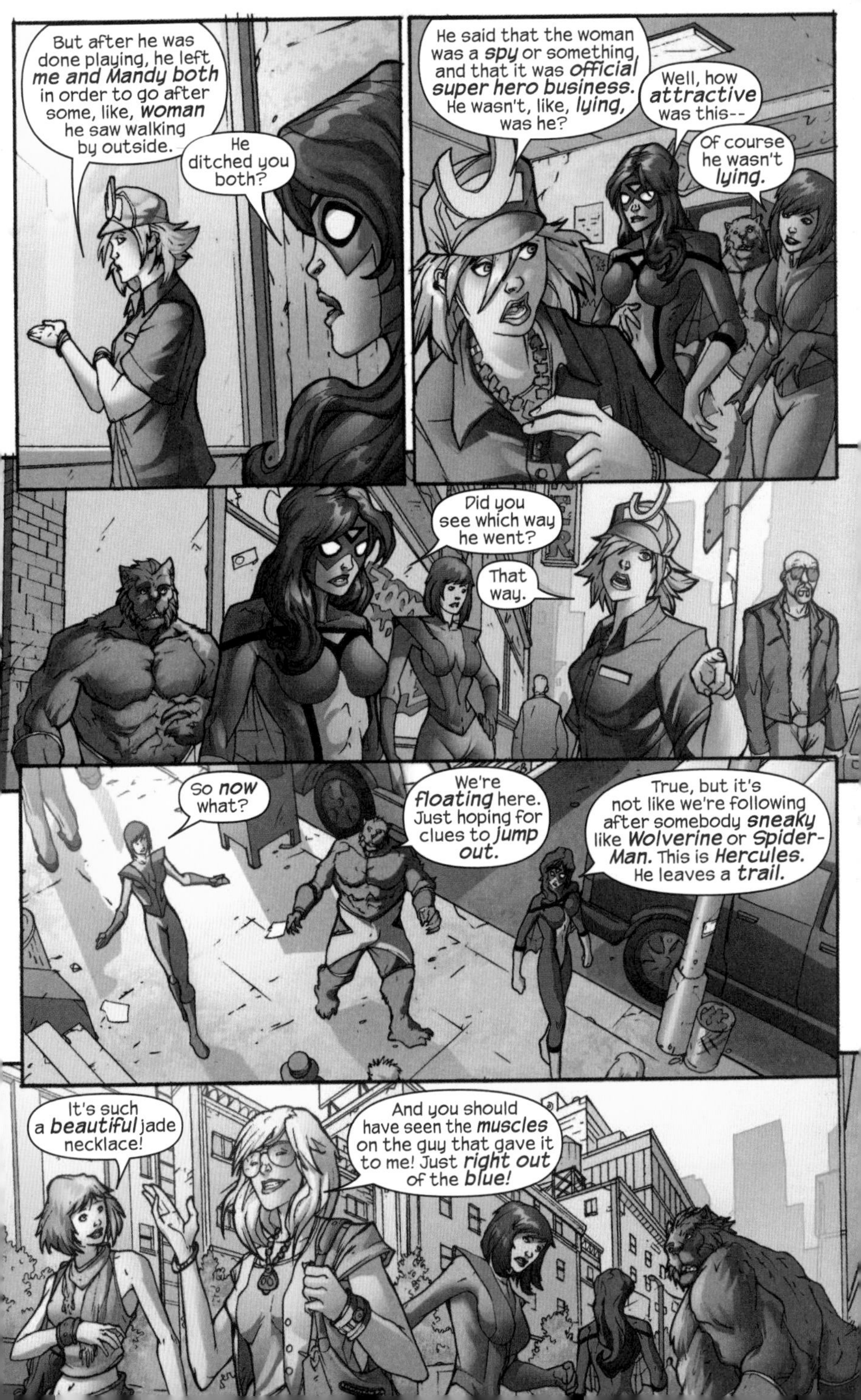
But after he was done playing, he left me and Mandy both in order to go after some, like, woman he saw walking by outside.
He ditched you both?
He said that the woman was a spy or something and that it was official super hero business. He wasn't, like, lying, was he?
Well, how attractive was this--
Of course he wasn't lying.
Did you see which way he went?
That way.
So now what?
We're floating here. Just hoping for clues to jump out.
True, but it's not like we're following after somebody sneaky like Wolverine or Spider-Man. This is Hercules. He leaves a trail.
It's such a beautiful jade necklace!
And you should have seen the muscles on the guy that gave it to me! Just right out of the blue!

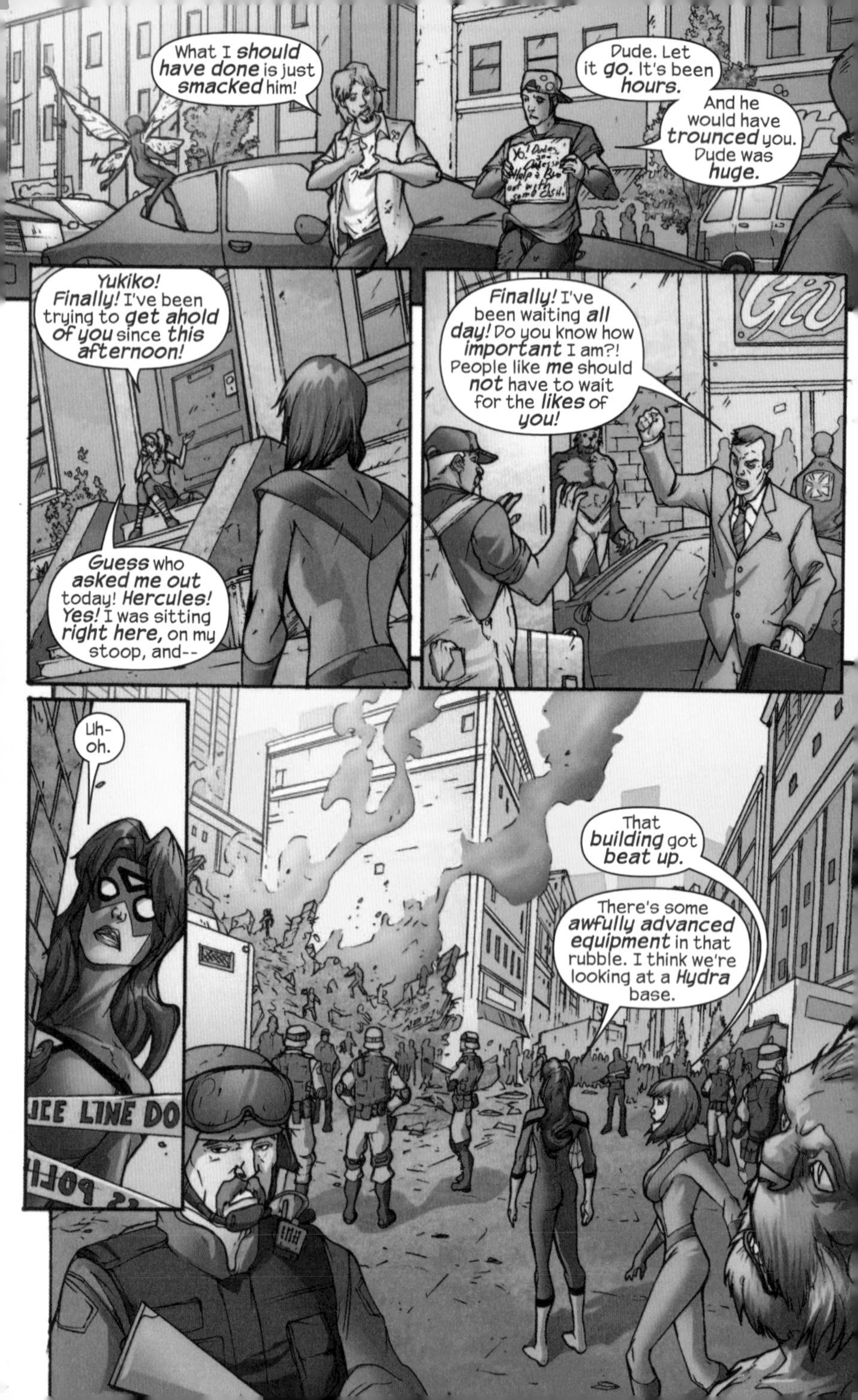
What I should have done is just smacked him!
Dude. Let it go. It's been hours.
And he would have trounced you. Dude was huge.
Yukiko! Finally! I've been trying to get ahold of you since this afternoon!
Guess who asked me out today! Hercules! Yes! I was sitting right here, on my stoop, and--
Finally! I've been waiting all day! Do you know how important I am?! People like me should not have to wait for the likes of you!
Uh-oh.
That building got beat up.
There's some awfully advanced equipment in that rubble. I think we're looking at a Hydra base.
ICE LINE DO

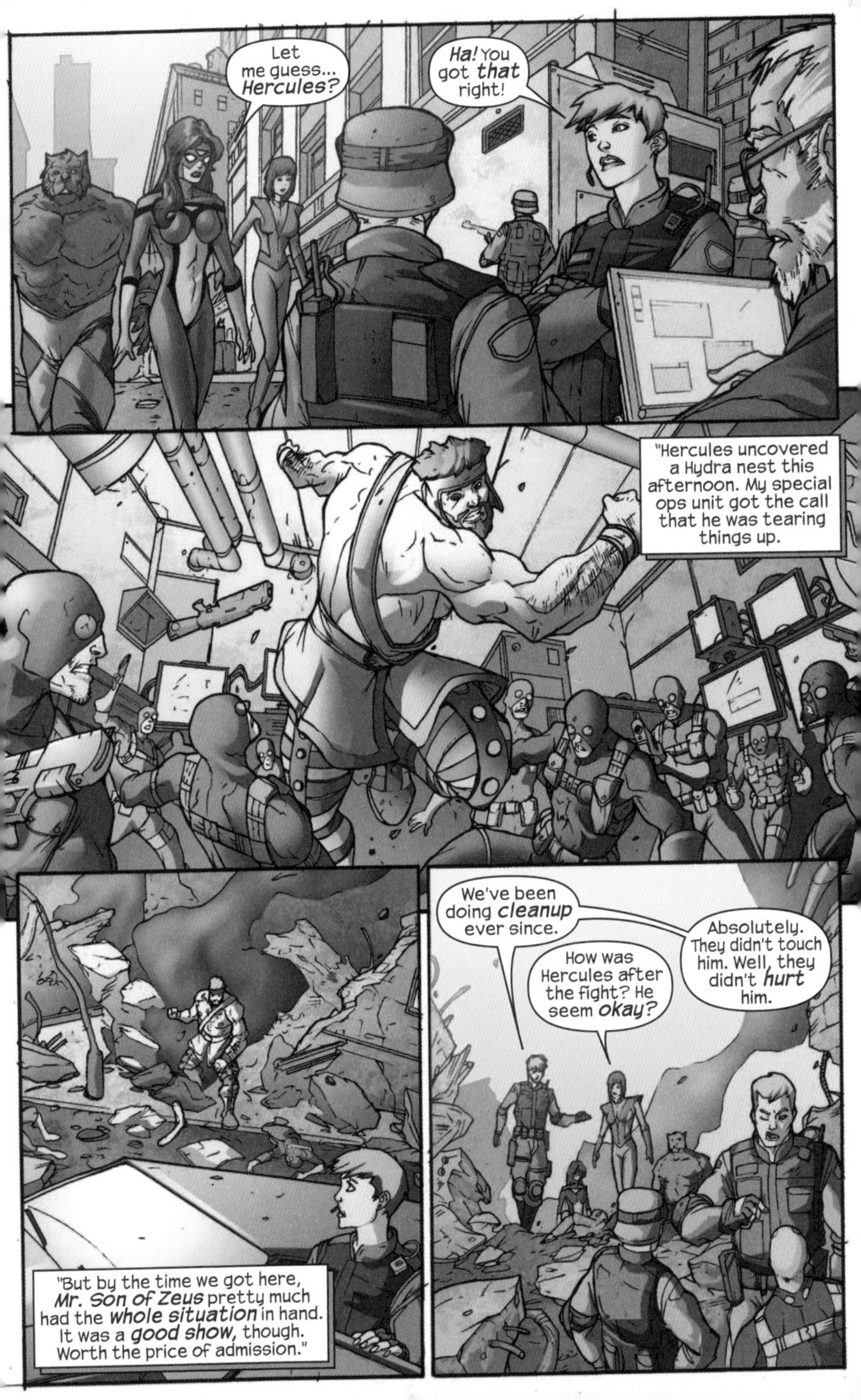

Let me guess... Hercules?
Ha! You got that right!
"Hercules uncovered a Hydra nest this afternoon. My special ops unit got the call that he was tearing things up.
"But by the time we got here, Mr. Son of Zeus pretty much had the whole situation in hand. It was a good show, though. Worth the price of admission."
We've been doing cleanup ever since.
How was Hercules after the fight? He seem okay?
Absolutely. They didn't touch him. Well, they didn't hurt him.

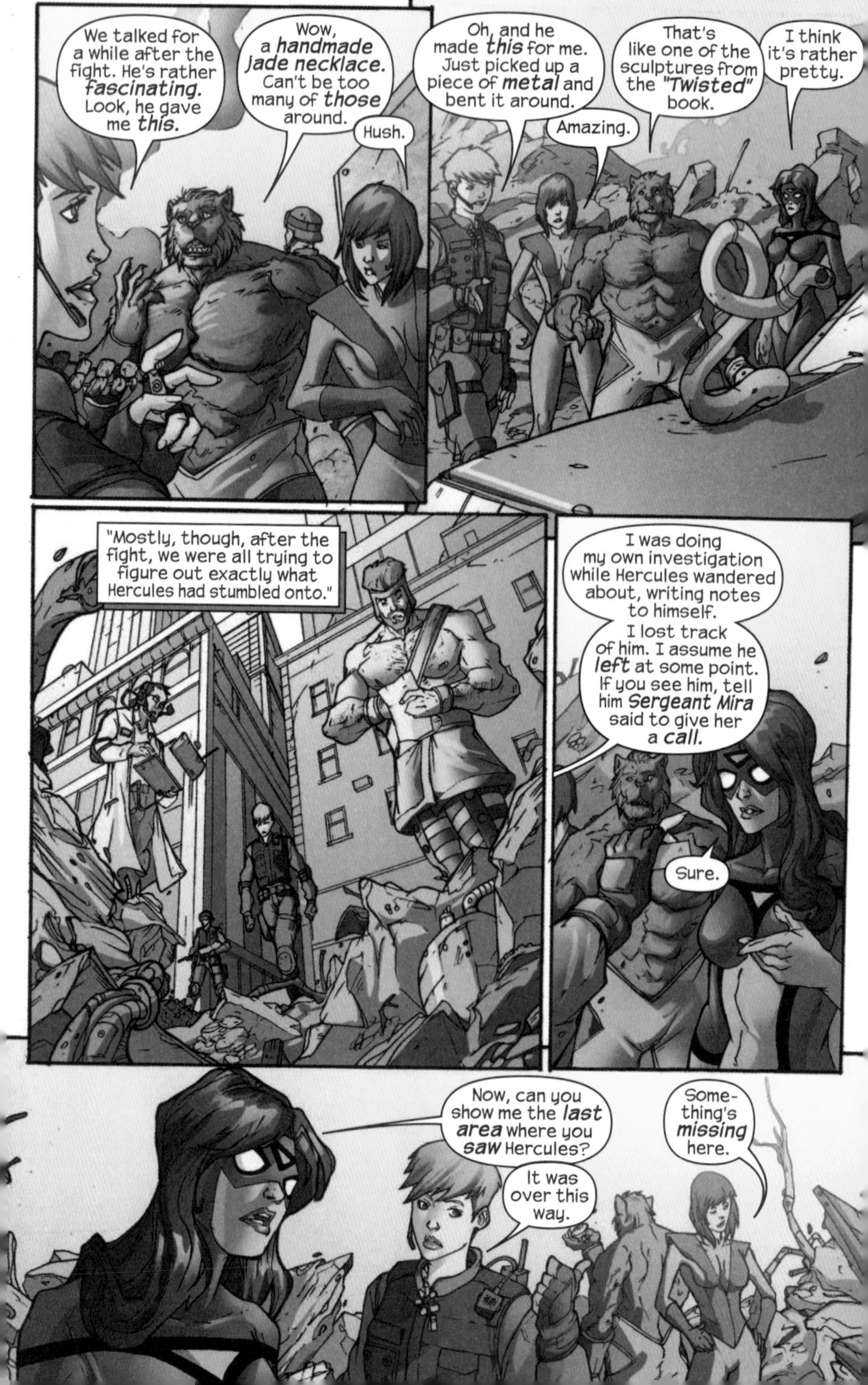

We talked for a while after the fight. He's rather fascinating. Look, he gave me this.
Wow, a handmade jade necklace. Can't be too many of those around.
Hush.
Oh, and he made this for me. Just picked up a piece of metal and bent it around.
Amazing.
That's like one of the sculptures from the "Twisted" book.
I think it's rather pretty.
"Mostly, though, after the fight, we were all trying to figure out exactly what Hercules had stumbled onto."
I was doing my own investigation while Hercules wandered about, writing notes to himself.
I lost track of him. I assume he left at some point. If you see him, tell him Sergeant Mira said to give her a call.
Sure.
Now, can you show me the last area where you saw Hercules?
It was over this way.
Some-thing's missing here.

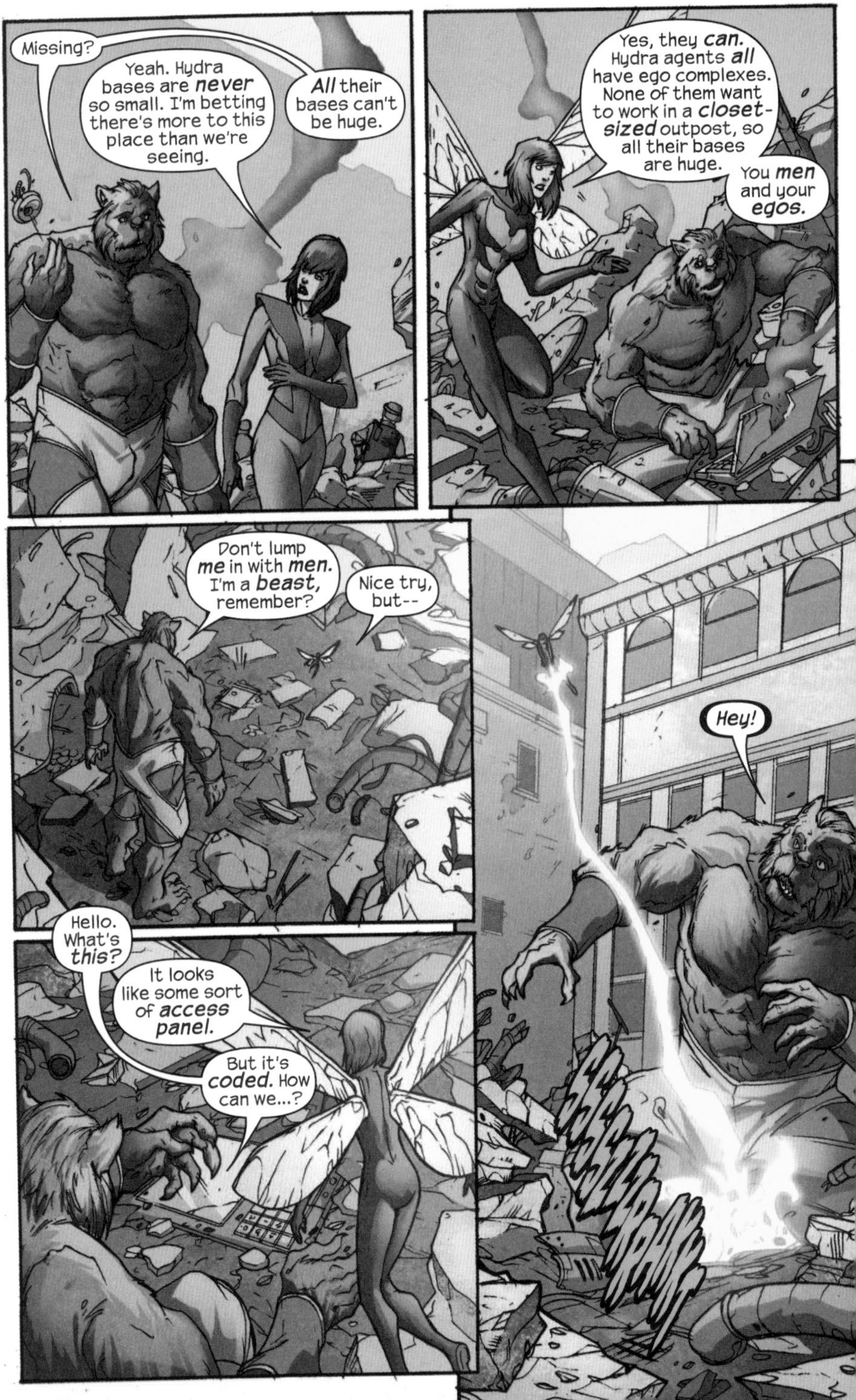
Missing?
Yeah. Hydra bases are never so small. I'm betting there's more to this place than we're seeing.
All their bases can't be huge.
Yes, they can. Hydra agents all have ego complexes. None of them want to work in a closet-sized outpost, so all their bases are huge.
You men and your egos.
Don't lump me in with men. I'm a beast, remember?
Nice try, but--
Hello. What's this?
It looks like some sort of access panel.
But it's coded. How can we...?
Hey!

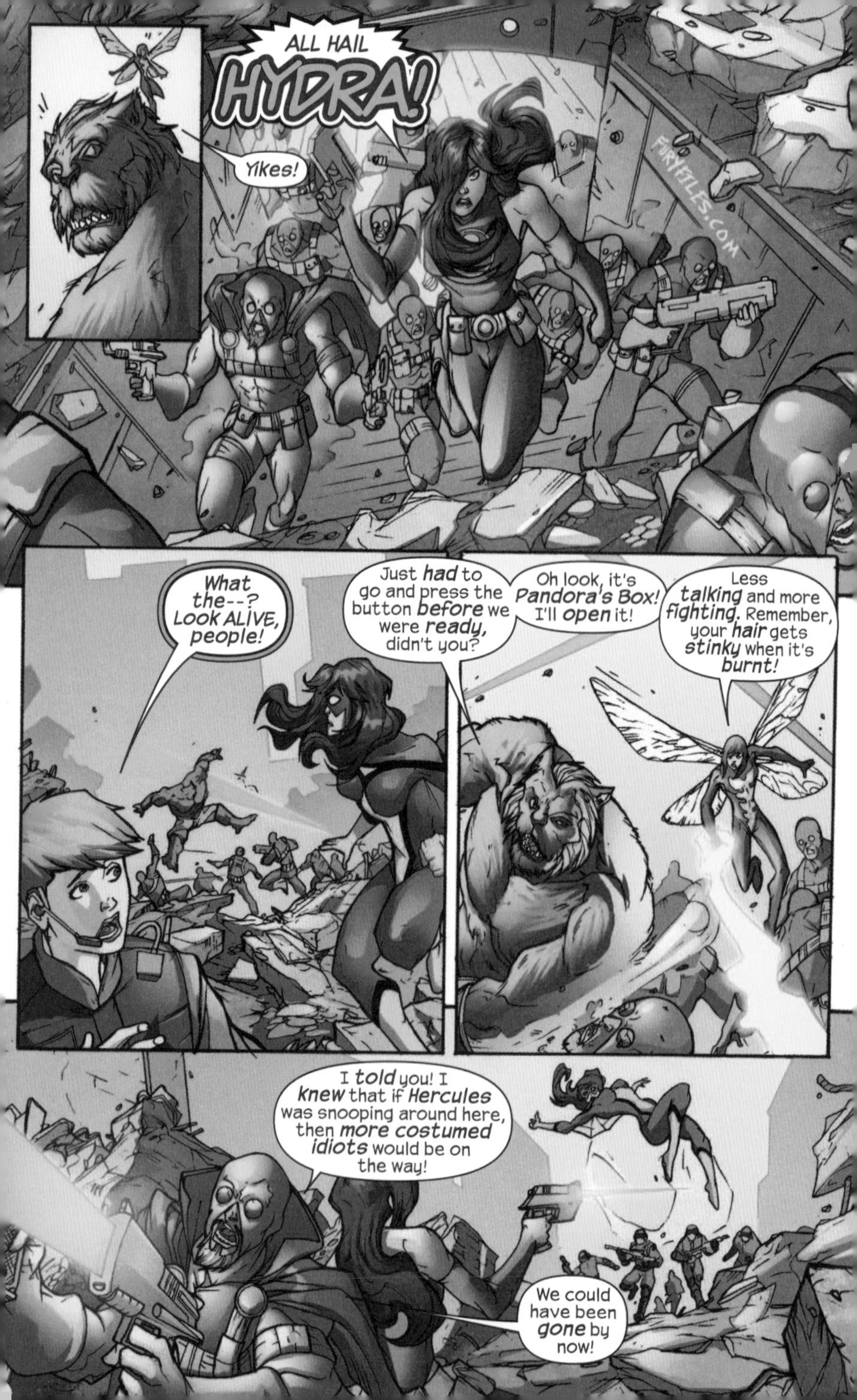
ALL HAIL HYDRA!
Yikes!
What the--? LOOK ALIVE, people!
Just had to go and press the button before we were ready, didn't you?
Oh look, it's Pandora's Box! I'll open it!
Less talking and more fighting. Remember, your hair gets stinky when it's burnt!
I told you! I knew that if Hercules was snooping around here, then more costumed idiots would be on the way!
We could have been gone by now!

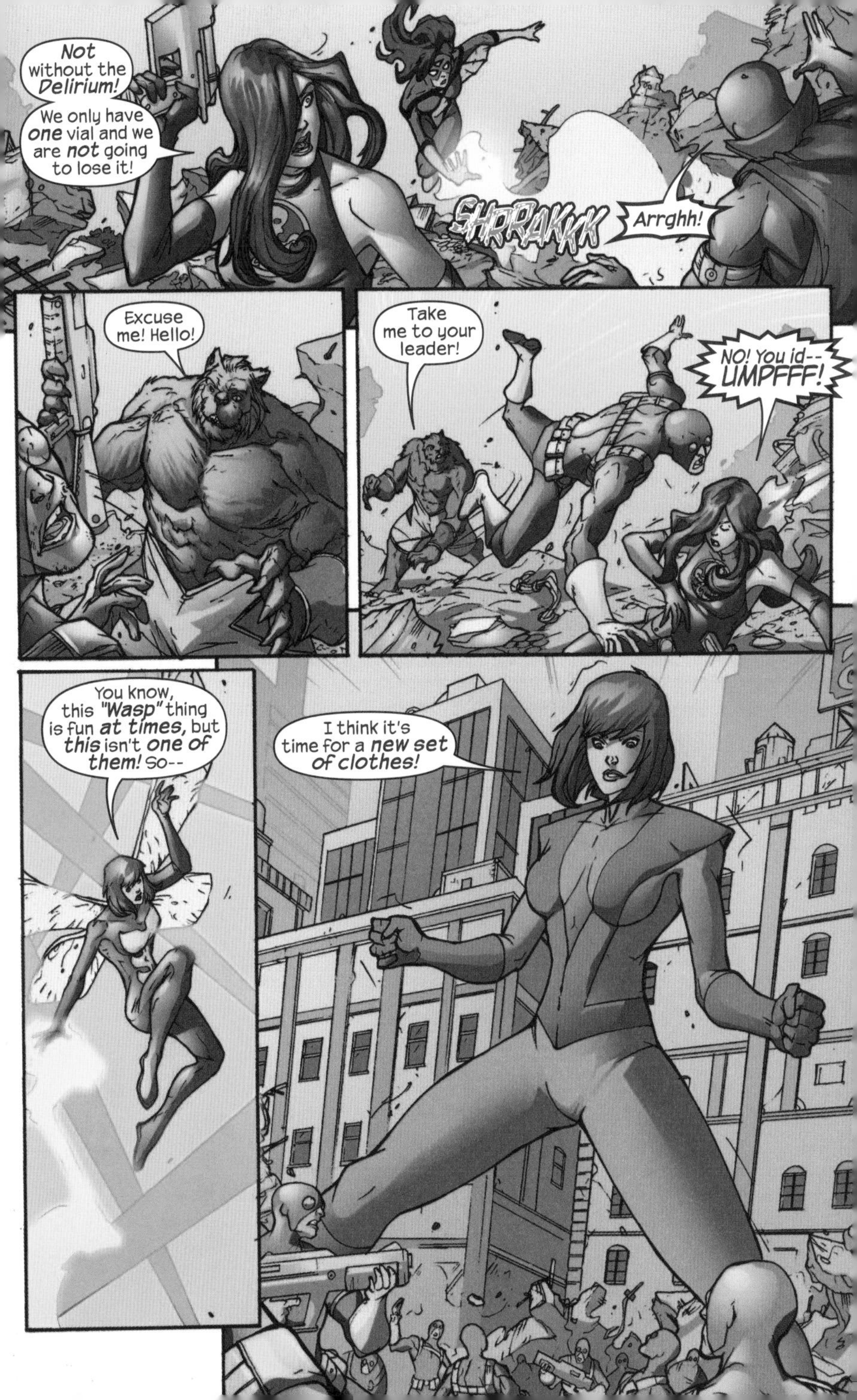
Not without the Delirium!
We only have one vial and we are not going to lose it!
SHRRAKKK
Arrghh!
Excuse me! Hello!
Take me to your leader!
NO! You id-- UMPFFF!
You know, this "Wasp" thing is fun at times, but this isn't one of them! So--
I think it's time for a new set of clothes!

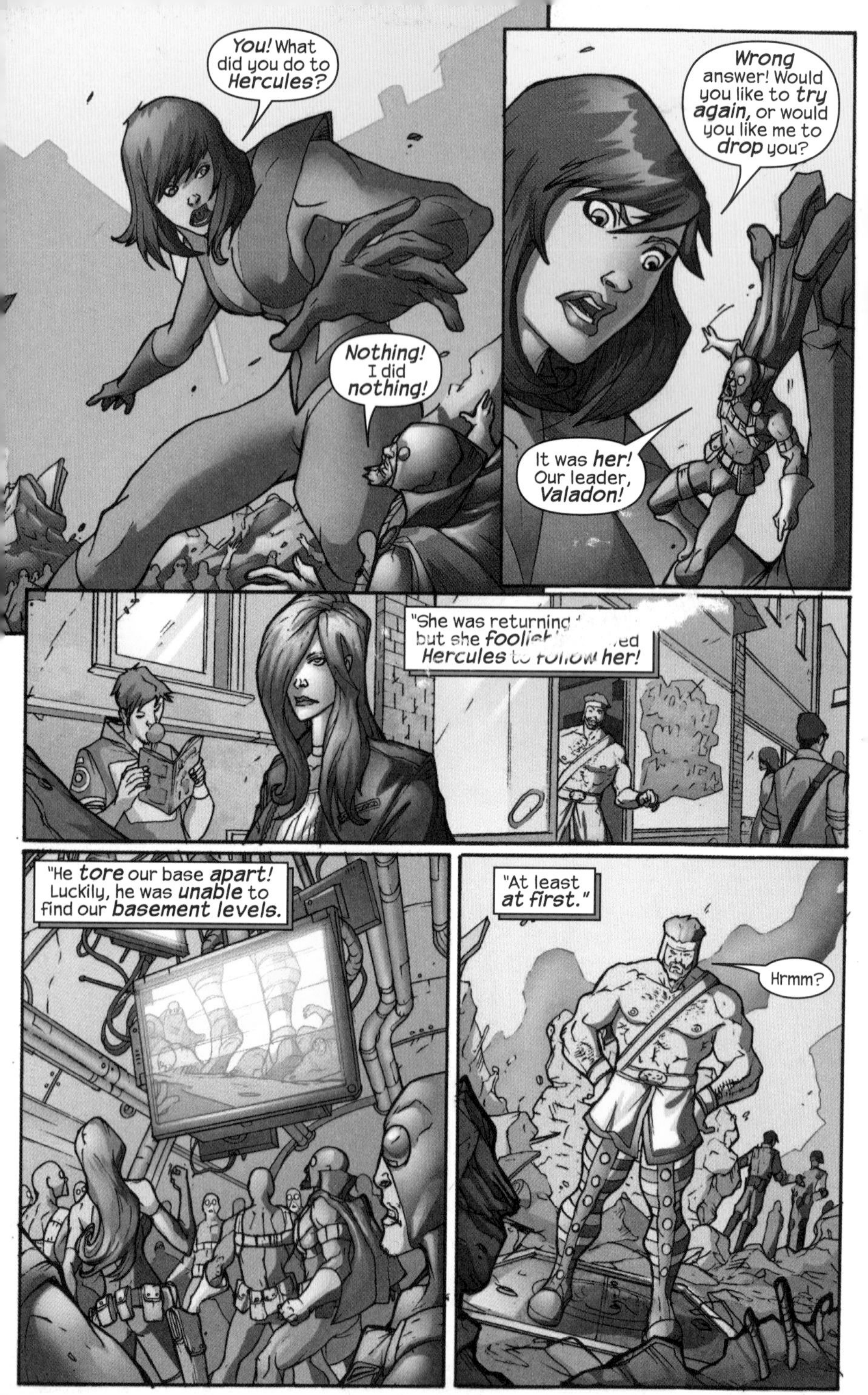
You! What did you do to Hercules?
Nothing! I did nothing!
Wrong answer! Would you like to try again, or would you like me to drop you?
It was her! Our leader, Valadon!
"She was returning
but she fooli
ed
Hercules
her!
"He tore our base apart! Luckily, he was unable to find our basement levels.
"At least at first."
Hrmm?

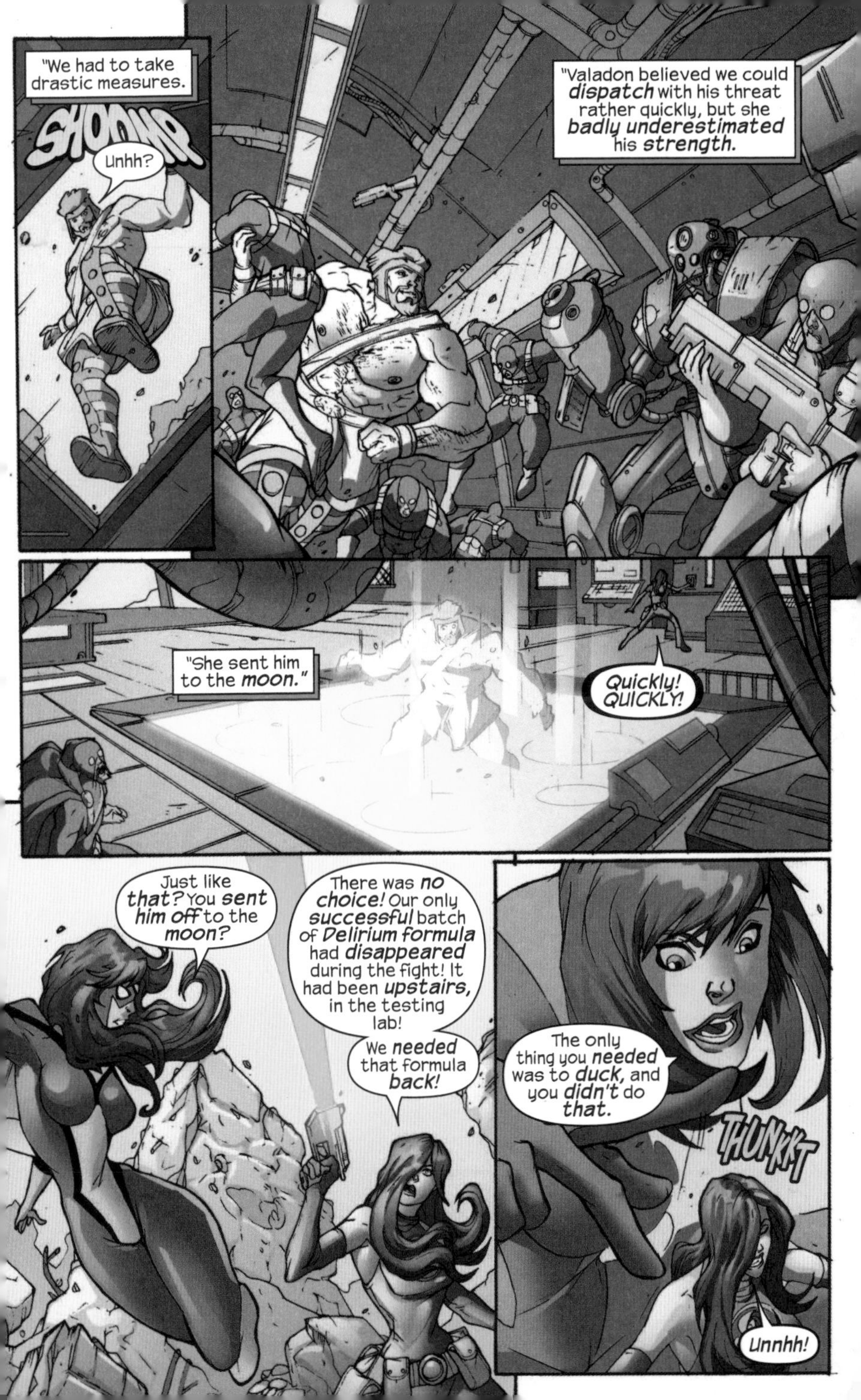
"We had to take drastic measures.
SHOOMP
Unhh?
"Valadon believed we could dispatch with his threat rather quickly, but she badly underestimated his strength.
"She sent him to the moon."
Quickly! QUICKLY!
Just like that? You sent him off to the moon?
There was no choice! Our only successful batch of Delirium formula had disappeared during the fight! It had been upstairs, in the testing lab!
We needed that formula back!
The only thing you needed was to duck, and you didn't do that.
THUNKKT
Unnhh!

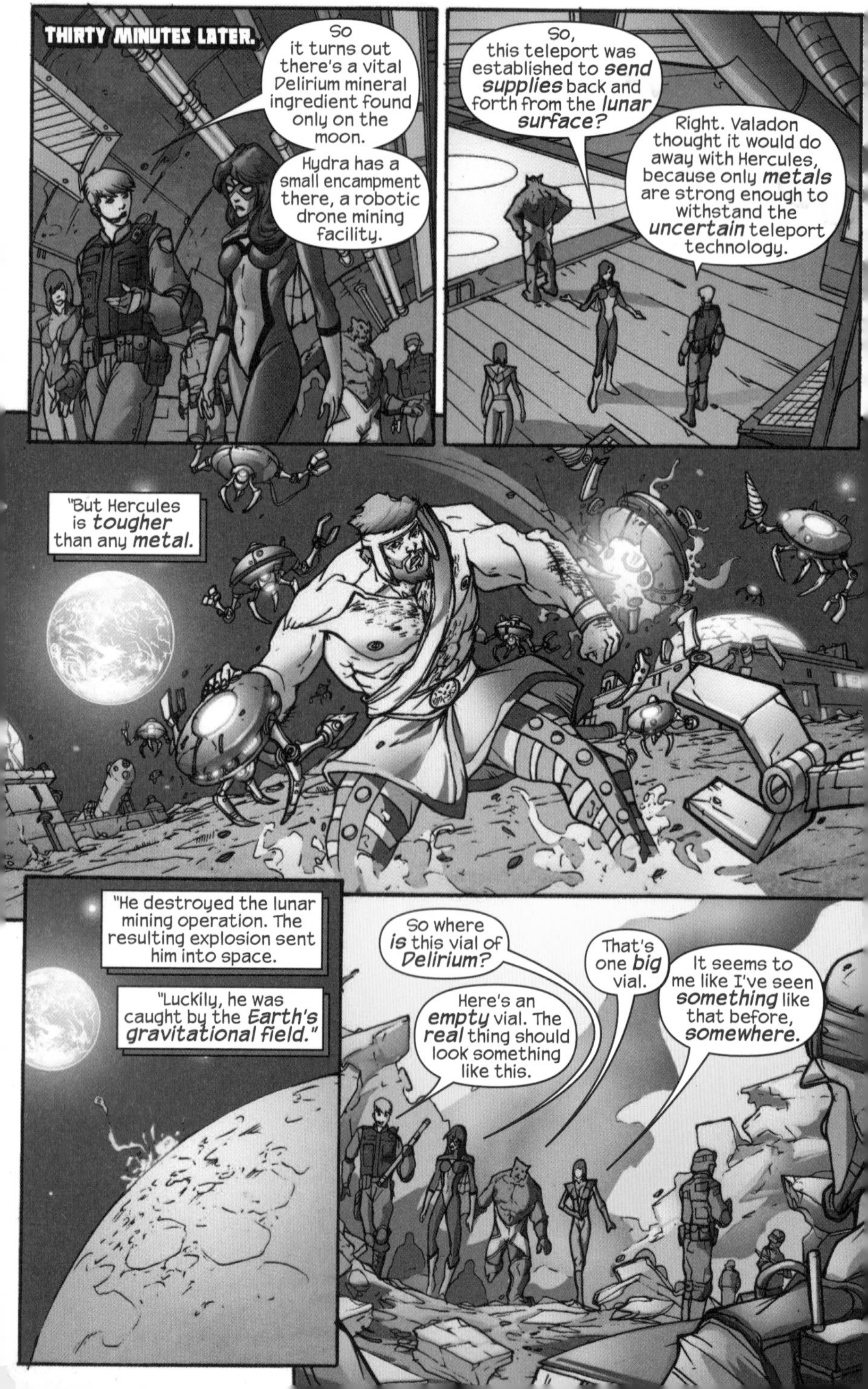
THIRTY MINUTES LATER.
So it turns out there's a vital Delirium mineral ingredient found only on the moon.
Hydra has a small encampment there, a robotic drone mining facility.
So, this teleport was established to send supplies back and forth from the lunar surface?
Right. Valadon thought it would do away with Hercules, because only metals are strong enough to withstand the uncertain teleport technology.
"But Hercules is tougher than any metal.
"He destroyed the lunar mining operation. The resulting explosion sent him into space.
"Luckily, he was caught by the Earth's gravitational field."
So where is this vial of Delirium?
Here's an empty vial. The real thing should look something like this.
That's one big vial.
It seems to me like I've seen something like that before, somewhere.